NILO &
DEMETRIUS

ALSO BY BRUCE STORES

CHRISTIAN SCIENCE: Its Encounter
With Lesbian/Gay America,
iUniverse, 2004 (260 pages)

THE ISTHMUS: Stories From Mexico's Past: 1495 to 1995,
iUniverse, 2009 (373 pages)

NILO &
DEMETRIUS
Brothers in Classical Greece

BRUCE STORES

NILO & DEMETRIUS
BROTHERS IN CLASSICAL GREECE

iUniverse books may be ordered through booksellers or by contacting:

*iUniverse
1663 Liberty Drive
Bloomington, IN 47403
www.iuniverse.com
1-800-Authors (1-800-288-4677)*

ISBN: 978-1-5320-6799-0 (sc)
ISBN: 978-1-5320-6798-3 (e)

Library of Congress Control Number: 2019901859

Print information available on the last page.

iUniverse rev. date: 02/2/2019

Dedicated to the ancient Greeks who
gave so much to the world.

Contents

Before It All Began

Wisdom begins in wonder.

— **Socrates**
470 – 399 BC

In the fifth century BC, Europe's southeast corner became the locus for the most creative and imaginative society the ancient world would know. Its grandeur was unique. Few nations could begin to challenge its civilization in any of the fields of architecture, art, astronomy, debating, education, government, history, literature, mathematics, medicine, military might, music, philosophy, rhetoric, science, sculpture, and theater. But how could that be?

Most of its land was inhospitable. Fertile ground was scarce. Most of the soil's thin layer was joined with rocks, limestone, and sand. The non-porous limestone held little moisture. With modest to slight rainfall, the dominant vegetation was shrubs. And there were other difficulties.

The climate favored mild winters, but also long, hot, dry summers.

All rivers too shallow to navigate.

Many prominent mountains (though not the highest in Europe) rise majestically, seemingly almost perpendicular from the ground, in row after row after row. They impede land travel. They also isolate settlements and restrict communication. Two-thirds of Greece is covered with mountains.

As with all civilizations, every Greek city-state had enemies. The Macedonians, Persians, other Greek city-states, and later, the Roman Empire, forced them to put much effort into their military prowess even as they labored to build their city-states.

These were the harsh conditions of Greece. To eke out an existence was doable. But cradling the most enlightened civilization the ancient world had seen, stretches the imagination.

How did they do it?

The answer came from learning to make the most of what they had. In this way, the Greeks, and most notably, the City-State of Athens, surpassed their neighbors to a high degree.

First, they turned to the sea. The sea was everywhere. Far from being a barrier, the sea helped in many ways. It enabled them to travel, to communicate, and to find an abundance of food. It opened wider vistas. It helped them settle in distant places. It proved a better way to transport themselves. In the process, the Greeks became excellent seafarers. The advantages of the sea were abetted by geography.

An array of peninsulas stretch out from Europe's southeast corner. Beyond them lie thousands of islands and islets. They abound from the continental limits of Europe to the easternmost end of the Aegean Sea. Nearly every spot in Greece lies within fifty miles of the sea. And vice-versa. Sea travelers in the Aegean and Ionian seas were rarely more than fifty miles from land.

Mastering the sea made it possible for the Greeks to be superb trading partners. They hungered to obtain grain, their most sought-after commodity. Greeks also imported wheat, wood, pork, slaves and glass. As to exports, they offered pottery, wine, metalwork, olives, and olive oil. Trading also had the benefit of exposing Greeks to promising places to settle.

Greek settlements branched out wherever the sea would take them. That included Asia Minor, the north African coast, Italy, and all the way to Spain. Wherever they went, they carried their culture with them.

The second component to their success was beneath the ground. Abundant deposits of ores were found under the surface. Discoveries of gold, silver, copper, iron, zinc, and lead enhanced the life of the early Greeks dramatically. They made possible the use of metallic weapons, tools and countless artifacts that revolutionized warfare as well as daily life. But metals weren't the only riches under their feet.

They also discovered marble—lots of it. It was as if the gods favored them that Grecian marble became the most famous in the known world.

Of course, getting marble and metallic ores from the ground involved much effort. Extracting metals from the ground predates recorded history. From the earliest days of known history and long before life was chronicled, the Greeks took to mining. Historians say it may have occurred far back in the Neolithic period (9000 BC). In the eighth or ninth century BC, according to Homer's poems, they already knew how to refine ores to get pure metal by melting them (smelting). They were able to forge metal into desired shapes using hammers and tongs.

As to what they found, the most important was likely the discovery of vast silver deposits in the rugged mountains near Athens. Extensive, luxurious, veins of silver did much to bring about the classical era. Silver made possible their formidable navy. Their dominance of the sea, paid by silver, helped defeat their enemies.

A third element was less tangible. But it may have been their most important. It was something the Greeks found neither from the sea nor the land. It came from deep within themselves. They brought it to bear upon nearly every aspect of life. Its name was *agon*. The idea of *agon* was that it was possible by way of an intensely competitive spirit, the Greeks could achieve near perfection in body and mind. *Agon* (root word for agony and antagonist) gave a stimulus to the individual to succeed in every endeavor beyond what other cultures could do. It pushed the individual to extremes. It was based on the competitive principle anything can be achieved. Its central expression was sports, making the *gymnasia* a significant arena. Without *agon*, the *gymnasia* ("naked exercise" in ancient Greek) would not have held such a high position. Even the smallest city-states and towns had at least one *gymnasia*.

Agon is perhaps best described by Jacob Burckhardt in his work, *The Greeks and Greek Civilization*, published (first in German) in the late nineteenth century:

Agon was a motive power known to no other people the general leavening element that, given the essential condition of freedom, proved capable of working upon the will and the potentialities of every individual. In this respect, the Greeks stood alone. (See bibliography.)

Possibly the clearest and most classic example of *agon* followed the battle of Marathon in 490 BC. One of the objectives of the battle of Marathon was to preserve Athens' fledgling democracy. At the battle's conclusion, the Greek messenger Pheidippides was chosen to run to Athens (about 25 miles) to deliver the good news of triumph. It took every bit of human stamina to arrive in the briefest amount of time. On arrival to Athens all he could say was, "We were victorious." He then fell, dead from exhaustion. His feat inspired the marathon races of today (26.2 miles), first introduced at the 1896 Olympic Games.

Apart from athletics, music, and poetry were among the essential expressions of *agon*. They gained in grandeur due to constant pressure from that motive force. Competitions took place at major festivals. Boy choirs, lyre players, and poetry recitations were among the most common.

In theater too, tragedies and comedies were refined as to their quality due to *agon*.

Another expression of *agon* was debating. Cultivating proficiency in debating was one of the ways they excelled in educating youth. Part of this was by teaching the nuts and bolts of debate techniques and rhetoric from an early age. This would serve them well as adults in the General Assembly, at symposiums, and other forums. Contests at festivals were common to determine the best debaters. Participants pushed themselves near the edge of their limits, again due to *agon*.

The Greeks also saw the educational process as an art. They believed its methods could be honed to produce the best possible schooled men. While a boy's early instruction (ages seven to twelve) was often inferior, adolescent citizens could opt for a superior education. This stemmed from the discovery of a one-of-a-kind didactic. It enabled citizen teens to make a once-in-a-lifetime decision. Each could choose a young adult mentor. This became one of the most remarkable types of teacher-student relationships that ever existed. It was unique. The Greeks called the mentor an *erastes*. His student was his *eromenos*. The *erastes* educated his *eromenos* one-on-one while their curriculum was exceptional. For sure, academics were taught, but also how-to-live in society.

In this setting, learning how to get along with others in social, business, and political environments held a prominent place. The *erastes* made connections for the *eromenos* with talented people. These were mainstay duties of all *erastai*. But the most unusual aspect of the *erastes/eromenos* pairing came neither from what was taught nor the teaching itself. It was their relation to each other. They were lovers. It was as if the erotic element of their relationships fortified their competitive motivation (*agon*). This may have had much to do with the Greeks' road to success. Such relationships usually continued until the *eromenoi* entered the military. Their *erastai* were not much older. Their relationships could start after completing their military obligations. In many cases, they remained good friends for life, though usually not as lovers.

Armed with rich manifold benefits of the sea, buried treasures of marble and large, rich veins of precious ores, strengthened with superior methods of education and the impulse from *agon*, the Greeks were prepared to become the most advanced culture the ancient world would know.

Unfortunately, the grandeur of classical Greece was short-lived. Fighting among city-states, the plague, and the failure of city-states to unite, took their toll. They destroyed each other. But while the city-states, their governments, and their militaries went down in flames, Greek culture more than survived. It attained the supreme honor. Greek enlightenment was to be cherished and immortalized by even its fiercest enemies, most notably the Roman Empire. And two-thousand, five-hundred years later, its institutions of architecture, art, government, philosophy, science, theater, and more, remain studied and cherished all over the world.

What follows is fiction. The writer's endeavor, however, was to maintain a narrative faithful to the spirit that was classical Greece.

CHAPTER 1

Nilo And Demetrius

Knowledge which is acquired under compulsion
obtains no hold on the mind.

— **Plato**
427–347

"Nilo," his teacher called out. "You must do better with your sums. You'll never achieve proficiency if you don't improve."

"I'm trying," replied Nilo. *The teacher's right. I must do it correctly,* Nilo told himself. *I must erase the wrong numbers.* Nilo had written them on his wax tablet. The tablet's length was nearly the distance from the small boy's elbow to his fingertips. He could erase wrong numbers with his stylus smoothing its surface. The teacher again repeated the dictation. Nilo tried to write accordingly. *I don't think I'm getting any of this right,* he told himself.

Sharing a wooden bench with four boys, balancing his wax tablet in one hand while writing with the other was tiresome—what a difficult day. *Nothing's working for me. Arithmetic, reading, writing, music, even my poetry lessons, all give me fits.* Concentration was difficult for Nilo. Such a long day for the eleven-year-old boy.

A voice behind him called out, "Pay attention. Pay attention."

Sitting behind him in the classroom was the family slave Chamus. As with all boys from aristocratic families, Chamus had to be there. Eleven-year-old boys like Nilo are prone to be inattentive, even rowdy at times. Chamus's presence tried to prevent or stop Nilo's unruly behavior. That was his job. But today, Nilo's problem wasn't rowdiness; it was his wandering thoughts. *I wish we were in the* gymnasia *now. There I could think about anything while running in the breeze. Running is freedom.* Idle thinking on this day was also reflected in a silly tune which unfortunately he was singing aloud, albeit softly.

> The bells of our town,
> The children hear them,
> Let them ring prettily,
> Din, dan, don.

His singing was heard by others, including the teacher.

Aghast at Nilo's inattentiveness, the teacher struck him with a long cord. Such punishment was common in the school.

"Ouch." the boy yelled, taking the pain on his thinly covered back.

"Pay attention." cried the teacher.

"Yes, yes," said Nilo moving his slouching posture to an upright position.

Although education was considered essential, the elderly teacher, who was also the school's owner, was a social inferior. He was poorly paid. He brought no enthusiasm to his classes. He was strict. He taught by rote. Memorization was the order of the day. For these reasons Nilo's father continually asked Nilo about his studies. "How did it go today?" was a common question. His father also felt he had to reinforce the school's instruction. The primary challenge for Nilo's father, however, was his son's pessimism.

The school day's too long for me, thought Nilo. *It feels like jail. I can't grasp it all. I've had enough education. I need to be free—free from my father's overbearing concern and free from the school he makes me attend. How can I find my freedom? Am I too young to leave school?*

There was a bright spot, however.

Nilo felt energized every day during physical education. Here he was gifted. He loved wrestling. He loved running. Except during inclement weather, physical education was held outdoors in the *gymnasia's* courtyard. Time spent there was his happiest time of day. Time was allowed for him to run considerable distances outside the confines of the gym. He relished the freedom he felt by running without his tunic in the open air with the other boys. So much he would sometimes say, *Thank you Sparta* to himself and sometimes out loud. That's because he knew Sparta was the first settlement in Greece to include total nudity in their athletics. From Sparta, the idea spread to other Greek city-states. The small *gymnasia* Nilo attended served the private school for ages seven to twelve years. It included ample open space for running, wrestling and other forms of exercise. This *gymnasia,* however, didn't include a bathhouse. But the problem had long been solved. Instead of constructing a bathhouse, it was decided to locate the *gymnasia* next to a small, but fast-moving stream. Nilo had carved out his space at the side of the water where he relished sitting at the end of class. He loved feeling water splash over him in the outside air. He was curious about his body. He often spent time in the stream examining himself. He was particularly fascinated by his tiny blond hairs that covered not only his torso, his arms and his legs as well. He couldn't see his back but imagined hundreds of small hairs covering him there as well. He tried to imagine what he might look like in a few years after these tiny hairs had grown out and turned dark. *Will they all grow longer? Will they cover my entire body? How will that look?* He wondered. *Will I be attractive to anyone?* Meanwhile, he liked himself as he was.

For Nilo, there was little apart from physical education in the school experience he enjoyed. He saw the educational ambiance as unfriendly. Neither he nor his family knew what to do. Fortunately, he felt his formal schooling was nearing an end. He would soon be twelve years old. On the positive side, Nilo came from an upscale aristocratic family. He had many friends. He was endowed with strikingly good looks that surpassed youthful beauty. Both he and his older brother Demetrius were unusually attractive boys.

For boys and adolescents in the fifth century BC classical Greece, physical beauty might seem an asset. Not for Nilo. Neither for Demetrius. So attractive were these boys they had to be counseled by their family to be always careful. "When you're outside your house, know your surroundings," his father told them. "You must always know who's watching you." Although it was illegal for an older boy or adolescent to touch a boy before his teen years, dangers persisted. The not-too-distant history of Nilo's school illustrated this.

Not long before, young school boys were at the mercies of older youth and young men. Older boys and men routinely took sexual pleasures at the expense of the younger ones. They did so with impunity. Stories of abuse from those days abounded. Nilo heard many. So, while the young boy was not always pleased Chamus had to sit in his class to prevent his comportment from being a problem, he felt safer having the family slave walk with him to and from school. As to the abuse of earlier years, the school knew something must be done. New laws were made. While harsh, draconian to some, the new school policies were a direct reaction to the formerly all too permissive situation. It was a case of one extreme following another. The new laws existed solely to protect the children. They consisted of four parts:

1. Schoolboys were required to have a family slave be with them from the time they leave home in the morning and return from school in the afternoon.
2. No one over age twelve was allowed inside the school while young boys were there, except for teachers, teachers' sons or brothers or sons-in-law. The death penalty awaited violators of this law.
3. Gym supervisors could not allow adult males to take part in any way with boys in their building. If so, he too would be guilty of allowing seduction of boys.

4. Schools had to be on total lock-down before dawn and again closed tight when darkness fell.

The school day was nearly over. Nilo was putting away his writing and drawing materials. Like most days, he would walk home with his neighborhood friend, Theous. Nilo, Theous, and Chamus left the classroom together and were soon out on the passageway. Like many slaves working for aristocratic families, Chamus was a protector. He had been with the family for many years. He was well-trusted by Nilo's parents. He was responsible for seeing the boys remained safe on their daily walk to and from school. There were too many vultures (adolescents and young men physically attracted to school-age children) who reputedly could corrupt them. Nilo saw them as he did most days. *Why don't they stay away?* Wondered Nilo. *They should know they won't get their satisfaction from me.*

Although Chamus was with the boys, the ever-present lurkers on the passageway would not stay silent—never. But they made their presence known from a safe distance. Campus and the boys long ago learned to ignore taunting in the passageways. That didn't deter the hollering.

"Hey there, beautiful boys. We want to make love with you."

"You pretty, lovely boys. You are soooo cute. You look like gods. Come to us. We can make you happy."

Their conversations among themselves began when Chamus asked the boys what they learned in school. Theous was excited about melodies he learned on the lyre. "Hey. Let me sing one for you," he said.

Clap, clap, clap your hands and play,
Daddy's on his way.
Is he bringing something with him?
Yes, a little bag of cookies.

Clap, clap, clap your hands and play.
All the children are playing,
Clapping and dancing,
Tra la la, tra la la.

Chamus wanted to animate the boys about the upcoming Panathenaic Festival. Their participation would mean much. As it was, Chamus the slave dominated the conversation that day. "There's much we need to do to prepare for this event," he reminded the boys. "And we can do much to glorify our City's patron, the goddess Athena."

"Yes, yes," said Nilo finally becoming excited. "I'm looking forward to entering the running contests. That's all I want to do."

Theous too, said his family would participate in the events. Theous was also a runner and would be entering the same running contest as Nilo.

As they rounded a bend in the passageway, their respective homes came into distant view. The boys, as usual, handed their tunics to Chamus to hold while they raced the remaining distance.

Chamus cried out, *"Alpha, beta, gamma—**GO**."*
And the boys took off.

Today, Theous won. But not by much. The boys said, "Goodbye" to each other and went to their respective homes.

Nilo had mixed feelings every day as he approached his house. *Father cares so much for me. I'm happy about that. But he wants to know everything. He always asks about my day. He wants to dominate my life. But I need my freedom.*

As Nilo entered his house, his father was there as usual to greet him.

"Good afternoon," said Nilo's father. "Did you have a good day?"

"Hello. I don't know. Today was slow. Mostly we worked on writing, doing our sums and had some music on the lyre. That was in addition to our time in the gym."

"How'd you do?"

"Well, to be honest, I'm not learning as fast as I should. The teacher is strict. The music, the sums, and the letters take too much concentration. I can't keep up with the class. I'm sorry."

"Okay. We can talk about that. I can give you some pointers. Demetrius has a big interest in music. He knows the lyre. Perhaps he can help."

"But Demetrius doesn't like to help me," said Nilo. "He treats me like a little kid who doesn't know anything. When you tell him to help me, neither of us like it because we both know he doesn't want to."

Due partly to their six-year age difference, Demetrius and Nilo were not particularly close.

"But you're brothers. You need to be concerned about each other. You should also know your brother will soon enter military training. You must understand. He's concerned with that."

Nilo was smaller than average for his tender age of eleven. He was also nearing the end of his formal schooling.

From there, Nilo could continue his education with a tutor who would teach him during the day. But Nilo was not enthralled by education. "I know I'll be facing a tough future," said Nilo. "But my family, my friends, and improving my running are all I care about."

"I understand that. You put much effort into running. You've been doing that for a long time. Your running will pay off someday. But it's also important to plan your life's goals. You mustn't avoid taking care of that. We'll talk more tomorrow. I need to spend time with Demetrius tonight. Perhaps we can talk after school tomorrow."

When his father left, Nilo went upstairs and knocked on the door to his mother's room. Women of the upper class usually spent their days indoors. They're either in the cooking area, the weaving room, or their bedroom. The main rooms of the house were the province of the men. Women rarely went outside. Slaves made the necessary trips to the market and did other errands.

"Come in," said Nilo's mother. "How was your day at school?"

"Okay, I guess. We mostly practiced our sums and music on the lyre. Our instructor pressed us hard on doing quality work."

"You know that's important, don't you?"

"The professor said, 'Writing and especially rhetoric are the keys to our future.'"

"He's right. I'm glad he's pushing you to excel. That's the Greek way. We call it *agon*. It forces us to do our best.

"By the way, I asked Chamus to talk to you about the Panathenaic Festival. It's coming soon. Your father and

I would like you to be part of that. Perhaps you can be involved in some of the athletic contests."

"Yes. I want to. It's a chance to prove how well I can run."

"Well, the main reason for the contests and all the activities, is to glorify our patron goddess, Athena."

"Chamus told us about the Festival on our way home from school. We can attend many events. I want to be in the running races. I've practiced for a year. I'll be at a disadvantage because I'm the youngest in my age group, except for Theous. But I can keep up with the best runners. I know I can. With Theous in the same race, it will be exciting."

"We'll be proud of you no matter how you do. And what a big moment it will be. It'll be more than a festive time. You'll be competing with Greeks from all over the Mediterranean world. Beyond that, running in the Panathenaic puts you in good stead with our gods and goddesses."

"You know I'll try my best."

"Yes. I know that. And thanks for stopping by to see me."

While Nilo's mother was always supportive of her children, it was Nilo's father who gave them the most attention. He did this both as an advisor and a teacher. Nilo's father was close to his children, especially his sons. He was his children's teacher until they were seven. The boys then began formal schooling. Nilo's sister was taught by her mother instead of attending a formal school. That was the custom. Nilo's father educated his youngest son on the fundamentals of music, giving him beginning melodies to master. He also introduced him to the Greek alphabet and how to make simple sentences. Starting in the year before formal schooling began, he gave him simple lessons in personal etiquette. Getting along with others would be paramount to his future success.

Nilo's older brother, Demetrius, had also been taught and counseled by their father from an early age. In many ways, Demetrius looked much like Nilo. Both were short and shy, with radiant good looks. Demetrius was considered by his teachers as above average in academic work. He finished formal schooling at age twelve. He then began informal education with a personal tutor. Now his sights were set on fulfilling his compulsory military service.

Demetrius's feelings about military service were mixed. The thought of protecting Attica against its enemies fascinated him. But living together in cramped quarters with many others could be difficult. His father asked him to visit the Military Post. There he could learn the best ways to prepare for his obligatory service.

Demetrius would follow his father's advice. But first, he wanted to talk with his longtime friend, Clymus, who recently finished his military service.

In spite of a three-year age difference, Clymus and Demetrius had been friends for years. They shared ups and downs of growing up. They helped each other with school work from an early age. Demetrius excelled in music, while grammar was Clymus's forte. Clymus also excelled in athletics, whereas Demetrius was far less coordinated. The most profound difference between the boys, however, was their age. While being three years older isn't always too noticeable a difference with boys, the wisdom this brought Clymus was noteworthy. He had an innate sense of direction that was lacking with many of his peers. Demetrius, therefore, felt his friend could help him learn how to adjust to military life.

On arriving at his friend's large two-story house, Clymus welcomed him.

"What a pleasant surprise. I'm happy to see you."

"Likewise," said Demetrius.

"Anything special on your mind?" asked Clymus as he beckoned his friend to enter.

"Well yes, I have something on my mind." as he stepped into the spacious courtyard.

Clymus led Demetrius through the courtyard into the *andron* (symposium room). *Androns* are noted for having sofas on all sides. This was a space used not only for entertaining visitors, but for holding symposiums where adult men meet to discuss philosophy and politics. Many such events go on for hours, usually turning into drinking parties and social encounters. But today's discussion between Clymus and Demetrius would remain serious.

After the boys made themselves comfortable, Clymus said, "I'm glad you want to bring your concerns here. What's on your mind?"

"Well, as you know, I finished regular school several years ago. I haven't done much since then except having lessons from a tutor. Now it's time to enter military service. You've already had your two years as a *hoplite* (Athenian soldier), so I came to see you to get some pointers, such as what to do and not to do."

"Okay. That's a big question. It requires an even bigger answer. But please allow me to be frank about this."

"Why certainly. That's why I'm here."

"Okay. You probably know the Attica military requires our soldiers to be in top physical shape. I know you go to the *gymnasia* sometimes, but you're not in condition. I suggest you go to the gym all the way to your enrollment date and run every day. If you don't, the military's workouts will be too difficult. If you can do that, this is an excellent time to be a soldier."

"Why's that?"

"Because we're at peace. You probably know our chief adversary used to be Persia. Well, we kicked their butt. Not once, but twice.

"So, our chief enemy is no longer a problem. We don't believe the Persians will return. In addition to our increased military might, Athens created the Delian League. The Delian League is an alliance based on the island of Delos. It unites the navies of many city-states who agree to come to each other's aid if one of us is attacked. Its main purpose is to give notice to the Persians they should never again mess with Athens or our allies."

"I see your point. The League will protect us.

"I do have some other concerns if you don't mind."

"Sure. Go ahead."

"I was wondering how much time soldiers can have to be with their families and friends."

"Okay, but that's not an easy question. The reason is, there's no regular time for that. It all depends on what's seen to be the present danger to Attica. If other city-states are believed to be preparing to attack Attica, there would be little or no time off. If the reverse is true, you might be able to visit your family sometimes."

The conversation was temporarily stopped as one of the slaves entered the room. He was carrying two wide-brimmed bronze mugs of wine. They were diluted with water, a customary way to prepare wine in classical Greece.

"Thanks for the wine," said Demetrius, "and for all the information you've given me. It will help when my military service begins."

"I think you'll find your two years as a soldier will go fast. You'll soon be back with your family."

"Yes, I hope so," said Demetrius. "But could you share something from your experience?"

"Sure. It's not easy to fit two years of military service into a few minutes. But I'll try.

"I remember coming in with no idea of what was going on. So much to learn so fast. The army gave us rules as to how to conduct ourselves. Sharing small spaces with others requires cooperation. Then we had our jobs. Our spaces had to be always clean. There was no laxness about that. There were also kitchen duties. We took turns doing the cooking and kitchen clean up. Then we had our daily exercise routines. Those were the most tiring of our duties. The most difficult times were when some of the other city-states tested our resolve, and there were battle skirmishes along parts of Attica's borders. The recruits in their second year are stationed full-time along our borders. If a sudden skirmish developed with an enemy, they would be first responders to the attack. Fortunately, those didn't last long."

"It's exciting to know how prepared our City-State is. Thanks for sharing this. And is there anything else I should know about?"

"Yes, there is. Outside of military confrontations, the most difficult part is getting along with others. That's important. The tight spaces you'll be in make upsetting others almost inevitable. And vice-versa. You can't be too considerate of your fellow soldiers. You'll develop friendships and learn to be wary of some of the others. But as to friendships, you'll see relationships among some of the men. You may want to know something about that."

"Yes. I've heard about relationships from others. I have no idea if that's something I want to do or not."

"Being in a relationship isn't required. Not at all. But if you do, approach it gently. You don't want to start looking for a partner the moment you arrive. If you wish to have a relationship, let it happen gradually. Your commanders are open to that. Male-to-male relationships are an integral part of the life-blood of the military.

"One more thing. I'd advise you to visit the Military Post as soon as you can. There you can ask questions about how to prepare for your military service. You should especially want to know what equipment you're responsible for and what the military will give you. You might want to purchase your uniform at the same time. You'll be required to bring it with you when you report for duty."

"That's exactly what my father suggested. That's what I'll do." Demetrius picked up his wine cup for one last swallow. "I thank you for the conversation and your time."

"Think nothing of it. By the way, are you and your family planning to take part in the Panathenaic celebrations?"

"I think so. We've talked about it. My brother wants to enter one of the running contests. He should do well. He's a good runner. For my part, I'm not inclined toward athletics.

I may stay home or enter a musical contest." Standing up now, he said, "Thanks for everything. I've got to run."

Both boys said their goodbyes as Clymus showed Demetrius to the door.

Nilo was home waiting for his father. He wasn't looking forward to their conversation. He knew his father was intent on talking about his future. Nilo wasn't interested in continuing his education. He dreamed of having freedom.

As it was, his father wasted no time when he arrived After they sat down, Nilo's father began by asking, "How do you feel about your next few years?"

"I don't know. I haven't given it much thought."

"Your formal schooling will be over soon. You're almost twelve-years-old. You need to know how you'll continue your education. The question is how to do it. You haven't been happy with your present school."

"That's right. It's because I can't get interested. The school is boring. The teacher doesn't care about the students. There has to be an easier way."

"You might be right about your teacher not caring. But there's something you must know. Succeeding in life never comes by finding the easiest way. Looking for the easiest way isn't the Greek way. Succeeding is hard. It involves self-discipline—a great deal of self-discipline. That's the Greek way. Look at Athens. We have the best temples and the best sculptors in the world. We have the best philosophers, artists, historians, debaters, and government the world has ever seen. That wouldn't have happened without *agon*. We know we're the best. Through our endeavor for excellence, we succeed in all we do. And you my dear, you too can be the best in anything you want to do. We can help you by finding the best tutor we can get."

"But I don't want a tutor. If he's strict, I can't learn."

"Well, maybe we have to find the right teacher for you."

"But you know I don't want that."

"There may be tutors you will like. You need to know that. We have to see what's out there for you."

"But I'm telling you, I don't know how to do that. Anyway, I don't need a tutor."

"We can work together to find one you will like."

Nilo's father thought his son should become mentally ready for his next steps in life. He knew the coming years are critical. He believed Nilo should understand what his future experiences would be for the next six or seven years. His next few years or more would be with a tutor. Beyond that, he could continue with a tutor as his brother did. Or he could choose an *erastes* who would form a closer relationship with him.

"Okay," said Nilo's father, as he became more serious. "You're about to finish school. Your next teacher will be a tutor. His activities will be limited to teaching subjects you need to learn. That's all. He won't be foisted on you. You can choose your tutor. But as you don't know any, I'll help you. We can find someone compatible with you. You also have a say in choosing subjects. I say this because you have to think about your future. That means having a tutor for at least a few years. Then, if you want a different kind of teacher, you might want an *erastes*. He'd be more than a teacher. He'll teach you about all aspects of life."

Nilo heard about *erastes/eromenos* relationships from his peers. *It's one thing to know about it, but what's it like to go through that?* He wondered. *The idea of a stranger for a mentor is one thing. But a lover is something else. Anyway, I don't need more education. I need freedom.*

"First of all," his father continued, "You're much too young to enter a relationship with an *erastes*. You're not yet at the minimum age for such a relationship. You have to wait until well after you've begun puberty. That is, you have to wait for your body to change."

"Ah yes. When my voice changes and I start to grow?"

"Exactly. That happens well before anyone has an *erastes*. The problem is, we don't know when that'll happen. For most boys, the ages are thirteen to fifteen. For some, it's later than that. The gods determine this. But, even though you're not yet ready, that doesn't mean you can't learn about such relationships. That would give you more time to learn about having an *erastes*. Then it may be easier when the time arrives to decide."

"That sounds nice. But who knows if I'll get along with my teacher who'll be my tutor and maybe later my *erastes*?"

"Fair enough," said his father. "If you want to know more about this, here's what we can do. I can take you to where you'll see young men looking to be an *erastes* for adolescent boys."

"You can do that?"

"Absolutely."

"What kinds of places?"

"Well, there are many."

"Can you tell me of one?"

"Yes. Of course. One obvious place is the Painted *Stoa*. Do you recall the many times we've passed by there?"

"Oh yeah, I do. That's a gathering place on the north side of the *agora* (market). Isn't it the one where the back walls are covered with those famous paintings?"

"That's right. The paintings show events from Athenian history. You'll see many people there—mostly old men. They talk about whatever's on their mind. Occasionally a young man or groups of young men looking for an *eromenos* will be there before or after shopping in the *agora*. But it's not an ideal place for boys like you. You can be corrupted there. When you find yourself at the *agora*, you might want to stop by the *Stoa*. But don't linger there. There are better places. A *gymnasia* or one of the *palaestras* are places most frequented by young men cruising for an *eromenos*. I don't mean the type of *gymnasia* where you go to school. That's small. Only students use it. The public *gymnasia* is a place where many kinds of athletics are practiced. Most users are men and older adolescents. Then there are the *palaestras*. They're privately owned. Activities in the *palaestras* are limited to wrestling and boxing or a combination we call *pankration*. But don't go there alone. It can be intimidating."

"Are those places dangerous?"

"No. Usually not. But when the athletes see a young stud with exceptional good looks like you, well, they can give you a hard time. Some men have strong physical attractions to young boys like you. That's not bad. But it could make you nervous. I'll explain this more when we visit there."

"You want me to go to those places with you?"

"Yes, until you're older and feel comfortable in those settings. That's all. Tell you what. We should visit the *palaestra.* It's smaller and less intimidating for you. Later we can visit a *gymnasia.* As to finding a mentor, you must be careful. Finding a good *erastes* is a learning experience. Even though having one would be years away, it's helpful to know it about it now. These kinds of relationships have been proven to instill knowledge better and faster than private schools or any other way of teaching."

"But why do the friendships have to be intimate?"

"Excellent question. First, they don't have to. For intimacy to happen, there must be desire. Desire brings intimacy. That's important. Why? It's because intimacy promotes learning. We Greeks discovered education thrives best when combined with intimate feelings. It's true. Look at the great men of Greece: Socrates, Plato, and many others. Their learning had one thing in common. They all had personal tutors in their adolescent years. But more than teaching is involved. First the student, that is, the *eromenos,* feels tenderness from his *erastes.* When this works with erotic feelings, they relish their time together. This translates into better retention of what the *erastes* teaches his *eromenos.* Erotic feelings work that way. They greatly help in whatever profession one chooses. It makes no difference if it is teaching, or politics, even the military. This has been proved. We learned this from one of our dearest teachers of all: the philosopher Plato. When you're older, you're likely to read his well-known work, *The Symposium.* That's where he tells us:

> *While they are boys . . . they love men and*
> *like lying beside men and being embraced by*
> *them, and these are the best of the boys and*

> youths…The evidence for that is that it's only
> such boys who, when they grow up, turn into
> real men in politics.

"Plato mentioned politics as beneficial. But this has proved to be so in all fields.

"Now if we go to the *palaestra,* you'll see many who look like gods. Their bodies will seem that perfect. What you perhaps need most is awareness—awareness of how this happens. Would you like to do that?"

"Yes, if I go with you."

"Okay. We'll do it then. Are you able to go to the *palaestra* in the middle of the day tomorrow? It would be good for us to be there at its busiest time."

"Yes. I can be ready when you wish."

"Okay. When the sun's at the middle of its journey across the sky, we'll make our way."

"Thank you, father. It's late now. I'm going to sleep. See you tomorrow."

The two men went to their respected rooms for the night.

Nilo was tired. But sleep didn't come, at least for some time. He was worried about the *palaestra. Would I stand out too much,* he wondered. He knew he'd be uncomfortable if he were too conspicuous. *Would I be the youngest one there? Would they try to be physical with me?*

Nilo wasn't old enough to participate in such a place. He could go as an observer if accompanied by his father. But as his father said, it would be tamer than the public *gymnasia* which was more sophisticated by its membership, more robust activities and sheer size. He wondered why it's necessary to go to such places to find an *erastes* to teach him. *There must be a more natural way,* he thought.

In time, Nilo fell asleep.

In keeping with the suggestion by his father and Clymus, Demetrius went to the Military Post to prepare himself to be a soldier. He had seen the Post many times, but always from the outside. Still, he was impressed again as he looked up at the protective walls and the guards stationed beside the Post entrance.

He explained to the guards why he was there.

They asked him to wait while they summoned someone to give him a tour of the facilities and answer his questions.

Soon a uniformed young man came by. The soldier was clad in the typical Athenian uniform without the heavy battle armor. "Hello. I'll be glad to help you," he said. "You want to see our facilities?"

"Well, yes. And I'm also trying to find out what I need to do before starting my military service."

"You've come to the right place. There's not a lot to do before you begin your service, except, of course, the obvious. You need to arrive in good physical condition. That's important. It can't be stressed enough."

Demetrius didn't know whether to admit he hadn't been in good shape. *But maybe there's a better time to say that,* he thought.

"In addition to being in good physical condition before your military duty begins, you need to purchase a complete suit of *hoplite* armor. (*Hoplites* are foot soldiers having their type of heavy armor with their signature round shield.) You must bring this with you your first day of service. As to your first year of duty, you'll spend it as a trainee. We have a daily routine which you'll learn. We'll maintain that routine unless there's an enemy invasion, in which case you'll receive instructions on how to conduct defensive operations. Then in your second year, you'll likely be stationed along Attica's borders as a defensive soldier."

Demetrius didn't know what to expect from his visit. He was pleased his guide was friendly.

"We can go in now," said the guide. "Let me show you around."

The first stop was the cooking and dining areas. "Here's where meals are prepared. You'll be assigned to the cooking area from time-to-time. Everyone has their turn with chores with the food preparation and clean-up."

Demetrius looked at the rows of open pits for fires, some having grills. He also took a glance in the storeroom at the food supplies. In addition to the quantities of food, including dried fish, cheese, olive oil, and fruit he saw the many shelves where numerous *amphoras* (earthenware vessels with side handles) containing wine were lined up side-by-side.

Off to the side of the cooking area, Demetrius could see wide tables with benches where *hoplites* take their meals. He tried to imagine men gathering here and friendships being formed.

The guide said, "Here's where we take our meals. The morning meal follows our morning drills. It includes hard bread which everyone softens by dipping it in wine. Some days we have *teganites* for our morning meal. Those are flat cakes made with wheat flour, olive oil, and curdled milk. When we have enough honey or cheese, they're served to compliment the *teganites*. Then, there's our midday meal. Again, we have bread dipped in wine, but olives, figs, and cheese are also served. More than that, we're usually able to have dried fish a few times a week. Supper is our main meal of the day. It's eaten near sunset and consists of vegetables, fruit and fresh fish.

"Again, all *hoplites* have responsibilities in meal preparation. They take turns in the rotation. They also have responsibilities with cleaning up. Exact responsibilities are given when training starts."

The guide led Demetrius to the sleeping areas. He saw row after row of small cots lined up close to each other. He also noted small chests by each bed where *hoplites* keep personal belongings.

Ye gods. Could I ever live in such a tiny space and with so many people? wondered Demetrius. *Clymus was right about shared spaces.*

"Let's go on. I'll show you our battle equipment and uniforms."

"I'd like that."

"Okay, follow me," said his guide.

They walked together down a narrow corridor that slowly descended until they were below the level of the ground. They continued descending until they came to a heavy wooden door. The guide opened the door, and Demetrius was led into a dungeon-like room. Demetrius felt dampness in the air. They could not see well until their eyes adjusted to the reduced light which came from shafts where the ceiling meets the walls. When he could see better, he took note of large heavy rocks forming the walls. His guide took him into a side-room where weapons were laid out. *What an impressive sight.* Demetrius thought. Here before him was an assortment of daggers of various sizes, along with spears of many lengths.

"This is our weapons room. Feel free to pick them up to look at them," said his guide.

He picked up and handled some of the military weapons. These included daggers of various sizes and long spears. As he was examining their intricacies, his guide told him succinctly, "These are weapons of death. Do remember that."

That didn't excite Demetrius.

Soon his eyes fell on the longest spears of all. They appeared longer than his body. He went to lift one up. As he did, his guide said, "The spears must be held with both hands. Extra-long spears like these are used by front-line men in phalanx formation as they meet the enemy. The outstretched spears, close together, make a scene like a porcupine about to strike."

From there, Demetrius went on to notice the decorated round *hoplite* shields. He picked one up. He held it over his chest. *Would this protect me from a spear or a dagger?* Demetrius wondered. But he only had a brief time to ponder this. His guide was ready to take him to the next section where they would see the basic uniform.

He was shown the battle uniforms soldiers wear in combat. In the first section, he saw helmets. Demetrius's first impression was the ornateness and height of the helmets. Sensing his interest, his guide explained, "The size of the helmets has the effect of making soldiers appear taller than normal and hopefully, more aggressive. If one of our soldiers were attacked by a dagger or sword from above, the height of the helmet would help deflect the sword or blade attack. As you can see, topping off the helmets are these magnificent horsehair crests."

The guide picked up a cloth gown-like apparel. "Here's the basic uniform. As you see, it's a linen shirt. It covers *hoplite's* entire torso and more. The shirt hangs two hands width below the waist. For protection during battle, *hoplites* wear metal armor plates on their shoulders. Bronze breastplates cover their chests and stomachs. Finally, we have shin guards to cover the legs. Under battle conditions, *hoplites* carry their shields and iron-tipped spears for defense. Finally, they keep attached to themselves short daggers they keep in a leather shield to use in close combat. The average *hoplite* wears up to thirty-three kilograms (seventy pounds) of armor."

"That's all interesting. But why are uniforms and weapons kept down below and away from the rest of the complex?"

"Ah, good question. We keep them here in case of an invasion. If an enemy attacks the Military Post, the equipment is easier to defend down here. Now, tell me while we're here, do you want to buy your uniform? You'll need to have it when you report for duty."

"Yes, I'd like to do that. May I try one on?"

"Certainly."

When Demetrius removed his tunic before trying on a uniform, his guide expressed dismay. "Oh, ye gods. You're not ready to be a *hoplite*. You're not in physical condition. You must lose your flabby stomach. Your chest, your abdomen, and your biceps need to be much more pronounced."

"Yes, I know," said Demetrius. "I've been working out and running every day for a while, and I'll continue doing so up to my enrollment date."

"That's not enough. You should dedicate all the time you can before you come here. You need to push yourself as hard as you can."

"Your point's taken well. Thank you for letting me know."

By trial and error, Demetrius found the uniform that fit best. Finally, he said, "This one will do." He made the purchase.

The guide took Demetrius back through the central area. They were soon outside.

Once outside, they looked over the exercise area. "As you can tell, this resembles an outdoor *gymnasia*" explained the guide. "The *hoplites* practice athletic activities designed to coincide with battle-type maneuvers. Here they learn to use spears and catapults. Different maneuvers are learned that simulate hand-to-hand combat."

Demetrius could see a few men engaged in *pankration* (a blend of boxing and wrestling). Each man had a fake dagger to use on his make-believe enemy. Demetrius was impressed with the ferociousness shown by each fighter.

By now, Demetrius was feeling overwhelmed. *There's much to learn here. I wonder how the* hoplites *master it all. And I wonder how I'll ever get through it.* He thought he was at the end of the tour when the guide said, "There's one more area to see."

He was taken down a different corridor. There they came upon a second sleeping area. Demetrius noticed this one was not at all like the first one. The beds were wider. There was also more space between the beds. "Is this where the officers sleep?" he asked.

"Uh, no. It's not. This is a special area. It's reserved for the soldiers who are partnered. That is, they're either lovers or life partners with another soldier. You may think this is unusual for our army. I say that because we used to think such an arrangement wasn't fitting for the military. Now we're accustomed to it. Everyone accepts it without question."

"What changed your minds?"

"What changed our minds was the example set by Sparta. The Spartans have the best army in Greece. No army in any city-state compares to them. So, we decided to learn as much as we could from them. We studied their battles closely. In battles against Sparta, we saw one of the secrets for their success. They have a special battalion. It's superior from the rest of their forces. From observation during our battles with them and from interrogating our Spartan prisoners, we learned their superior battalion consists of partners who are lovers. It turned out these men do better in battle when they fight together next to their beloveds. That made no sense to us at first. But those soldiers aimed to exude utmost bravery under harshest battle conditions. In those situations, we learned a partner would never, ever, want to be perceived as a coward by his beloved. For these reasons we encourage partnerships and provide this special space for them."

Demetrius was glad his guide re-enforced what Clymus told him. *This debunks the old argument against men loving other men because they can't reproduce. My guide brings out excellent reasons for men to bond this way.* The entire afternoon was a teachable time for the young and impressionable Demetrius. He was taking it all in.

When the tour was over, Demetrius could more easily picture himself as a professional soldier. He would be an Attica *hoplite*. He was looking forward to his next major experience in life: a defender of Attica, with its City-State of Athens.

The next day, Nilo and his father left home in the middle of the day to observe the *palaestra* at its busiest time.

On the way, Nilo's father shared some thoughts.

"One thing that makes us Greeks what we are is our love for athletics and physical fitness. This makes our bodies more like those of our gods. In return, the gods reward us by looking more favorably on us. You're old enough now to begin caring about your physical conditioning in all ways."

"I'd like that."

"Some men take conditioning to heart. You'll see them right away. Others take a half-hearted approach to working out. They go over their routines for a while, then hang around with their buddies. Others do hardly any physical training at all. They're the ones who talk endlessly about whatever young, beautiful youths the see. Such idleness, while seeming harmless, is the scourge of our civilization. And above all, never appear anxious to meet a stranger.

Never. You must always appear to be involved with purposeful activity."

"Tell me, did you go to the *palaestra* when you were young like me?"

"I did when I was a few years older than you. When my growth spurt was evident, I couldn't wait to get started. My older brothers talked about the *gymnasia* often. They and their friends spent much time there. I was impatient. I couldn't wait until it was my time. What I learned was physical training is difficult. It takes effort beyond what you've ever imagined."

"Ay, you're giving me much to think about. I'm going to take it one step at a time."

"Good idea. Hey, we're almost there. The *palaestra's* up ahead."

What they saw was a rectangular colonnade building housing a series of covered porches. The covered areas served as shelters in inclement weather.

Nilo and his father entered the *palaestra* with its long exterior. There was a place inside the entrance for leaving one's attire. They laid down their simple one-piece garment by the others.

Like his brother, Nilo enjoyed being where he had freedom from his tunic. As they passed through the entranceway, Nilo now unclad, noticed the many men and youth turning their heads to see him. He even overheard a whispered voice saying, "Ay. That's the cutest one I've seen in ages. He's still a babe, though."

Nilo had been long accustomed to having heads turn wherever he went. His good looks were always noticed.

Father and son walked together down the colonnade passing different rooms: lecture room, bathing area, social area, storage, and others. Then they entered the wide courtyard.

The main feature they saw was a wrestling pit consisting of loosened dirt. As there was a pair of older adolescents engaged in wrestling, they found a bench and watched the action. There were others nearby waiting their turn to wrestle. They took notice of the muscularity and sounds of the grunts and groans coming from the wrestlers. What impressed Nilo the most was their appearance. He said to his father, "I've seen a lot of young men before with good builds and muscles like these. But I've never seen so many in one place. Some of these men look as if they could be gods, immortal gods."

His father laughed a bit and said, "These men have been coming here for years. They worked hard to develop their bodies. The good part is, you can look like that too. If you decide physical training is the choice you want to make, you can have a body as glorious as these men. But have no doubt about it. It takes work, training and much time to have a quality body as these men have."

They noticed a new match was about to begin. Father and son saw the wrestlers starting their preparation by applying olive oil over their bodies. They did this to prevent sand from entering their pores. The wrestlers then dusted themselves with a fine powder.

Rhythm was another component of wrestling. The combatants practiced and competed to flute music.

Another feature of wrestlers was maintaining their hair cut short. This was to keep their opponents from having something to grasp. Sometimes they wore a skullcap for the same reason.

The activity reminded Nilo of wrestling bouts he engaged in at school. Wrestling and running were the main activities where Nilo excelled. He knew his instructions well. The wrestler's objective was to throw his opponent to the ground from a standing position. A point was scored for a fall. A point was also scored when a wrestler's back or shoulders touched the ground. Three points were required to win a match.

Nilo soon realized he was the youngest in the *palaestra*—no children anywhere. He would've got up and left, but for his father's presence.

As for Nilo's father, he hadn't been inside a *palaestra* in many years. He lost contact with those he associated with. Now with the pungent odor of fresh sweat permeating the *palaestra*, the idle chatter, and groans from the wrestlers, Nilo's father more easily recalled his younger years. This is where he first met his *erastes* in this same place so many years ago. His name was Axios.

Talking to Nilo again he said, "Ah. The golden days of my youth, would you believe, they're coming back to me."

"You came here often?"

"Well, yes. But that was a long time ago. I was a loner here. I didn't know anyone. I was learning my routines; trying to get in shape and then remain in good condition. Because I was a loner, one of the trainers took a liking to me. His name was Paraxus. He showed me the ropes. He gave me helpful hints for training."

"He became your *erastes*?"

"Oh no. He already had his *eromenos;* someone I didn't know. But it was because of Paraxus I eventually found my *erastes*."

"Did he come up to you and introduce himself?"

"Not exactly. It went like this. It was warm outside, and especially inside the *palaestra*. Beads of sweat were falling off everyone. The instructor worked our group hard that day. It was for the approaching evening when we couldn't see, he ended our session. Then everyone headed for the baths. The baths were crowded, as you might expect on a hot day. It was then someone called my name. I looked up, and there was Paraxus. He came with a few friends. One of them, who looked younger—he may have been his *eromenos*, but I didn't know. Anyway, they had been working out and as the rest were rinsing sweat off their bodies. I hadn't seen Paraxus in a while. After our initial chit-chat, his younger friend slipped away. Then he introduced me to his other two friends, Axios and Comitas. Both were pleasant and friendly. But it was Axios who stood out. After our initial greetings, it was Axios who continued our conversation. 'I haven't seen you at the *palaestra* before. Are you new here?' he asked. I was shy then. I didn't know what to say. But I must've said 'yes.' 'Is this your first time here?' he wanted to know. 'Do you want to be a wrestler or perhaps a boxer?' His questions went on and on. When he looked into my eyes, I had to look to the ground. That's what I'd been taught to do. 'A youth should never act too interested,' my father would say, 'because by doing so, one would be considered easy prey.' Then before leaving, Axios asked if I planned to return to the *palaestra*. When he learned I didn't, he suggested I return the same day next week. 'We can talk more then,' he said. I didn't give an exact answer saying, 'I'm not sure.' or something like that. When it was time to say goodbye, Axios took one long look, deep into my eyes. That was something I'll never forget. I believe he also wanted to fondle me because he kept looking at me down there. But perhaps he thought better of that. After all, we just met."

"Did you return the next week, as he asked?"

"You know, I didn't know what to do about that. On the one hand, I didn't want to lose his friendship. But on the other, I couldn't allow myself to come across as being too interested. It was a difficult decision. There were some good reasons, though, as to why I eventually decided to go. First, as I said, I didn't want to lose his friendship. He seemed like a kind man, one who takes an interest in his friends. That was important. He was also a good friend of Paraxus. That meant much to me. That seemed to say he was a decent man, one who wouldn't take advantage of an adolescent. So, considering all this, I went to the *palaestra* the day he wanted me there. However, I wouldn't go early. I waited till late in the afternoon, an hour before the sun began to fall behind the mountains. Again, I couldn't seem anxious. When I entered the *palaestra*, I saw him in the wrestling pit. He was with a workout partner. I was sure he didn't see me. But I was able to see his body in a clear light. The body oil he used, his muscle tone and body tan all seemed to conspire to make him look like something special. His years of training did him well."

"When did he see you?"

"It was a little later. But yes, our eyes eventually met."

"Did you go over to where he was?"

"Oh no. I could never do that. But soon after he saw I was there, Axios came by. He said he thought I wasn't coming that day but told me how happy he was that I did. And from then on, he always wanted to be near me. I felt the same way but couldn't show that. That would've cheapened me, as a potential *eromenos* and as an individual. Axios wanted to take me places, do things for me, and he brought me gifts. He went on like that until I said he could be my *erastes*."

"How did you feel about that at the time?"

"Well, I enjoyed the attention, of course. At times I wished I didn't have to play hard to get. What I wanted to do most was curl up in his arms. But I had little choice in that. We must do what a decent adolescent in Athens must do, which is to act discreetly. But finally, he won me over. Then both of us were happy. I never regretted being his *eromenos*."

"What made you decide to give in?"

"Well, our society-scripted activity had pretty much played out. But there was more to it than that. I didn't want to be his *eromenos* because he would be a good provider and was enjoyable to be with. I had to know if he could be a good mentor, teach me how to get along in society besides being able to teach traditional academics. When I learned he could, I was willing to share my life with him, at least for the next several years."

"Wow. That's so fascinating. I'm glad it worked out for you."

The information Nilo was receiving made more interesting what he saw. He saw those serious about their training and the non-serious alike. Then he asked his father, "How can I tell if someone is looking for an *eromenos*?"

"No need to worry about that. The older would-be partners always make the first move. That way you'll know who they are. Besides, an attractive boy like you will never have to worry. When you're older, you'll meet men who have an interest in knowing you. Be patient. The most likely reason they haven't come this way is that I'm here. A prospective *erastes* doesn't want to be involved with a family member until after he becomes his *erastes*. Then it's important for both the *erastes* and the adolescent's father to know each other. In most cases they become friends. That's the way it is in Athens."

Sensing there was nothing more his son could learn at the *palaestra*, Nilo's father suggested they leave. They did. They picked up their cloak and tunic by the entranceway and left the premises. But before he could cover himself, Nilo felt a hand below his waist. He felt a hand clasp his genitals while giving a gentle squeeze. As this was clearly unexpected, he cried "Whoa," and the uninvited hand released itself.

At this point, his father said, "Ah, you've been groped. I should've warned you. This is common at the *palaestra*. But you'll get used to it. Believe me; you will."

For his part, Nilo was unable to speak. As they were descending the few stairs leading down from the wrestling school, his attention was again diverted. This time it was piqued by commotion on either side of the stairs. He listened to their voices.

"Oh, how lovely the wrestlers are today."

"Oh yes. Watching them hold their partners—that is so sensual. How pretty they are. What I'd give to be able to hold them as firmly as their partners. Each one is more beautiful than the other."

Another one said, "These men are divine, lovely, and ever so sensuous. Seeing such young men is as much a delight to us mortals as they must be to our gods. But oh, if we could touch them."

For Nilo, this type of talk wasn't new. He heard it almost daily on his way home from school. But he never entirely got used to it. Knowing boys like him and young men are thought of as sexual objects was an uncomfortable notion. He conveyed his concern to his father. "Is it always like this outside the *palaestra*?"

"I'm afraid it is. Many spend their days lurking around the *palaestra* to get any sights of the young men they can. They enjoy taunting the prettiest ones as they leave. And whenever they think they can get away with it, they'll try for a friendly grope. Sometimes they'll find in the crowd someone who'll go with them. Such young men are called a *pornos*. That is, they sell their bodies for money, but not for affection. In time, you'll get used to this activity outside the *palaestra*. It's normal for this place."

Back home, Nilo knew what he had to do next. He had to practice for his running competition at the Panathenaic Festival, now a week away. He was anxious to be in top condition for the event which meant so much to him.

Soon Demetrius came into the room. "Ah. I see you've returned from the *palaestra*. Did you enjoy your time?"

"Hi, Demetrius. Did I enjoy the *palaestra*? Indeed, I did. For the most part, that is. It was quite an experience seeing all those men working out. Some of what we saw, I anticipated, but other things were unexpected. I don't know what to think about those lurkers. I learned a lot anyway, thanks to our father. But there's a problem."

"What could that be?"

"Father showed me the *palaestra* because he believes it may be a good place to meet an *erastes* in a few years. But I don't need an *erastes* or a tutor. I've had enough education. Father's trying to force me to do something I don't need. I love our father, but why does he want to control me so much? I don't understand that."

"Father loves you, and so does mother. They want what they believe is best for you."

"What's best for me is my freedom. And what have you been doing?"

"Well, as you know, I went to the Military Post yesterday. My reason for going was to learn all I could about how to prepare for my two-year service. While the experience was helpful, I also learned how to prepare for it from my friend, Clymus. He already served. He insisted I get into good physical condition as soon as I can, certainly before my service begins. So, I have to start running and maybe someday even keep up with you."

"I'm happy for you. Let's pray we can both be stars. Meanwhile, we have to get ready for the Panathenaic games."

"Ah yes, the Panathenaic games. Yes, they're important. We're glad you're going to take part. What an honor that will be for Athena."

"And you, Demetrius? Are you doing anything for the games?"

"I'm not sure. As you know, I'm not proficient in athletics. But I might enter some of the musical or academic contests. I'll have a better chance to do well in those areas."

The next several days saw a frenzy of activity in Nilo's household. Most of this was in preparation for the upcoming Panathenaic games. Nilo's father was refreshing his memory of Homer. He would recite his orations to the public without using notes. For his part, Demetrius reviewed poetry to the gods he wanted to sing. All the while, Nilo was pushing himself to improve his speed for his race.

CHAPTER 2

The Panathenaic Festival

Hail, goddess and give us good fortune and happiness.

— **Homer's hymn to Athena**
between 12ᵗʰ and 8ᵗʰ centuries BC

With a few days before the Panathenaic Festival, nearly everyone in Athens was busily preparing for celebrations in their area of expertise.

Nilo's father was memorizing his recitations from Homer. He desired to recite from memory, not using notes.

Nilo's mother was rehearsing praises to the goddess Athena and other ceremonial roles where she would take part.

Nilo would practice his running up to two days before his contest. He felt he should rest the day before his race. He had been practicing for the past several months leading up to the competition.

Demetrius finally decided to sing poetry.

Nilo's sister would also sing praises to Athena.

Chamus, the slave, according to Athenian law, would not be allowed at the Festival, even if accompanied by the family.

All over Attica, citizens were working hard to ensure the Festival would run smoothly. Animals, mainly sheep, and bulls were rounded up for their march to Athens. The animals would be sacrificed in the massive slaughter known as the *hecatomb*.

Beyond the city gates, citizens in faraway *demes* (settlements) were making final preparations for traveling to Athens. Many had already begun the journey.

Two days before the Festival, the family gathered to ensure everyone was ready.

"I'm looking forward to it," said Nilo. "Preparing ourselves for the Festival is important. We need to show our goddess Athena how much we love her."

Nilo's father said, "I'm glad our family is committed as much as it is. We'll be getting up early, long before daylight on the Festival's first day.

"You may remember our route. First, we'll walk towards the City Gate. Marchers will make formations outside the Gate. If we're fortunate, we'll get a close-up look at the *peplos*, Athena's gown. It's so large it takes four women to carry the *peplos* in the procession's journey to the Acropolis. It took the women more than a year to complete the gown for our goddess.

"We also want to be in a good position to watch the procession as it goes from the Dipylon Gate to the Acropolis and into the Parthenon. After the procession, a significant time-honored activity is a sacrifice to our gods. It's called the *hecatomb*. Let me read from the *Iliad* what Homer said centuries ago about the *hecatomb*. Please listen.

> *They arranged the holy hecatomb all orderly round the altar of the gods. They washed their hands and took up the barley-meal to sprinkle over the victims [cattle], while [the priest] lifted his hands and prayed aloud on their behalf.*
>
> *When they had done praying and sprinkling the barley-meal, they drew back the heads of the victims and killed and flayed them. They cut out the thigh-bones, wrapped them round in two layers of fat, set pieces of raw meat on the top, and the priest laid them on the wood fire and poured wine over them . . . When the thigh-bones were burned and they had tasted the inward meats, they cut the rest up small, put the pieces upon the spits, roasted them till they were done, and drew them off: then, when they had finished their work, and the feast was ready, they ate it . . . As soon as they had enough to eat and drink, pages filled the mixing-bowl with wine and water and handed it round, after giving every man his drink-offering.*
>
> *All day long young men worshiped the god with song, hymning him and chanting the joyous paean. And the gods took pleasure in their voices.*

"On the day after the procession, we'll attend the other events, especially the contests: athletics, poetry, music, and others."

Soon the time came for the family to set out for the Festival.

On the morning of the Festival's first day, Chamus awakened the family one by one. He wanted them to have time to see the procession from the start. They readied themselves. Following their morning meal, they headed out.

Everyone was mostly quiet as they walked through Athens' passageways on their way to the Dipylon Gate in predawn hours. The closer they came to the City's center, the narrower became the passageways. So narrow, persons about to go outside would have to knock first on their door from the inside. That way, no one on the passageway would be hit when the door opened. From a distance, they could hear sounds coming from the *agora* and other places as most City dwellers were likewise making their way to the procession. From a distance, lights at the Gate from candles and torches were coming into view. "I can see the lights. I see them," shouted Nilo.

"Yes," said his mother. "We'll be there soon. Remember, don't act rowdy. We must always show respect to our goddess."

The family's conversation was interrupted by music from a small musicians' troupe. Tunes accompanied their singing on lyres and flutes. Emotions were getting high. The family was caught up in anticipation of the procession. The number of people on the passageways was increasing the closer they came to the Dipylon Gate.

"Will we see the start of the procession?" asked Nilo.

"We hope so," said his father.

Assuming they were all together, the family decided to continue getting closer to the action. They resumed pressing their way through the crowd. Demetrius wasn't with them. The family hadn't noticed that.

In time, they were unable to get closer to the Gate due to the tightness of the crowd. Nilo's mother said, "We have to watch the procession from here. It'll start shortly after the sun rises." At the same time, she was glancing around to see if her family was all with her. She counted everyone except Demetrius. She called his name.

No answer.

In a loud voice, she said, "Demetrius, where are you?" And even louder: "**Demetrius, we're here.**"

Again, no answer. Only a continuing buzzing from the voices of the crowd from every direction in the predawn darkness. They also heard the continuous music in the background.

Nilo's father added his voice speaking loudly, "**Demetrius, we're over here. We're here**."

Still, no answer.

"Where could he be?" asked Nilo. "Oh, this is awful." Nilo knew better than to cry, but he was apprehensive about his brother. "Demetrius! Where are you?"

His parents assured him, he'll be found. "As soon as the sun gives us light, we'll see Demetrius for sure," said his father. But in his heart, he didn't know. They knew much time remained for them in the darkness. Even the faintest morning light from the radiant sun was yet to be seen. What the family decided to do was remain where they were and not try to get closer to the Gate. "If we stay here," said Nilo's father, "Demetrius is more likely to find us. This isn't far from where we last saw him."

They waited. And they waited.

In time, came the dawn. With it no sign of Demetrius. The Panathenaic Way, however, was in view. They knew the procession was about to start. The crowd became less congested. Finally, Nilo's father agreed they should take themselves closer to the procession.

As they drew nearer to the Panathenaic Way, they first heard music signaling the departure of the procession from the Dipylon Gate, the main entrance to their City. Soon they would see the marchers. Though still anxious about Demetrius, they, like everyone else, were getting caught up in the excitement of the onset of the procession. It was instilling a deep sense of honor and piety. Then the marchers came into view.

"I can see them," screamed Nilo. In a short while, the first marchers would pass Nilo and his family.

The first in line were the priestesses and other Athenian women carrying gifts to be offered to their goddess. A piously profound hush in the crowd was apparent as they went by. Included were four women bearing the *peplos,* the folded-up gown to be offered to Athena. The women spent considerable time the past year weaving the robe. A significant event in the temple would be delivery of the *peplos* to the much larger-than-life statue of their goddess.

Following the women were animals to be sacrificed: sheep and cows.

Next came the *metics* (resident aliens). They were wearing their distinctive purple robes. Their extended arms carried trays containing cakes and honeycombs to be used as offerings to the gods. The *metics* weren't citizens. Therefore, they would not be making the offerings. Only Athenian citizens could enter the temple.

The *metics* were followed by musicians playing the aulos (a reed instrument with finger holes), the kithara (forerunner of the guitar) and the seven-string lyre, the most popular instrument in Athens.

At that moment, Nilo yelled out, "Look! Look! Behind the *metics*. There's a huge ship coming toward us. It's moving on land! And it's so big."

Nilo's father said, "Yes. That ship's called a *trireme*. It's by far the best ship in Athen's navy."

When it came closer, Nilo was enthralled by the Athenian *trireme*, which for purposes of the procession, moved on wheels.

Nilo's father said, "Would you believe that ship can have as many as one-hundred and seventy rowers at any time?"

All Nilo could say was, "Wow! What a beautiful ship."

Next in the procession came groups of elderly citizen men wearing white robes. They excitedly waved their olive branches to the noisy crowd.

The next contingent drew more than usual excitement from the crowd. These were the chariots. Two horses led each chariot. The chariots were arguably the most exciting of the contingents in the procession. The beautifully painted chariots held two men: a driver and his companion. They conducted themselves in the procession in a similar way as they do in the contests, albeit slower. In the procession, as in the contests, the companion would leap out from the back end, then run briefly on the ground beside the chariot while trying to maintain the same speed. Then the runner would jump up and re-enter the chariot, even while it was speeding. To the bystanders, this was a fantastic feat. This gained many oohs and ahs from the adoring crowd. Of all the components in the procession, the chariots, by far, commanded the most attention from the idolizing crowds.

Then came the military. The Athenian infantry, cavalry, and naval squadrons, in full uniform, all marching in-step together, made notable appearances.

Holding up the end of the procession were ordinary Athenians. They were grouped by their respective *demes*.

Many of the spectators joined in at the end of the procession. They were all moving towards the Acropolis. Others preferred to go by less congested passageways, which is what Nilo's family did. They decided to take a nearby narrow passageway that would also take them to the Acropolis. For them, it was a more natural way to move about.

But they hadn't forgotten Demetrius.

Concern for Demetrius was turning into a sense of fear for what may have happened. Nilo and his sister were crying. Their parents didn't know how to comfort them. Nilo's parents felt a need to keep a closer watch on their other son and daughter. They drew them near so Nilo and his sister were flanked closely by them on either side. They also stopped talking about the Festival. Their thoughts were centered on Demetrius, not the prestigious ceremonies engulfing their City. There was silence among the family members. Everyone knew what the others were thinking. They talked about going home. That would be difficult. The press of the crowd was surging strongly towards the Parthenon. They had to follow.

After passing through the *agora*, the procession continued forward with the pressing crowd behind it.

"The crowd is pushing hard," cried Nilo. They were going with the crowd—pushing until they found themselves directly behind the Acropolis at the Propylaea. Here was the main Gate to the Acropolis. This was the end of the line for *metics* (foreigners), and other non-citizens, as they weren't allowed to enter the Acropolis. "I'm being crushed," said Nilo referring to the crowd's thrust.

Surprisingly, almost as soon as Nilo said those words, the pushing abated. That's because nearly everyone was captivated by the sight beyond them. Even those who couldn't go farther could see ahead. On the other side of the Gate, they saw preparations for the massive animal sacrifices and prayers. There at the east end of the Acropolis, the mass sacrifice (slaughter) of one-hundred bulls known as the *hecatomb* was taking place on the large altar. Again, Nilo's father spoke up.

"These animals came here from all over Attica and from other nearby city-states. These are sacrifices to our patron goddess Athena and her father Zeus, King of all the gods and goddesses."

It was a major logistical maneuver getting the animals up to the main altar where the slaughter took place. Men with knives looking more like daggers were cutting the animals' throats. The bulls were on ropes and pulled toward the slaughtering point. They were held in place by ropes in a confined blood-splattered space so their throats could be safely cut. At the same time, men were in place handling removal of the manifold carcasses. The meat from these animals would be divided among the many *demes* whose representatives had come to participate. Those bringing smaller animals to be sacrificed held on to them until they entered the Parthenon.

After having a good view of the rich *hecatomb*, the crowd moved on. They continued until they were near the high altar in front of the Erechtheum.

The Erechtheum was an ancient Greek temple on the north side of the Acropolis. It was dedicated both to the gods Athena and Poseidon. Its name derives from a shrine dedicated to the legendary Greek hero Erichthonius. Having taken a good look, the crowd pushed again.

The crowd continued until it reached the Parthenon. A respectful silence overcame the crowd entering the Parthenon. They looked on in awe as they watched the *peplos* carried by four girls. Their movements were accompanied by musical sounds from the aulos and the lyres. They saw the *peplos* being set down gently next to the awe-inspiring, much larger than life, marble statue of Athena.

From there, those having sheep to sacrifice waited in line to perform the act with prayers and music. The solemnity of the event was apparent to Nilo. He looked on in awe. Particularly inspiring to him was the animals' owners getting "permission" from the victims to be sacrificed. This was accomplished by dripping water on the heads of the sheep. This caused their heads to bob up and down. That was taken as a sign of permission from the animals for their sacrifice. This would be the last of the ceremonies conducted inside the Parthenon. So ended the procession. From there, the crowd left the Parthenon dispersing in different directions.

At that point, the family's thoughts again returned to Demetrius. Nilo spoke up. "It's not right to be here while we're worried about Demetrius. We've got to go home now."

No one objected.

As they began making their way through the narrow passageways, not a word was spoken. Talking was pointless. As before, everyone knew the others' thoughts.

Nilo's father started thinking of the people he knew who might help him find his son. They would undoubtedly aid the family in their time of need. *But how to contact them? Everyone was here at the Festival.*

As they approached their home, each one was looking for possible signs of Demetrius. No signs were seen as they entered their house. The one person remaining in the house was Chamus. For his part, Chamus didn't see or hear anything from Demetrius. Before long, he too was feeling the same grief as the others.

At this point, everyone wanted to be left alone and went to their respective rooms. Some tried to sleep. They couldn't. An hour later, Nilo's father decided to talk to everyone. He would speak to them one at a time. He went first to Nilo's room.

"May I come in?"

"Sure," said Nilo. "But can you tell me how we'll find my brother?"

"We're working on that. We're trying to learn all we can do. The problem is, because of the Festival, it's impossible locating anyone to help."

"I see," said Nilo, brushing back tears.

"Later today, I'll look for friends who work for the government. They may have ideas."

"What do you think happened to him?"

"I don't know. There are many things it could be. He might be in the crowds looking for us. We must be patient. We'll find ways to look for him. We can also say prayers to Athena and other gods."

"Yes! That's what I've been trying to do. Do you think she's watching the Festival? They're mostly for her."

"I don't know, but I expect in some way she is. So yes, I think so."

"Then maybe she knows where Demetrius is and what happened to him."

"You're right. Maybe she does. If that's true, she'll have Demetrius back with us at the right time. Now I must reassure the others. You didn't sleep much last night. Please try to get a good nap."

After consoling other members of the family, Nilo's father wished there was someone he could turn to for support. It was tearing him apart inside that Demetrius may have met misfortune. He blamed himself for not trying harder to keep his family together. Now, he hoped, his help might come from the gods.

"Hear our prayers, Athena," he prayed. "We are your loyal subjects. Please hear our prayers."

CHAPTER 3

What Happened to Demetrius?

Even the darkest night will end, and the sun will rise.

— **Victor Hugo**
1818–1885

On route to the Panathenaic festivities, a primary concern for the family was finding a place to watch the procession. When one was found, they stopped. But even there, catching the view wasn't easy. Each had to strain his neck. As Nilo was the shortest, his father placed him on his shoulders. The next shortest was Demetrius. He couldn't see over the crowd. He looked around. Soon, he saw someone leaving his position on top of a small mound of dirt. Instinctively he went there. He didn't tell his family. *At last! At last! I can see what's going on,* said the happier Demetrius to himself.

There was much to see.

What held Demetrius's attention above all were the chariots. He could sense the courage it took to be a companion to the drivers. He tried to imagine what it might be like at competitions when more chariots participate and at a faster speed.

The two-wheeled chariots are small. Each one holds a driver and one other person: his companion. As the chariots drew closer, Demetrius could see the drivers' companions leap off from the back of their chariots onto the ground, all at the same time. *Incredible,* thought Demetrius. The companions then ran beside their chariots. Then daringly, they jumped up and back onto the horse-drawn chariot, again in unison. The horses, together with the runners, stirred up voluminous amounts of dust. Some of it drifted deep into the crowd. Demetrius, like the others, was absorbed in this event. His eyes remained fixed on the drivers' companions. But his attention was about to be diverted.

While he was captivated by watching the chariots, he felt an arm close behind him. He thought it was from the pressing crowd. He also felt an arm over his shoulder. At the same time, a hand covered his mouth. He was forced to go from the mound of dirt to a position several meters away. The crowd nearest Demetrius didn't take notice. They too were engaged by the chariots, while at the same time trying to avoid the ubiquitous dust.

Demetrius was taken to where he was surrounded by a small group of men. They took him through the pressing crowd. It seemed to Demetrius they went several blocks. Then the youth was taken through a wooden door into a small room. The small room led to a larger space where Demetrius would remain for some time. In addition to the men who brought him to the space, others were already there. They were waiting for "a good time."

As Demetrius was brought into the room, he heard a loud voice, "What have we here?" asked one of the men excitedly.

Demetrius was "escorted" onto a small platform about eight inches (twenty centimeters) high. One of the men grabbed Demetrius's simple tunic. He pulled on it until the boy was bare in front of them.

"Ah! Look! Look what the gods have given us: a splendid specimen of beauty. We'll take great delight in this gift from the gods," said one of the men.

"No." said another. "He's not a gift from the gods. He *is* a god! He came to us from Mount Olympus. Where else does one find such beauty?"

Without arguing further about who the boy is or where he came from, the men began touching him. Their hands soon spread over all the contours of his body.

Demetrius was trembling with fear. Finally, the quivering youth spoke. "What are going to do with me?" he asked with a tremor in his voice.

"We do the talking here," said one who appeared to Demetrius to be the leader. "You stay quiet unless we tell you to talk."

The men remained in an excited state while one of them brought out wine for all to drink.

Demetrius noticed there were a couple of two-person sofas at the side of the room. These were the same as those in symposium rooms in aristocratic homes.

"I'll have him first," said the man who Demetrius thought to be their leader.

Demetrius was taken to one of the sofas.

The others watched in delight as they filled their cups of wine. This wine, however, was not diluted with water as was the custom.

Demetrius was afraid. He was shaking with fear. *Will I live through this?* he wondered. *What is my family thinking about my disappearance? Can they do anything?*

He was forced to lie down on one of the sofas and follow the commands of the one who appeared to be the leader.

The ordeal with the presumed leader was difficult for Demetrius. Never had this happened to him. It seemed forever before the man was finished.

When the presumed leader was done with the youth, others came to be "with" Demetrius. They took turns one-at-a-time. Later, the adolescent was used by two men at a time. His body was reeling with pain. It seemed the awful nightmare wasn't going to end.

When there was a lull in the activity, Demetrius was asked to take wine.

"No!" he said firmly, "I don't like wine."

"You will drink," the men said.

The men continued drinking while forcing Demetrius to imbibe the wine as well. The strong wine they gave Demetrius was not diluted with water.

"Oh, my gods, hear my prayers to you," said Demetrius in a whispering voice, heard by himself, and he hoped, the gods would also hear his pleas. "Please deliver me from this ordeal. I beg you."

The gods neither responded nor did they come to his rescue.

Eventually, the men got tired. Some were drunk. They began lying down on the floor or sofas. Though it was daytime, they went to sleep. They were awake all of last night preparing for the "event."

For Demetrius, sleep didn't come. He sat there for what seemed forever. All around him the others remained asleep. The adolescent walked around. The door that brought him into the room was securely closed. There was no way to escape.

It wasn't until hours later, one of the men aroused himself. He was hungry and found something to eat.

He sat down beside Demetrius. Soon he began talking with the young man in a low voice. He put his arm over Demetrius's shoulder. "I'm sorry for this, for what we did to you."

"But, then why? Why did you do it?" Demetrius begged to know.

"You must understand my dear, how much you mean to us. We don't have opportunities to be with someone as delicate, as youthful, as innocent and one so full of beauty like you. It's so important for us to have fulfillment that can come from someone like you. You've got to understand. Please, try to understand."

"I don't know if I can," stammered Demetrius as he tried to say something more but was unable.

"I hope you'll find it in your heart to forgive us."

"I have to ask the gods about that."

"Perhaps that's all I can ask. Now I have a favor to ask you."

"A favor? A favor from me? You all do whatever you wish to me without asking. Why do you say you want a 'favor?'"

"The truth is, I don't like to force myself on anyone. But sometimes I must, as there's no other way. But to tell you the truth, I enjoy being with an adolescent like you much more when he also wants to be with me. But now, I'm too old to be anyone's *erastes*. I can't get their favors, especially not from the beautiful adolescents of Athens such as you."

Demetrius was taken aback by the openness of this man. He asked the stranger, "What kind of favor do you want?"

"Will you kiss me?" the man asked.

The answer surprised Demetrius. The man can come across like a human being after all. He was not acting like the animal he and the others were before. Nevertheless, he knew the man was still seeking gratification. Only he was doing it in a nicer way.

On the other hand, Demetrius's concerns centered on when he'll be free. *When will this nightmare end?* he desperately wanted to know. Meanwhile, he had to deal with this man who was still a stranger to him.

There was a moment of silence before Demetrius could answer the simple question, "Will you kiss me?"

Demetrius said, "Yes. I will kiss you." After everything he'd been through, he thought, *What more can a simple kiss mean? How could that hurt?* Demetrius then drew near the man. He placed his lips over those of the stranger. Not hard, and not soft either. Just a normal kiss.

"Thank you," said the stranger. "Thank you so much. And may the gods bless you." He then gave Demetrius an embrace which Demetrius didn't try to block.

"Here, here," he said. "Have some food. This is mine, but I want you to have it."

"I'll take part of it," Demetrius said. "You have the rest. I'm too distraught to eat much."

"I understand," said the man. "By the way, my name is Bacchides."

"I'm Demetrius."

More silence. This time it was for several minutes. Demetrius was still hurting. Also, he was fearful of what might occur next.

Demetrius asked the stranger, "What will happen when the men wake up? Do you know?"

"No. I don't know," said Bacchides. I don't make decisions here." Then Bacchides took a good look around the room. Although it was early in the evening, he saw everyone still asleep. They were up the entire night before. He thought a moment. Then he whispered to Demetrius, "Would you like to leave?"

What a surprise! thought Demetrius. Without further ado, he instantly said, "Yes, yes please," he whispered back.

"Okay. Stay quiet and follow me."

They both got up and walked into another room. Demetrius didn't have his tunic. That wasn't important now. He looked in the back room through the dim light. At that moment he couldn't understand why they were going there. There was no way he could see to go outside or to another room. He was confused. But Bacchides continued into the room with Demetrius beside him. He went over to a large tapestry on the wall. He pulled on it slowly. This revealed a small door. At that same moment, they heard stirrings from the other men. Bacchides opened the door and whispered to Demetrius, "Go and run fast."

Demetrius said nothing as he left fast and ran hard as Bacchides told him. Then he disappeared into the depths of the night's darkness.

Demetrius was still in pain. He found himself in a narrow alley. He was lost. All around he saw an unusual amount of trash, leftovers from the celebratory crowd. There were no lights anywhere. It was eerily quiet and dark. He continued in the same direction until he came to a passageway. It was a bit wider than the alley. Far ahead he saw stragglers from the day's festivities. When he caught up to them, he asked for and received directions that would take him home.

It was difficult for Demetrius to walk from the pain of his ordeal. He persisted until he arrived home. He reached for the door knocker. He hit it hard against the door, knocking three times.

CHAPTER 4

Reunited

Divine justice will extinguish greed, the
son of hubris, lusting terribly,
thinking to devour all.

— **Herodotus, Greek historian**
Circa **484 BC – 425 BC**

It was evening. Nilo's father encouraged everyone to eat. The family remained depressed. Too little eating and sleeping worsened their depression.

"What are you going to do?" asked Nilo.

"I'm still praying to Athena to show us our way, that is, what we must do," answered his father. "This isn't easy. We must be obedient to our goddess above all else. If there's a way for Demetrius to return, our goddess will show us the way."

"I hope he's alive," said Nilo.

"We all do," said his father.

Conversation stopped as there was a knocking on the front door. Chamus, the slave, went to see who's there.

Everyone else held their breath.

Chamus opened the door wide enough to see.

It was a neighbor, the father of Theous, Nilo's schoolmate.

Chamus opened the door wider. He let him in.

"I heard the bad news. I came by to see if there's anything we could do," Theous's father said.

"Thank you," said Nilo's father. "I wish there was something any of us could do. If there is, we haven't learned what it might be."

"I'll help you pray."

"We appreciate that."

"I also know people who work for our City. If there was a crime, a kidnapping, or any foul play, it's their job to deal with that. I'll contact them in the morning if you'd like."

"Yes, yes, anything, please. And would you like to share our food?"

"No. No thank you. I must be on my way. I'll contact you after I meet City officials. I'll tell you what they say." And then he was gone.

Nilo began sobbing, "I want my brother! I want my brother!"

"Please Nilo, please know we'll do everything to find Demetrius. That's a promise," his father said.

"I know you will. But I'm so unhappy."

"We all are. You must know the situation will be resolved."

Time passes.

There was another knock on the door. Once more Chamus went to see who's there. Again, he would open the door wide enough to see. Before he could, a voice said, "It's me. It's me, Demetrius."

Chamus opened the door as wide as he could, beckoning the beleaguered youth to come in.

He was dirty. He was naked. He was tired. His body bore sores.

Before any family members could say something, Demetrius said, "I'm tired. I don't want to talk. I must lie down."

Without saying more than, "I'll help you," Demetrius's father, and Chamus, carried the young man to his room. They laid him on his bed.

"Anything you want?" asked his father.

Demetrius said, "Yes, could you bring water."

Chamus immediately brought him water. He also gave him a wet cloth to put over his forehead to cool his temperature.

Demetrius's father said, "You don't have to talk. We'll talk when you're ready. Now you can rest or sleep. Chamus will be outside your room all night. If you need anything, call his name."

"Thank you and thanks to our dear goddess Athena. I'm grateful to her and happy to see you all. I must rest now. Good night."

"Good night Demetrius," and his father left the room. He went to be with the others.

Everyone's joy for Demetrius's return was palpable.

"I can't wait till Demetrius is better and can talk," said Nilo.

"We all feel that way," said his father. "But we have to give him time to get well. If Demetrius doesn't feel like talking when he wakes up, we shouldn't question him. We'll soon know what happened. What's important is he's alive. He's home again. Now we can start thinking again about the Panathenaic contests. I'm sure Demetrius wants us to be involved. It's our way to thank Athena. Now let's get some sleep."

Following the father's advice, they all went to bed.

Remarkably, everyone fell into a deep sleep. Fears about Demetrius had disappeared. Calm and reassurance returned. But then, in a few hours, sobs and unintelligible sounds were heard from Demetrius's room. The noise woke up his father. He raced to his side.

"Are you okay?"

It appeared the young man wasn't awake. In his sleep, he was turning and making sounds that couldn't be understood. But from out of a cacophony of loud and unintelligible noises, his father deciphered a few words:

"No. No. Not again, please!"

It took a while before his father figured out what was going on. Demetrius was having a nightmare. By way of his dream, he was reliving the horrible infliction that befell him the day before.

"You're safe now. You're home with your family. We love you. We're going to take care of you."

The young man didn't hear the words of reassurance. He remained asleep.

His father stopped talking. He stayed by his bed with his arm extended over his son.

Nilo and his sister came to the doorway. Nilo asked, "What's going on? Is Demetrius okay?"

"I think so," said his father. "Dreams like this are normal. He'll be alright soon. You can return to bed. We'll talk in the morning."

Before the children could leave, Demetrius cried out again. "Don't do that. I beg you." And again, he turned his body.

This time his father decided to wake him. *He shouldn't have to experience that pain again,* he thought. He rubbed the young man gently on his back. "Please wake up, Demetrius. It's a bad dream," he said.

Demetrius did not awaken.

Then his father called to Nilo who remained in the doorway. "Please bring me another cloth soaked in cold water. He still has a fever."

Nilo returned with the wet cloth. His father placed it on Demetrius's forehead.

Again their father asked Nilo and his sister to leave. "Now you two return to your rooms," he said. "We'll talk in the morning."

The children did as their father asked.

The wet cloth must've affected Demetrius as he stopped his frantic screaming. He was breathing normally. His father kept an attentive watch as his son drifted into a regular sleep. While things were looking better for the young man, his father didn't leave his bedside.

Nothing changed until hours later.

Demetrius opened his eyes. It was still dark, but he was able to look around. *I'm home! I'm back!* he gleefully thought. *How wonderful this is.* As he was gazing, he noticed his father asleep on the floor. *Ye gods! My father's here. He must've been here all night. Should I wake him? No. I'll let him sleep. My ordeal must've caused a strain for everyone.* Demetrius continued resting on his bed until his father began to stir. Demetrius sat up. He looked at his father. In a moment their eyes met.

"I see you're awake," said his father.

"Yes, and you are also."

"How are you feeling?"

"I'm rested, but a little confused."

"Are you hungry?"

"I can wait until the others are ready."

"Would you like to talk now?"

"If you mean what happened to me. No. I'm sorry. I can't relive that."

"That's fine. Take it easy until you're back to your normal self."

"Thank you. It's a happy feeling being with you."

From the doorway they heard a voice, "And we're also happy you're with us."

"Nilo! What are you doing up so early?" His father asked. "How long have you been standing there?"

"A few moments. I heard Demetrius's voice. I had to see him."

"Yes. I understand," said his father.

"Please come in," said Demetrius.

The brothers then reunited with a warm hug. "Ouch! Please be careful," said Demetrius. "My body still hurts."

"It's good to see you, Demetrius. We were worried about you. The gods were good to us in letting you come home."

"Yes. I knew you were praying for my safe return. And you're right. The gods didn't let us down."

By then the other family members had gathered at the door to Demetrius's room.

Demetrius's father said, "We're going to let you rest. We'll have plenty of time to talk. Chamus will remain outside your door. You may call on him for anything."

"Thank you, my dear family," said Demetrius. "I love each one of you."

Everyone left the room.

Downstairs they began talking about picking up their life from before the ordeal with Demetrius began.

"Are we going to continue with the Panathenaic Games?" Asked Nilo's sister to no one in particular.

"It depends on how everyone feels," said her Mother. "It may be a good idea as Athena is responsible for your brother's return."

"I'd like to go," said Nilo.

"So would I," said his Mother. "We could even go there today, that is, if everyone feels up for it."

"Yes," said Nilo. "My race is on today. Do you think Demetrius might come with us?"

"I don't think he's ready for that," said his father.

Before leaving for the Games, Demetrius's father made one more visit to his son's bedside. "We're going to the Games. Is there anything you'd like to say before we leave?"

"If you mean telling you what happened, no. I still can't do that."

"I understand. We'll try to return early." And he left Demetrius's room.

Demetrius stayed in bed all day. He slept intermittently. Chamus remained at his side. Meanwhile, the family left their home to attend the Panathenaic Games.

When they arrived at the Games situated by the *agora*, they were surrounded by a crowd waiting for the athletic events to start.

Other activities for this day had already begun. The family arrived during the musical and rhapsodic melodies. They consisted of both patriotic as well as religious offerings to their gods. Most conspicuous were those with their lyres, kitharas, and reed instruments.

The warming up on the instruments soon ended. So did conversations in the audience. They knew the formal music and singing were soon to begin.

Without fanfare, the singer and musicians took their places. They waited until the crowd quieted down. The singer had chosen for this day his rendition of the opening lines from Book I of the *Odyssey* by Homer.

With the hush of the gathered crowd, the singer began.

> *Tell me, Muse, of that man, so ready at need, who wandered*
> *far and wide, after he had sacked the sacred citadel of*
> *Troy, and many were the men whose towns he saw and whose*
> *mind he learnt, yea, and many the woes he suffered in his*
> *heart on the deep, striving to win his own life and the*

return of his company. Nay, but even so he saved not his
company, though he desired it sore. For through the
blindness of their own hearts they perished, fools, who
devoured the oxen of Helios Hyperion: but the gods took from
them their day of returning

The music continued as the singer paused. After a moment, he continued singing the melody.

Now all the rest, as many as fled from sheer destruction,
were at home, and had escaped both war and sea, but
Odysseus only, craving for his wife and for his homeward
path, the lady nymph Calypso held, that fair goddess, in her
hollow caves, longing to have him for her lord. But when
now the year had come in the courses of the seasons,
wherein the gods had ordained that he should return home to
Ithaca, not even there was he quit of labors, not even
among his own; but all the gods had pity on him save

*Poseidon, who raged continually against
godlike Odysseus,
till he came to his own country.*

The familiar singing was intended to put the audience in the mood for what was to follow, namely, the athletic events. The first event would be the men's race. The men were already in preparation. Some were doing their paces while others were applying olive oil to their bodies. Most were paired up in applying the liquid to each other's bodies. This would help their naked bodies shine while keeping dust out of their pores.

In addition to contestants using it to spread over themselves, olive oil had an essential role during the games. As an indication of value, in the fourth century BC, the prize for the victor in the *stadia* race (a six-hundred-feet-long foot race) in the men's category was one-hundred *amphoras* (ceramic jugs) of olive oil.

The men were asked to take their positions at the starting line.

The participants took their places with their barefoot toes tucked-in behind the starting line. Their shining, naked bodies bent forward slightly, anticipating the start of the race. At that exact moment a loud voice cried out:

"Alpha, beta, gamma—**GO!**"

The men took off.

Nilo, his father, along with everyone else watched intently as the men broke loose from the starting line. They made their way down the track. There were yells from the sidelines. Families were rooting for their favorite contestant:

"Faster, faster."

"You can do better."

"Don't slow down."

"Go, go go!"

And so it went, as the racers went 'round and 'round the track.

The air was filled with pervasive dust kicked up by the runners. Much of it went into the attentive crowd. Many turned their heads to protect their eyes.

All too soon the race was over. This race was not close, at least not for the front-runner. He came across the finish line a few meters before anyone else. Immediately a crowd formed around him. When the crowd was quiet, the winner cried out: "Thank you, thank you, everyone. Thanks especially to the gods who made my victory possible."

No sooner had the winner made his announcement when the race area was cleared of friends and families of its participants. Now other families and friends were gathering by the track. They came to watch the next race which was in the eleven to sixteen age range.

Nilo proceeded onto the track. He took his position behind the starting line. Once he found his place, Nilo looked at the other racers. He wasn't pleased. They were mostly older than him. He also noticed the fifteen and sixteen-year-olds with long legs and bulging muscles. He also spotted his good friend Theous at the other end of the runners' line-up. Looking at the well-built youths and young men, Nilo thought, *They must've been practicing for years. Is it possible I'll have a chance? Anyway, I'll know soon.*

The contestants readied themselves. For the second time this day, the announcer cried the familiar words: "*Alpha, beta, gamma*—**GO**."

The runners took off. Again, heavy dust was kicked up. It spread everywhere. For a moment no one could see how the runners were faring. But it was soon apparent Nilo was far behind the front-runner. Nilo, for his part, was determined to close the gap. *The gods are with me. I know that. I feel the* agon. *I can and will do my best.* He was determined to make his legs go faster as he was about to go into a turn. He went into the bend with his head held high. So high he didn't notice the small flat rock in front of him. The rock slipped away into the loose dirt when his foot stepped on it. Nilo tumbled to the ground. He wasn't badly hurt as he saw runners pass by. He got up a bit shaken. He tried to catch up in the race. Unfortunately, the others were too far ahead. Nilo knew he couldn't regain his position. He straggled off the track.

Immediately his father came to him.

"I'm sorry," Nilo told his father. "I disappointed you."

"No, you didn't," his father exclaimed. "It was a freak accident. It could've happened to anyone."

"I love you, but I embarrassed our family."

"You didn't embarrass us. You tried your best. And remember this was your first time in the Panathenaic races. You'll do better next time." But Nilo's father had a good idea of how the boy felt. His son was obsessed with doing well. Now he felt disgraced.

"We'll talk more about this and how you can make up for this in your next outing." But he didn't know if Nilo wanted to continue talking about his fall. He changed the subject. "I don't think you want to watch the other contests. Maybe it's best if we go home. We also need to clean up that nasty cut on your knee."

The family left the contest area and went home.

After tending to Nilo's wound, the boy's father went into deep thought about how he might best handle his son's situation. He pondered this for some time. Eventually, he decided to talk again with Nilo.

"Nilo dear, how are you feeling?"

"If you mean about that race, not so good."

"I'm sorry this is bothering you so much, but I do understand."

"My whole heart and soul looked forward to this race. I was expecting to do much better."

"Many people suffer heavy defeats in whatever endeavor they choose. Then they come back and surprise everyone with a stunning performance."

"Yes, but what makes you think that'll happen to me?"

"I don't know. Much of it has to do with your desire. Are you interested in continuing your efforts in racing?"

"I don't know. If I continue being made a fool of, not at all."

"But if you can become a successful runner, would you like that?"

"Absolutely!"

At this point, Nilo's father didn't know what else to say. He didn't contribute more to the conversation. Nevertheless, he kept thinking about Nilo's situation and how he might help his son overcome his severe disappointment. He also wanted to turn his attention to his other son.

Demetrius was asleep when the family returned from the Games. Later, when he awoke, he still hadn't heard how they went, and especially about Nilo's poor performance. As it was, Nilo gave him the bad news.

"I did terrible. I didn't even make it around the track once before falling. It's like I shouldn't try to be a runner anymore. There's no future for me in running. What keeps me happy is you, Demetrius. You're alive. You're home with us. For me, that means everything."

"Thank you for your kind words. But don't take your defeat so hard. You're a beginner. You were running against those much older and accomplished than you. Of course, losing is difficult. But you mustn't be so hard on yourself."

"I can't help it, Demetrius. I've done badly in school and in almost every subject. This is a stain on our family. Running was all I could do well, or at least I thought so. I've let my family down in every way. And how are you feeling?"

"I'm better thanks. All this sleep has helped. I hope to join the family soon and lead a normal life again. Father wants me to discuss the ordeal I had, but I'm nowhere near ready to do that."

"I understand. Try to get more rest. We'll be here if you need anything."

"Thank you. And can you ask father to come here?"

"Sure. Talk with you later."

Downstairs Nilo talked with his father. "Demetrius is wide awake now. He's doing much better, but he's still not ready to discuss what happened to him. He said he wants to talk with you."

Father thanked Nilo and went immediately to be with Demetrius. When he was at his bedside, he asked about his condition, and if he had enough food and sleep.

Demetrius said, "I'm okay," Demetrius lost interest in talking about himself. He was more interested in impressing on his father how hard Nilo was taking his loss at the

Panathenaic Games. "My brother is depressed. He feels he disappointed his family, his friends, and most of all, Athena. He doesn't feel like he has a future. Here he is, about to enter his youth, the most exciting years in life and he's devastated by what happened. The truth is, I don't know how to help him. It seems words don't mean anything. He seems resigned to his failure. I wish I knew what to do."

"Yes. I sense that too. And to be honest, I don't know what to do either. But I promise you I'll give this much thought, perhaps talk with Athena. She's our goddess of wisdom, you know."

"Yes, I know. That's a wise decision. There has to be a way to help Nilo."

"Yes, there must be. And you Demetrius, perhaps you should be resting again. We're praying you'll soon be able to get up and be with the family."

"I hope so. Thanks for everything."

"So glad you're feeling better. We'll talk more soon." Demetrius's father left his room.

CHAPTER 5

A New Course for Nilo

*Falling is not a failure. Failure comes when
you stay where you have fallen.*

— Socrates
Circa 470 – 399 BC

As the days passed, thoughts and concerns of the family turned less on Demetrius and more towards Nilo. While Demetrius still couldn't share the experience of his abduction with anyone, he was gaining strength and appetite. He was up with the family and living more like he was before his nightmare experience.

It was Nilo with whom the family's concern became focused. He remained in a deep depression. The boy continued feeling he had no future. School remained a problem. He had less enthusiasm for running. No one knew how to help him. It was in this atmosphere Nilo's father, more than anyone else, took Nilo's situation to heart.

After days of contemplation, long talks with Nilo, and regular prayers to Athena, the boy's father realized neither he nor any family member was able to improve how Nilo was doing. This awareness became the catalyst that would bring change.

If I can't do anything for Nilo, there must be someone who can. This thought invigorated the boy's father as he realized he didn't have to depend solely on himself nor his family to resolve Nilo's condition. *But who? Who can I turn to for help?*

There was no immediate answer to his question. His thoughts turned to friends and those he knew in the government. No one special came to mind. He considered checking out philosophers in the *stoas*, but he believed they wouldn't get far with Nilo. Then something happened that took his attention away from Nilo and back again toward Demetrius.

One quiet afternoon Demetrius came to his father. He asked, "Can we talk?"

"Of course. You know we can discuss anything whenever you like. What's on your mind?"

"Thank you. I want to tell you I'm ready to discuss my ordeal."

His father was taken by surprise. "In the name of our gods, I wasn't sure you'd ever be ready to talk about that. But yes. I'm more than willing to listen to you if you're sure you want to share your experience. But there's one thing I'd like to do first." He called for his slave Chamus. When Chamus came into the room, he was told to ask the father of Nilo's friend Theous to see if he might come over to listen to Demetrius discuss his ordeal.

Demetrius's father explained to his son, Theous's father "has ties with the government. He has friends and acquaintances among them. More importantly, he knows Athenian laws. It would be helpful if he could hear your story."

In a brief time, Chamus returned with Theous's father.

"I'm glad you could be here," Demetrius's father said. "It's important for you to hear what my son has to say."

"Thank you. I understand how you feel. Everyone wants justice to be served."

They went to the *andron* (symposium room) to hold the conversation.

Theous's father was offered a place on a sofa and sat down.

Demetrius's father opened the conversation. "Okay. Let's get right to the subject. We left home early in the morning to see the Panathenaic procession. We were enjoying the groups in the procession. We were especially excited when the chariots came by. Everyone's attention was riveted on them. We had moved closer to the action, but unknowingly, without my son. My wife was first to notice Demetrius wasn't with us. She called his name. There was no response. We took turns calling for him. But no answer. How could we look for him in a crowd so wedged together? It was impossible. We stayed put for a while. Later we followed the procession up to the Acropolis. We saw the *hecatomb* and other activities. That was fascinating. For a while, it took our thoughts away from Demetrius. We saw everything. When the formal activities were over, we came home. We were hoping Demetrius would be here. But he wasn't.

"Now, Demetrius, it's your turn. Could you begin when you were separated from us?"

"Yes. I'll be glad to. As we were watching the events, I removed myself from the family to a short distance away. That was because I was looking for a place to see everything as I'm shorter than most of the crowd. I found a good spot. Then like the others, I immediately got caught up in the excitement of watching the chariots."

"Ah yes," said Theous's father. "We all got caught up with that. Go ahead, Demetrius."

"Okay. Several men, I don't know how many, came behind me. One twisted my arm and put his hand over my mouth. They dragged me several blocks and through a door and into some rooms. Then they put me through the worst ordeal of my life. They put their hands all over my body. They did all kinds of things to me."

Theous's father interrupted and asked, "Sexual things?"

"Yes, definitely," answered Demetrius.

"Did you want them doing that to you?"

"No. Definitely not!"

"How long did that go on?"

"I don't know. It seemed like hours. They were taking turns. Sometimes two of them were going at me at the same time. The pain was severe."

"No need to continue what they did to you. I'm curious how it ended. Did they simply let you go?"

"No. It wasn't like that. They were drinking a lot. It was undiluted wine. They forced me to drink with them. Then they fell asleep. They didn't sleep the previous night because they were planning this activity. I couldn't sleep. The pain was too much. However, one of them woke before the others. He befriended me. He apologized for their behavior, including his own. He even told me his name. It was Bacchides. He opened a door for me before the others woke up. He told me to run. I went directly home. You know the rest."

Theous's father, acting somewhat surprised said, "We may have a case here. You all may know when someone does as he pleases with another person without his consent, it's a serious crime. It's called *hubris*. The penalties for *hubris* are severe. I will report this. You will hear from me. It might be that you'll be asked to give descriptions of the men who abducted you."

"I'll be happy to do what I can," Demetrius said.

"We'll be in touch then."

Demetrius and his father said in unison, "Thank you, thank you."

After Theous's father left, Demetrius felt a load fall away. "I'm glad I told you," he said to his father. "It's not like it's bottled up inside me anymore."

"I'm happy to hear that. Now you can get on with living."

While Demetrius was improving, Nilo's situation was far from being resolved. The boy remained depressed and appeared to have little ambition.

It was clear to their father where he should devote his attention. He decided several days ago he'd try to find someone who could help his son. No one came to mind. *How can I help Nilo?* He pondered. He knew among the Athenian aristocracy there are men of great renown. *These are men who mastered many emotional ups and downs of day-to-day challenges that keep others behind in life.* But how could he tap into those resources? He thought of persons who crossed his path during his adulthood. He had listened to philosophers expounding their beliefs in the *stoas* and the *agora*. That's not what he needed. Names of former acquaintances crossed his thought. None fit his need. His pursuit turned to those who gave him sound advice in his younger years. Still, he couldn't come up with an answer. He had to lower expectations. Eventually, he decided to check out an old friend Axios, his former *erastes*.

He knew from the start Axios didn't meet the criteria for the many tasks of a tutor and trainer his son desperately needed. That was certain. But he also knew that Axios over many years developed contacts with those in educational circles. While Axios himself wasn't the one he was after, he felt he was more than qualified to suggest who that person might be. So, he went looking for Axios. As it was, it took him some time to find him. They hadn't been in contact in recent years. But by asking numerous acquaintances, he was eventually led to the home of his former *erastes*.

After a knock on his door and a brief wait, the door opened.

"Axios, my friend, how are you?"

"So good to see you. What a wonderful surprise." The two former lovers shared a warm embrace. "Please come in."

Axios took Nilo's father into the *andron* where he was invited to sit down. The men exchanged pleasantries and got caught up on their lives. After which Axios said, "The years have been good to you. You have no idea how happy I am to see you."

"The truth is, I've wanted to see you for a long time. As you know, we played an important part in each other's lives for many years. You were good to me. You taught me about life and much more. I couldn't have had a better *erastes*. Most of all, you were the best friend I ever had. While I wanted to see you before now, too many things got in the way, mainly responsibilities to my family."

"Ah yes. I understand. And I wanted to see you, too but didn't know how to look for you. But here we are. I'm so happy to see you."

At this point, Axios's slave entered the room with two wide-brimmed brass mugs of water-diluted wine.

"Oh, thank you."

"It's a pleasure, my friend."

Nilo's father then explained the reason for his visit. "Axios, the reason I came by is to ask your advice. Years ago, you were helpful to me when I needed to know about many things. Now again, there's a big question mark in my life. I have no idea what to do."

"And what may that be?"

"You certainly know for Athenian families, the most important thing in their adult life is their children are successful. That they lead a happy and rewarding life."

"Oh absolutely. Yes."

"Well, my youngest son seems headed towards failure. He lost his ambition. His school work's been a disaster. I don't know what to do about that. The one bright spot in his life was running. But he did a devastating performance at the Panathenaic Games. That destroyed his morale. He has no interest in going forward. And even before his poor performance, he didn't want to continue his education. I've talked with him many times. There seems to be no hope. I'm looking for someone who can help him academically, which he desperately needs, and instill in him his former love for athletics, especially running."

"Ye gods! There's much in what you said. Getting someone to improve his life, especially someone who doesn't want to improve, well that's a tall order, my dear. I don't know if I can help you or not. But that's not to say I won't try. You're a good friend. I'll always do what I can for you. It warms my heart to see a father with so much affection for his son he would do anything to get him on the right road. But let's be clear. Your son may be beyond help. But we don't know that. We have to assume he can be helped."

"Thank you. Do you have immediate thoughts on how you might help?"

"No, I don't. But I do believe there are people out there who can help. My sense is you prefer this to be one person who both tutors him academically and someone who has talent in the *gymnasia*. However, if he's looking for an *erastes*, please know I can't help you. It's your son who decides who his *erastes* will be, should he someday decide to have one."

"Oh gosh no. Nilo's way too young to have one, much less to even look for an *erastes*. He's shown no interest in having a loving companion or even a tutor. In a few years, sexual interest may kick in. That would be well after his growth spurt. Certainly not now."

"Okay. That'll make our search possible. However, this may take time. I'll get on this and see what we can do. You must also know some adults will be wary of working with your son. As you know, it's illegal for adults to be physically intimate with twelve-year-olds. Even if everything is innocent, a close working relationship can cause concern. At any rate, we need to stay in touch. Let's see how things go."

"That's fine. I'll see you as often as you wish."

"I know you will. I'm grateful you came by. It's not good for old friends not to see each other."

"Thank you, Axios. Thank you very much. You're still the kind, generous and friendly person you've always been.

You gave much meaning to my life during my formative years. I adore you for that. May the gods be with you."

"And also with you. Goodbye."

"Goodbye."

At first, Axios didn't know where to start in his search for an education helper for Nilo. Like Nilo's father, Axios too would seek advice from others. He knew some of the philosophers who enjoy hanging out at the *stoas*. He would try to see some of them. Since the philosophers at the *stoas* are usually occupied in conversations with onlookers, he would seek one at his home. His name was Osiris. *I haven't talked with him in a few years,* he thought. *But maybe he'll remember me.*

When he reached his house and knocked on his door, Osiris opened the door. He responded warmly. "Hello, Axios. What a surprise! I haven't seen you for a long time."

"It's good to see you. I was hoping you had a little time and perhaps we could talk."

"For you, yes. Come sit down." As the men walked to the *andron*, Osiris asked, "What brings you here today?"

When the men sat down, Axios explained what was on his mind. He told him about Nilo and that his father wanted the best tutor possible for him, especially one who would be sensitive to the boy's needs. "He hasn't adapted well to the school where he was sent. There must be a better way."

"Indeed, there must be. And no doubt there is."

"That's why I came to see you. It's important for my friend to find the right one. And I know you're in contact with many philosophers and other highly educated men."

"Okay. First, let me thank you for thinking of me in this way. I'm humbled you feel I might be able to help. And do you know what? It's possible I might be able to do that.

Here's what I can tell you. I happen to know a certain man who is gifted. He's gifted with the knowledge of philosophy. He was once a student of Plato, our master of that field in Athens. But he has more to offer than that. He's a sensitive man. He takes his students' feelings into account like no one I've ever known. His knowledge of mathematics, as well as traditional subjects, that is, reading, writing, and music is superior. His name is Lukos. He's from the *Deme* Kolonai."

"How's he regarding physical education?"

"As far as athletics and the *gymnasia* are concerned, I must say no. He has some talent there but not like his academic areas of learning. I suggest for physical education, you find someone else."

"That's fine. No one's an expert in everything."

"Oh, and something else. Lukos happens to be a student of the history of the Grecian people. He's self-taught in that area as so little of that is taught in our schools."

"Well, if Lukos and Nilo work together, we'll have to see what interests Nilo the most."

"Yes. That's the way to go. How would you like for me to set up a meeting with you and Lukos?"

"That may be a good way to begin."

"Okay then. I'll get back to you soon."

"Thank you, Osiris, for your time. Thank you so much."

Meanwhile, Demetrius was still waiting for Theous's father to give him a report on what the officials and Athens Assembly might do with his case. All the while, the officials were searching for Demetrius's abductors.

Demetrius was now eating a light meal of bread with honey. He was resting on a sofa while eating from a low table with the rest of the family. They were catching up on whatever news was available to them of wars far away and events with the Athens' Citizens' (democratic) Assembly. When there was nothing more to say of those happenings, Demetrius asked his father, "What else can we do to help Nilo? I want to help my brother any way I can. It hurts to see him depressed about life. There will be time before my military service begins. I won't spend it all exercising and running."

His father answered Demetrius by sharing what's been done so far. He concluded by saying, "and anything you can do to help will be appreciated. Perhaps we can see what we can all do together."

Demetrius agreed. Then he left to do his running and exercise routines.

The next few days were unusually quiet. Nilo's father was waiting for news from Theous's father as well as getting word from Axios about a possible tutor for Nilo. Meanwhile, he broached the subject with Nilo of meeting with a prospective tutor.

"You want a tutor for me?" said Nilo in a surprised tone. "I told you I don't want a tutor. I don't need a teacher of any kind. You know how it's been with my schoolmaster."

"I do. But your new tutor won't be a schoolmaster. He'll be working with you alone."

"That could be worse. He might expect more from me. I don't want to do it," said Nilo. Then in a louder voice, he said, "No. I'm not going to do it!"

"But you must give him a chance."

"How do you know he won't be any better than my schoolmaster?" cried Nilo. "I'd hate that!"

"Okay, you're right. I don't know. But let me say this. My friend Axios is well suited to find a tutor for you. I asked him to help because he knows many in the business of education. He agreed to find someone for you. Axios knows your situation. I talked to him about how things have gone for you. I don't think he'll waste your time finding someone who's not sensitive to your needs."

"Most teachers are pushy. They say I need to know this, and I must know that. They get angry when I don't learn as fast as they want me to. Anyway, I don't need school. I can read and write and do basic sums. I can return to running and exercising. All good Greek boys and youths run and exercise. Maybe I can be more like them."

"Nilo, please. Your whole future's at stake. Imagine, if you can: you could be a politician or a philosopher, or whatever you want. But you must have a decent education. All I ask is you give a new teacher a chance. That's all."

Nilo didn't know what else to say. He shrugged his shoulders and looked down at the floor.

"Believe in yourself Nilo. You can do great things. If your new teacher isn't someone you like, I promise you don't have to stay with him. We can continue our search until we find someone you like."

"I don't know," said Nilo. And with that, the conversation ended.

Meanwhile, Axios met with Lukos, who said he'd be happy to meet with the prospective student and his father. A meeting was arranged to take place in Lukos's home in the *Deme* Kolonai. Following that meeting, Axios notified Nilo's father that he and Nilo could meet with Lukos at his home.

CHAPTER 6

Lukos, The Kind Teacher

No man should bring children into the world who is unwilling to persevere to the end in their nature and education.

— **Plato**
427–347 BC

"No! I don't want a tutor. I've had enough education. So, no!"

Nilo saw no future in continuing his education. He told his father bluntly and forcefully he didn't want to see a possible tutor. But even though he decided not to go to such a meeting, he eventually gave in to his father's pleadings. "Okay, I'll go. But I doubt he'll be someone I want to spend time with."

On the appointed day they went to the *Deme* Kolonai and approached the home of Lukos. They knocked on his door.

It was a few moments before someone came. This gave father and son time to look at the exterior of the large two-story home. As with most Athenian houses, even among aristocrats, Lukos's residence appeared undistinguished on the outside. But while the home itself was plain enough, they couldn't help but notice the solid front door. It was made of the most beautiful dark wood available. The door also stood out by having numerous inlay carvings. These were likenesses of prominent persons in Athenian history. "They're so pretty," said Nilo, as the fingers of his right hand wandered over one of the more intricate designs.

Nilo's father was about to comment on one of the images. But at that moment the door opened.

Standing before them was a relatively tall man with broad shoulders. His beard was cut close to his skin. His face was attractive with a pronounced jaw and a high forehead. He displayed an infectious smile and piercing eyes. His eyes were drawn immediately to the boy in front of him. "You must be Nilo," said the man. "And of course, your father. Hello, and welcome to both of you. Please come in."

"Thank you," said Nilo and his father in unison as they entered the spacious house.

As is the custom for Greeks in entertaining visitors, they went directly to the *andron* where they would talk. And talk they did.

"My name is Lukos Kolonai," the man said, "I'm thrilled to meet both of you. I hope you'll feel at home here." Now talking to Nilo's father, he said, "As you know, I met with your friend Axios. He spoke highly of both of you. He told me something about your situation, but perhaps I need to hear directly from each of you." Looking more directly at Nilo's father, he said, "Why don't you go first."

"I'd be glad to. First and foremost, I'm a family man. I have a wife, a young daughter and two sons: Demetrius who is eighteen and will soon begin his military service and Nilo, who is now twelve. I love them and want the best for them. I taught my children until they were seven. At age seven, both boys went to a traditional school. Demetrius did well at the school, but unfortunately, my youngest son did not. Nilo, as you know, had challenges with education. Schooling hasn't worked out. We need something unique that fits his interests and personality. My sense is he'd be better off with a tutor. Someone special. This requires a knowledge of traditional academics, of course. But also, someone who can develop a real concern for the boy. Someone who can understand him and help him find his life's calling. I think you know what I mean."

"Perhaps I do. So Nilo, I' d love to hear how you see your situation."

"Okay, but I'm going to tell the truth. And I don't think you want to hear it. The truth is I don't like school. I never wanted to go to school. I don't want a tutor either. I'm sorry if that's not what you and my father want me to say. And don't ask me what I want because I don't know what I want. I don't even know what I'm good at. Maybe I'm not good at anything."

After a pause in the conversation, Lukos responded. "Thank you, Nilo. Thank you very much. First, I like it when someone tells the truth, that is, to say what's on their mind. You may know many boys don't like doing that. They want to tell you what they think you want to hear. That doesn't help. Maybe you can tell me what your interests are. How do you like to spend your free time?"

"I like to spend my time with my family and my friends. I like to because they love me, and I love them. But I'm not sure whether I love anything else. But I can't say for sure because there are many things I still don't know about."

"Well, that's interesting. Interesting indeed. Tell me please, would you like to know something about what you said, 'are the many things you still don't know about?'"

"I can't say because I have no way of knowing if I'll like them or not."

"Fair enough! Tell you what. What do you think of this? Why don't you come to my house every day for one week? We can look at and go over many things in life you haven't been exposed to. Maybe one or more subjects might excite you. If so, then maybe you'll want to continue coming to my house."

"What makes you think I'll like something?"

"I don't know. That is, I don't know if you will like the things we'll spend time with or not. But if there's a chance you'll discover something you love, wouldn't that be worth coming here?"

"Ummm, maybe."

At this point, Nilo's father interjected, "My guess is Nilo would like to visit you daily for a week. I think he knows you might have something he can be excited about. It's not certain of course, but it may be worth the effort. What do you say Nilo?"

After a brief pause, Nilo said, "I don't know, but maybe I must try something sometime, so I have nothing to lose in coming here. But only for a week."

"Oh, that's wonderful Nilo," said Lukos. "You've opened yourself to possibilities. Good for you. Why don't we start in three days? That'll give me time to get ready for you."

Nilo's father said, "That will be fine. What do you think Nilo?"

"Well, okay I guess."

"Fine," said Nilo's father. "Well, that does it then. Nilo will be here early in the morning on the third day from today."

"Well, I'm so happy. I look forward to our time together Nilo."

At that point, all three stood up and began walking toward the door. Nilo's father said, "We were impressed with the carvings on the outside of your door. Did you make those yourself?"

"No, I didn't. A friend of mine made them. An excellent carpenter he is."

"Well, he does outstanding work."

When they reached the door, Nilo and his father said their goodbyes.

When father and son returned home, they found all was quiet. Nilo's mother was upstairs in the weaving room working on a new garment while his sister was beside her carefully watching and learning from her.

At first, it seemed Demetrius wasn't home, but then he seemingly came up to Nilo out of nowhere. He said, "Hello. Glad you're back. By the way, I'm going for my run. Would you like to run with me?"

That was a friendly comment, but it hit Nilo hard. It made him realize he hadn't been running since his fiasco at the Panathenaic Games. At first, he didn't know how to respond. But after reflecting on his request, he thought, *Why not?* Then he said, "Yes, of course. I'll be glad to run with you."

The two brothers left the house and began running on the passageway. It was raining. They didn't care. What was unusual about this was it was one of the few times in recent memory they did an activity together. After all, they were six years apart. In the course of running, it didn't take long before Nilo was well ahead. The months of practicing for the Panathenaic Games gave Nilo an advantage. His brother had only been running for a few weeks. When he looked back, he saw Demetrius slowing down. He wasn't in condition.

When they were together again, Demetrius was huffing and puffing. "I have to practice more if I'm going to make my grade in the military," he said. "A lot more!"

Despite Demetrius's lack of practice, Nilo found a degree of confidence coming back to him. He saw his daily running and exercising hadn't been in vain. He indeed had attained stamina. Now he felt he could return to his daily regimen of running and exercises while no longer thinking of himself as unworthy. But from then on, Demetrius never again asked Nilo to run with him.

On returning home, they met their father while drying themselves from the rain. He wanted to speak with Demetrius. "A government messenger stopped by while you were gone. He brought good news for you," he said.

"It must be from the military," said Demetrius. "They may want me to report sooner than they first said."

"No, the message isn't from the military. It was from someone representing our Citizens' Assembly. They think they've found the men who violated you."

Looking surprised, Demetrius said, "That *is* good news."

"Yes, and they want you to go to the *agora* to identify the men. At the same time, there will be a preliminary hearing before a magistrate."

"How interesting. I wasn't sure they'd ever find those men. Thanks for the information. I'll plan to go there."

"One suggestion. You might want to ask Theous's father to go with you. He knows much about Athenian laws. He could be a big help. And I believe he'll want to go with you. He was upset about what happened."

"Excellent idea. I'll ask him."

When Demetrius approached Theous's father, he found him more than willing to go along.

"Justice must be served," he said.

They decided to go immediately to see the magistrate at the Assembly headquarters in the *agora*.

When the men walked together to the Assembly headquarters, they were caught in a heavy rainstorm. It had been raining several days in a row, so this was not surprising. The rain didn't deter them. Their mission was much too critical. When they arrived at the Assembly headquarters, a representative took them to see the men suspected of gang-raping Demetrius. They went to the room where the men were held. There, at first sight, Demetrius was struck with the contrast from how the men looked during the time of his ordeal and the way they appeared now. He also realized he couldn't recall the faces of the men involved. What Demetrius did remember was the man he perceived to be their leader and the man who befriended him. Those he could identify. The others were a blur.

Demetrius and Theous's father were asked to remain for the *anakrisis* (preliminary hearing) before a magistrate.

They agreed. Demetrius and the accused leader of the rapists stood in front of the magistrate. Both Demetrius and the suspected leader were asked to take an oath. Demetrius had to swear his accusation was honest. The leader, however, declared they had the wrong persons, and he and the others were innocent. When they were finished, a date was set. The representative told Demetrius they'd try to extract a confession from the others and the trial could be held as early as next week. The two men promised to attend so they could testify against the suspects.

———

The night before Nilo was to have his first class with Lukos, his father approached him. "Can we talk for a moment?"

"Certainly," said Nilo.

"I'm concerned about your meeting with Lukos tomorrow."

"Why?"

"Well, if he comes to feel you're disinterested and show a lack of desire in being tutored, he may want to cancel his agreement with you. Then where will you be? And what's going to happen to your future?"

"But what if what he wants to teach me isn't interesting, then what can I do?"

"Whether what he teaches you grabs your attention or not, you should comport yourself well tomorrow and in all your classes with Lukos. This is what I want you to do. Please listen carefully.

"First, give your tutor a chance. Don't go with the idea you won't like what he teaches. To succeed, you must have an open thought. Lukos is widely recognized as an outstanding tutor. If you give up on him, another opportunity with someone as skilled as he is might not happen again.

"Second, while you listen to his lectures, ask yourself, what is he trying to say? What does he want me to know? Capture in your thought precisely what he's saying.

"Third, under all circumstances do everything you can to keep your mind from wandering. I know the temptation to think of other things can be strong. But if he senses you aren't listening, Lukos will be unhappy. More importantly, you won't be learning.

"Fourth, feel free to ask questions. You're his lone pupil. Therefore, asking questions won't interfere with his teaching. That will show Lukos you're at least listening. And questions from you may show him he hasn't explained something well. If so, Lukos needs to know that.

"Fifth. You'll be using your wax tablet, as you did in school. Try to write down important points to review them later. It's easy to forget. If you review what he says, it'll be easier to retain what he says. Read your notes soon after class. Refresh them in your mind, so you'll remember if he asks you questions from a previous class. If you want to go over with me what you learned from Lukos every day, we can do that too.

"Finally, What I've said is important. Your success may depend on these classes. Do your best. I can't ask more than that."

Nilo answered, "I know you want me to do well. I like that you care so much about me, but I don't know if I can do all you've asked."

"Take it one day at a time. When what I asked you to do are habits, they'll be easier. I swear to that. Now it's time to get a good night's sleep."

Father and son shared an embrace, and Nilo went to sleep.

The next day seemed like a good omen for Nilo. While it had been raining much of the past week, this day was nearly cloudless. After a simple morning meal of porridge and bread, he headed off to Lukos's house. As decided by Lukos and Nilo's father, the boy's slave would not go with him. Lukos felt Nilo could maintain order by himself. Also, the passageways to Lukos's house seemed relatively safe for him.

On arrival to Lukos's home, Nilo knocked on the door. Again, it would take a few moments before Lukos would answer. Meanwhile, the boy again found himself entranced by the historical figures carved into the door. But he didn't understand what they were about.

When Lukos opened the door, he was all smiles. "You're here, my friend. I'm so happy."

"Good morning Professor Lukos."

Nilo thought it strange someone as well to do as Lukos wouldn't have one of his slaves answer the door. But he didn't say anything about that. As in most Grecian homes of aristocracy, the front door opened into a large courtyard from which all downstairs rooms connected. Nilo, led by Lukos, went directly to the place where the boy would be taught. They followed the central courtyard until they came to the instruction room which Nilo thought was plain and simple. Nilo was offered a nondescript sofa to sit on. What an improvement this was over the hard-wooden bench he shared with other students when he last attended school. He was also surprised Lukos provided him with a low three-legged table. It was placed in front of the sofa. This was unconventional. But as Nilo would come to see, Lukos himself was a nonconformist. Nilo saw the table as a big improvement. It meant he had a place for his writing tablet. He no longer had to hold it with one hand while writing with the other.

As to lighting, the door to the courtyard would be kept wide open allowing sunlight to enter the windowless room.

"Please sit down," said Lukos, gesturing with a sweep of his arm.

Nilo sat down. And as he did, Lukos pulled up another small sofa which he placed near Nilo's. He sat down and began talking. All the while Nilo was looking around the room. He wanted to see if there were cords or whips Lukos might use on him. As it was, he saw nothing like that.

Lukos opened the conversation.

"Good morning my friend. Welcome again to my home. I'm glad you're here. We're going to have an enjoyable time together while we discover many new and interesting things. That's what education is. It's a continual discovery for oneself about the world we live in and its many dimensions. There's no limit to our learning in this adventure together."

What a surprise for Nilo! Classes in his former school began with words like, "Sit down and be quiet." "Sit up straight." "Pay attention and listen, or you'll be punished." *Is Lukos for real?* Nilo wondered. *Is it possible I might like being here? This man's treating me like a human being.*

Lukos then asked Nilo, "Could you tell me what subjects you were studying in your former school?"

"Oh sure—that's easy. Mostly, we studied math, writing, and music together with poetry which we sang. Occasionally, we had lessons in drawing."

"Okay—as you remember, you, your father and I decided to let you study with me for one week. After that, we'll decide if we want to continue. With that in mind, I suggest we don't cover traditional subjects. That's because I want to introduce you to a wider range of subjects. Then, after a week, if we decide to continue our arrangement, we can include more traditional areas of study, such as math, writing, poetry, and music."

"Oh! I also went to a small *gymnasia* at my school. There we had exercises, running and wrestling."

"Good! Physical education is important. It needs to be in every curriculum. But if you continue running every day, that will suffice for this week. If you return after this week, we can arrange for *gymnasia*-type activities in your curriculum."

"Okay—but what kind of subjects are you going to teach this week?"

"Thank you for that question. The subjects we'll discuss this week will come from both of us. This will depend largely on your interests, that is, what you'd like us to talk about. Here are some of the subjects. You can tell me the ones you like the most. They are architecture, astronomy, government, Greek history, hunting, philosophy, religion, and theater."

"Hmm. So many! How many can I choose?"

"Well, if you make many choices that would lessen the time, we spend with each one. If you choose only a few, then we can go more detail with each one."

"Could you repeat the list of subjects?"

"Certainly. They are (speaking slower this time) architecture, astronomy, government, Greek history, hunting, religion, philosophy, and theater."

"Hmm. Architecture sounds good because we have many beautiful buildings in Athens. I'd like to know how they were designed. And astronomy. I'd love to know about the stars. My father has friends who go hunting. That's exciting too. But all the others are interesting, so I don't know what to say."

"Yes, Nilo, I understand. That was a difficult question. Let me give you some thoughts. As to architecture, that's a complicated subject. We probably couldn't do it justice in one week. As to government and Greek history, perhaps we can include them as one subject as they're related. Hunting's a wonderful subject too as most young men become involved with that. But due to your age, you won't be hunting for several years. You won't have a chance to use what you learned in the classroom. Religion, medicine, philosophy, and theater: they're all good choices. Why don't we go for three options?"

"Okay. I've made my decisions. I want to study history and government as one of my choices. Also, religion and philosophy. Are those okay?"

"Those are excellent. I'm proud of you for making such good choices. I hope you'll find them interesting. And if you find one is boring, we can remove it and switch to something else."

"Sounds good to me. I want to do it that way."

"We've spent much time in our discussion of what to study. Now the sun is high in the sky. That means there's not enough time to do all the coursework we'd like to do. How about we do one subject today?"

"That sounds good."

"Okay. Before we do, can you stand up please?"

Nilo stands up.

"Now stretch your arms as high as you can, as I'm doing. At the same time, raise your feet, touching the floor only with your toes. Good! Now try as hard as you can to touch the ceiling like I'm doing. Keep trying; keep trying. Excellent! Now let's stretch our arms sideways as far as we can. Okay, now make circular motions with your hands and arms. Keep that up for a couple of minutes. Good. Now let's bend our knees while we stoop down so low, we can touch the floor. Now stand up. Stoop down. Stand up. Stoop down. Stand up. When we've done that ten times, we'll sit back down."

"I like getting up. Sitting down so long hurts my bottom."

"I'm glad you like it. We'll try to do that a few times each day. Otherwise, we might get sleepy besides having sore bottoms."

"Ha-ha, okay."

"History is a subject you chose. Greek history that is. What that means is the history of all the people in the world

101

who speak our language, the language of the Greeks. So, we're not limiting our study to the people in Athens or even Attica which is the land that surrounds and is controlled by Athen's City-State. Now, do you have any idea what the word 'history' means?"

"I think it means what happened before about our people. Something like that."

"Well, yes. Maybe it would be easier to explain what it would be like if we had no history—no history at all. So, let's pretend nothing's been written down to tell what's happened before. So here we are on the Greek peninsula. No one knows how long our people have been here. No one knows what our people have done. We do know something about what's happened since we've been alive. We've also heard some things from our parents and others, especially older people. They've told us what's happened in their lifetime and from what they know from folks older than they, who might be dead now, about what happened in their lifetimes.

"Have you ever played the children's game where ten or more stand in a line? The first one whispers a sentence to the second person. The second person whispers to the third person what he thinks the first person said and so on till you get to the end of the line?"

"Ha-ha, yes. It's funny."

"What happens?"

"We played that game in school. What happened was what the last person said isn't anything like what the first person said."

"Yes, and like you said, 'It's funny.' But when we're dealing with our history, Greek history, one person telling something to another person is more serious. You've undoubtedly heard of Homer who wrote the *Iliad* and the *Odyssey*."

"Oh, yes. Everyone's heard about Homer. Many persons have studied, and some have even memorized Homer's stories."

"That's right; they have. Homer's work covers a lot of Greek history both about us mortals and of our gods. But for centuries there was no writing for us to read Homer's stories. They were simply told from one person to another person like when you played that game in school. Homer's stories were also handed down that way from generation to generation. And again, they weren't written down. And for that reason, we don't know for sure what's true and what's not true about anything we read from Homer. But at the same time, Homers' works are almost all we have for much of our history."

"When did they begin to be written down?"

"Good question. It deserves a good answer. Long ago the Greeks' ability to write was entangled with and dependent on other elements of our history, especially our wars and how they affected our economies. Briefly, this is how it went.

"The first invention of writing didn't take place in Athens or any Greek-speaking area. It happened in Egypt. Later, writing came to Greece. But the ability to communicate by writing was lost, or nearly lost, in our Dark Age, because our economies were going downhill. But knowledge was still passed on. It was passed on by one person talking with other persons and from them to others. That's what we call 'oral tradition.' Writing wasn't regained again until about 300 years ago. But it didn't happen until after the Greeks were able to use an alphabet we borrowed from the Phoenicians. Having an alphabet, the Greeks learned to write again. With this ability, Homer's works started to be written down. That's fortunate because we have them now for our learning and enjoyment."

"Wow! That's much to think about."

"Yes. And I gave you the briefest account about that. Now I see time is moving. We've got to keep going.

"When all the subjects of learning are discussed there may be a tendency to prioritize them. That means when some will say one subject is more important than another one. At present, many believe politics and debating are the most important. We sometimes are aware of this when we visit the *stoas* and, of course in our Citizens' Assembly where decisions about conducting affairs of Attica are debated. Without a doubt, politics and debating are important. But so is math. Can you imagine having a society with an economy and no one knows how to add or subtract? So, we agree math too is important. And when we sift through other academic subjects, we see they're all important. But often one or more subjects are put down as being less important than others. One that's considered less important is history."

From here, Lukos details the work of the pioneers Homer and Herodotus in chronicling Greece's history.

"Homer wrote down events that happened long before he was born. He wrote in poetry, and his verses were usually sung instead of read.

"Another person who wrote about events that took place before his lifetime is Herodotus. Herodotus is known as the 'father of history.' His life work was to ensure that human achievements may be spared the ravages of time. And that all their noble attainments with their glory, be kept alive. It was also most important to him to give reasons why they went to war."

From there Lukos went into the beginnings of Greek civilization. He discussed the Mycenaean people who may have had the first civilization that could be considered Greek. That's because they had a high level of community organization. They developed art, writing, and put a structural organization in their military. And they had a high level of trade around the Mediterranean Sea. They also helped unify the Greek people in the areas of religion and language. Then came the Dark Age.

"The Dark Age was punctuated with a decline in the Mycenaean control and culture. The art of writing, for example, was lost. But some things like language and religion did not disappear."

Nilo was listening as carefully as he could. Although he was sitting on the sofa, he found difficulty sitting in the same position. He wanted to recline his head back, but he knew that might signal to Lukos he wasn't paying attention.

Lukos sensed this and said it was time to stand up again and move his arms around and around. They continued doing exercises for about five minutes. Then Nilo sat down again.

Lukos then went into the foundations of Athens history, especially how the goddess Athens became the patroness of their City-State, and in doing so, gave her name to the *polis*.

It was a long class, but Nilo found Lukos's teaching "incredibly interesting."

At the end, Lukos said, "That's all for today. I look forward to seeing you tomorrow. By the way, don't forget to do your running today."

"I won't. Thank you Professor Lukos. Thank you for your interesting class."

Lukos and Nilo walked together through the courtyard to the front door. Lukos opened the front door for Nilo. But instead of sending him on his way, he pointed to the carvings on the door. "Would you look at these carvings? The men engraved in these panels are important persons from Greek history. We can look at the lives of some of these men tomorrow when you return. We also need to begin discussing philosophy and religion. And as you will see, they're somewhat related. Thank you again for coming. Do enjoy the rest of your day. Goodbye Nilo."

"Goodbye Professor Lukos. Thank you for everything. See you tomorrow."

While walking home from Lukos's house, Nilo knew his father was going to ask him about his first day with Lukos. Nilo wondered what he should say.

Nilo was right. On returning home, his father wanted to know how his first day went with Lukos.

"How did it go today?" was the first thing he asked as his son walked through the doorway.

Although Nilo had given thought to his father's concern, he still hadn't formed an exact answer. Nilo wondered if maybe Lukos tried hard to win his favor because it was his first day and perhaps the following days would be more difficult. So, he gave his answer casually, "Oh, it went okay, I guess."

"You guess! Don't you know?"

"I said it went okay. But there are five days left to go. At the end of the week, we should have a good idea."

"Can I ask what you learned?"

"Yes. And that's the good part.

"I learned about the early history of Greece, the history of writing and something about the history of writing the history of Greece. Lukos made the class interesting. While he was good for me today, I don't want to judge him, or his teaching based on one day of class. Also, we spent much class time deciding what we'll study this week. What we decided was Greek history, government, religion, and philosophy. Today, there was only time for history."

"Good enough and thank you. I'm glad it went well for you. I hope you enjoy the rest of your week. By the way, did you take many notes on what you were learning today?"

"Uh, no. Not one note. I was so interested in what Lukos said I forgot to take notes."

"Well, we can remedy that. Would you mind taking out your tablet and jotting down what you can remember? Then we'll discuss it together."

Nilo did as his father wished. "The first thing we talked about was history itself. What it is. And how fortunate we have a history that's written down. History that isn't written can change every time someone tells another person about it, so we don't know if it's true or not."

From there they reviewed what Lukos said about the Mycenaean people being the first Greeks, about Homer who wrote about them, their discovery of our gods, and the end of the Mycenaean civilization. After that came the Dark Age.

Nilo's father asked him questions and added here and there to what Lukos told his son. When they were finished, it was time for Nilo to take his run for the day.

Before Nilo left, his father asked one more question. "Did Demetrius tell you about his court appearance set for next week?"

"No. But he said he was going to the Assembly's headquarters. He would try to identify the men who accosted him."

"Okay, well, he's going to Court next week for his trial against the men who violated him. Is this something you might be interested in attending?"

"I don't know, but maybe it won't be important how I feel. If I have classes with Lukos next week, the Professor will want me to attend his class."

"Okay, well, have a good run."

"See you later."

The next morning Nilo's father came into the room where his son was having his morning meal.

"Father, you have your cloak with you. Are you going somewhere? It's so early."

"Yes. I'm going to school with you."

"You're going to attend my class?"

"No, no. I need to see Lukos. That's all. And I might as well go with you, so we can talk before your class."

"Ah, okay."

After their morning meal, father and son walked briskly to Lukos' house.

"It seems strange not having Chamus with me every day," said Nilo.

"That's a sign you're growing up. Growing up is one step at a time, and leaving home alone is a big step."

Nilo loved the idea of getting older whenever it gave him more responsibility. He also felt that way about studying with Lukos. The professor treated him more as a peer than someone he looked down on. Indeed, he was growing up.

After they knocked on the door of Lukos's house, Nilo pointed to the panel of engravings on his front door. "Lukos said we're going to talk about some of these people in class today. They're famous persons in Athens' history."

In a moment the door opened. It surprised Nilo and his father it wasn't Lukos in the doorway. He was an adolescent. He looked to be a few years older than Nilo. *Quite an attractive youth to be a slave*, Nilo's father thought. *With such beauty, he could easily pass for an aristocrat.*

"Please come in," the adolescent said. "Lukos is waiting for you."

The youth led them into the room where Lukos was waiting and then excused himself.

"What a nice surprise to see you," Lukos said, upon seeing Nilo's father.

"Good morning Lukos. I hope you don't mind. There's something I need to discuss with you, and I decided to come with Nilo. I promise to be brief. I don't want to interfere with your class."

"I understand. I'm glad you felt it was okay to see me. What's on your mind?"

"I know you and Nilo haven't decided to continue your class after this week. I hope you will. Nilo was happy about your first day. What I want to talk to you about is something else."

"Oh?"

"Please know, I didn't come to tell you how to run your class. Not at all. It's that a golden opportunity for both of you has come up. I wanted to know if you might be interested in taking advantage of it. It's like this. I have another son. He's several years older than Nilo. His name is Demetrius. Back when we were watching the Panathenaic Procession, he was kidnapped by a group of men and taken to a place several blocks away. There he was held for many hours and gang-raped by these men. The men have been captured. They're in jail now. Their trial will be next week. I was wondering if you might be interested in attending the trial with Nilo. My son told me the concept of government and how it works is one of the subjects you'll be studying. Therefore, it seems like this may be an ideal way to teach Nilo how our court procedure works. Nilo will no doubt be interested in how his brother's case unfolds. He would be eager to learn how our court system works. What do you think?"

"Well, this is a surprise. But first, there hasn't been a decision yet as to whether Nilo and I will continue studying together after this week. But if we do, yes of course. I'd be happy to consider your proposal. And you're right. It would be an excellent opportunity for both of us. Nilo can learn more about government in Athens at the trial than I can teach him in the classroom. We can discuss the proceedings when we return to the class."

"I'm glad you feel that way. I believe Nilo will decide in a few days whether he wants to continue studying with you. Then if you also agree to continue, then we can plan on . . ."

Nilo interrupting said, "We don't need to wait a few days to decide about next week. I want to continue next week with Lukos."

"Bless you Nilo. And may the gods be with you," said Lukos. "That's such a nice thing to say. And I can tell you both I'd like to continue teaching Nilo."

"That settles it then," said Nilo's father. "I'll let you know about the details and when we need to be in Court. There's no need for me to stay longer. You need to get on with your class."

CHAPTER 7

New Crisis for Nilo

*Do not train a child to learn by force or
harshness; but direct them to it by what
amuses their minds, so that you may be better
able to discover with accuracy the
peculiar bent of the genius of each.*

— Plato
427–347 BC

Nilo returned home later from his class than the day before. His father was understandably concerned. But when Nilo walked in, all his father could say was, "Hello, how did it go today?"

"Hi. What a day! We did so much. Lukos was excited about attending the trial next week. We talked about that a lot. The class was so interesting Lukos forgot about the time. We finished later than we were supposed to."

"Could you tell me more about what he said?"

"Sure. Lukos told me how the court system came to be the way it is today. He discussed the days when the tyrant Draco made all the decisions regarding crime. But his laws were harsh. Someone could get the death penalty for stealing a cabbage or pinching an avocado in the market. That's' why we refer to harsh laws as draconian. Later when Salon was in charge, he brought civility to judging those suspected of making a crime. Salon introduced common sense laws. His main contribution was making laws that put Athens on the way to democracy. That was when the Assembly of Citizens began meeting to make laws. As to criminal cases, magistrates had the most power for a long time. But Salon established a court of appeals to overcome whims of magistrates and their sometimes abusive decrees."

"That must've been interesting."

"Lukos made it interesting by being excited about it. So excited he forgot more than the time. He didn't bring up stories about the engravings on his front door as he promised. I forgive him because I learned a lot. Tomorrow, we're going to discuss the trial system as it is now. That'll help me understand about Demetrius's trial."

"It does sound like you did learn a lot."

"Yes, and I can't wait till tomorrow."

"You might want to know Demetrius has been busy working on his speech. Theous's father is helping him. But no matter how many persons help him, Demetrius is the only one allowed to deliver his speech."

"It will be exciting seeing my brother talking to the court before all five-hundred and one jurors. You and Lukos will be there too. I wonder if he'll be nervous. I know Demetrius will win."

"We'll look forward to it."

"Okay. I'm going running. Talk to you later."

When Nilo returned from his run, he went directly to Demetrius's room. "How're you doing today?"

"Oh, hi. I'm fine, thanks. And you?"

"Fine. I was wondering how the presentation for your trial is coming along?"

"Oh, well, we're working on it. Theous's father is helping a lot."

"You might want to know my Professor is interested in your trial. We're going to attend. We'll watch it together. Then we'll talk about it in class."

"Oh, wonderful. I'm happy you'll be there. Father told me about Lukos. He's impressed with him. Now tell me this: do you think Lukos would give a supporting testimony?"

"I don't know. But I'll ask him."

"It's heartwarming to know you and father will be there. I'll be plenty nervous. I've never spoken to a crowd like the Assembly of Citizens."

"I know you'll do fine," said Nilo and he left the room.

As Nilo went to bed that evening, it took him longer than usual to fall asleep. His thoughts were fixed on the classroom. *I must be the luckiest guy in the world. I have a teacher who cares for me. He wants me to learn. I'm so, so, happy.*

The next time Nilo sees his teacher, he's brought into the classroom by Luko's slave. As he enters the room, he's startled to see things are different. This time the sofas of his teacher and his are closer together. Lukos is sitting down. This is odd, thought Nilo as he sees his teacher's tunic is no longer covering the top half of his body. He wears his tunic

114

as if he were attending a symposium. Nilo takes a long hard look at Lukos's bare chest. *He's in fantastic shape*, he thought. He also gets his best view ever of his biceps. *This man must spend far more time in the* gymnasia *than I imagined.*

For his part, Lukos wastes no time getting started.

"Good morning Nilo. We've got a lot to cover today. It's important for you to have a good understanding of how the Citizen's Assembly operates before we go to Demetrius's trial. When you enter the trial arena, you're likely to be awed by so many jurors. The reason there are so many (which is normal for charges of *hubris*) is that it's more difficult for that many men to be corrupted. Bribing five-hundred and one jurors isn't easy."

"Yes," said Nilo. "But don't you think it'll be difficult for Demetrius to convince that many people the accused persons violated him?"

"Here's the thing." Lukos gets up and sits down next to Nilo on his sofa. "It's like this." He puts his arm around Nilo and looks deep into his eyes. Then he bends over to kiss the boy. The moment their lips touch, everything goes dark.

Where is everything? Nilo asks himself as he abruptly sat up on his mattress. *Oh, ye gods! I've been dreaming.* As he recalled where he was in his dream, he cried, "O' why couldn't that be true? Why couldn't it? It has to be true." Nilo remained awake for a long time before crying himself back to sleep. He continued fantasizing about his dream after he woke in the morning. He was able to console himself only by thinking his dream might come true that day.

The next morning after Nilo left for his class with Lukos, his father was thinking about how thankful he was his son was learning about the legal system. He was also glad

Nilo has a teacher gifted in knowledge and personality. *The gods have been good to me*, he thought. *There must be a reason for that. Perhaps someday I'll know what it is.* He thought about this for a long time.

An hour or so later when Nilo's father was still contemplating about his son's good fortune, he heard the front door opening. *That's strange,* he thought. *Who would be coming here at this hour?* He went to check. What he saw was a subdued Nilo.

Demetrius was nearby.

Nilo said a barely audible "hi" to them. He went directly to his room.

Demetrius and his father looked at each other in a confused way. Finally, Nilo's father went to check on his son. He knocked on his door.

Nilo said, "I don't want to talk to you or anyone."

Nilo's father decides to leave his son alone. But much later when Nilo didn't come down for the evening meal, his father was determined to learn what's wrong. He went upstairs. "Nilo, can we talk? I need to know what's happened to you."

After a period of silence, Nilo's father simply called his son's name in a loud way, "**Nilo!**"

Without saying a word, Nilo opened his door. He looked down at the floor the entire time, not wanting his eyes to meet those of his father's.

Nilo's father entered his son's room as the boy returned to his bed. "Aren't you going to tell me anything?"

"I don't wanna talk."

"Nilo, you've been crying. What happened today? Were you harassed on your way home from Lukos's house? Or did Lukos try to do something with you?"

"No, nothing like that. But I don't wanna talk about it."

Father remained in Nilo's room, and for a few moments said nothing. Then his father said, "Please talk to me. How can I help if we don't talk?"

"You can't help me. No one can."

Again, father respected Nilo's wishes to be alone. He left his room.

The next morning when Nilo still didn't come downstairs, his father decided to visit Lukos. He needed answers. He went to his house.

He knocked on the door. When Lukos opened the door, Nilo's father made no pleasantries. "What did you do to my son?" he demanded to know.

"I did nothing to your son. I was trying to teach him, nothing more. Then he got up and left. He didn't say why."

"He came home yesterday. He went straight to his room. He wouldn't talk to me. He cried all night. Something happened here. You must tell me what it was."

"What happened is we talked about how the legal system works in Athens. That's all. Honest. I was preparing him for what he would see when Demetrius goes to trial next week. Nothing was different. Well, Mikkos was in the class with Nilo. But that's all."

"Mikkos? Who in the gods' names is Mikkos?"

"The classes I've set up for your son were meant to be for Nilo alone. That's right. But when we changed our curriculum to include the legal system in Athens—well, that was something I wanted Mikkos to know about also.

I invited him to our class. I didn't think you or Nilo would mind having him here. I didn't. Now I'm sorry for not asking you and Nilo first."

"But who in the names of our gods' is Mikkos?"

"He's another student of mine. He's the same person who let you in the last time you were here."

"Okay, thanks. But why do you want to teach your slave?"

"Oh no! Mikkos isn't my slave—no. He's here because he's my *eromenos*. That's why I'm teaching him."

Raising his voice, Nilo's father said, "Your *eromenos*! Oh, ye gods! That explains everything."

"What do you mean, 'That explains everything?'"

"Oh, Lukos! Can't you see? Nilo may be in love with you. He may have even wanted to be your *eromenos* when he's older. If you told him Mikkos is your *eromenos* that could've upset him very much."

"Do you think so?" asked Lukos. "I had no idea he felt that way. I tried to be as helpful and understanding as possible. Nothing more."

"That's all it would take. Nilo's an impressionable boy. He's badly hurt. This comes after having a bad experience at his former school. On top of that was his failure to finish his race at the Panathenaic games. He's sensitive to all that. Now he may feel like he's a failure in love because he can't have you. I don't know what to say to you Lukos."

"I feel badly for you and Nilo. Believe me, and if I knew about Nilo's feelings, I would've never invited Mikkos to our class. And now if there's any way we can keep Nilo in the class, I hope we can do so with or without Mikkos."

"I doubt if there's anything either of us can do until I talk with Nilo and see what he wants to do. Then I'll let you know. I'd like him to continue with you. It's difficult finding a good teacher these days."

"Thank you. If there's any way I can help in the future, please let me know. I'm sorry to see Nilo hurt so much."

After the men said their goodbyes, Nilo's father went directly home.

While walking home, Nilo's father became deeply engrossed in thought about his son. *Now after finding such a good teacher for him, Nilo's overcome with grief. Could there be any way to help him?*

As he continued walking, he arrived at an intersection of narrow passageways. He heard a voice calling him. When he looked to one side, he saw Theous's father walking toward him from the intersecting passageway. He answered him, "Hello my friend." The men shook hands. They had an amicable conversation about many things, especially Demetrius's trial.

Near the end of their conversation Theous's father said, "Oh, and before you go on, I'd like to invite you to my home the third evening from today."

"Sure. I'd love to go. Anything special?"

"Yes. I'm sponsoring a symposium. I hope you can come. A few philosophers will be present, so you know there will be good conversation. You'll receive a more formal invitation when my slave makes the rounds of delivering them."

"I'd be delighted. I haven't been partying much these days, but I'd enjoy visiting with you and your friends. Is the symposium to honor a special event?"

"Yes, but please understand. This is something delicate between us. I hope it's not upsetting for you and Nilo."

"What possibly could that be?"

"Well, I didn't want to discuss this with you before. I know Nilo's accident in the Panathenaic race caused you and your son much grief."

"I don't understand."

"You left the athletic events at the Panathenaic Festival after your son fell and he left the race. I didn't want to embarrass you by telling you how well my son Theous did. It's his performance we're celebrating at the symposium. I'd never want to gloat over your misfortune. You've got to believe me because I wouldn't. On the other hand, I can't avoid inviting a good friend like you to attend our celebration. Besides, there will be much merriment from our being together. There will be nine of us attending for dinner with others arriving later. I hope you'll bring both your sons."

"Well, Demetrius for sure. But don't you think Nilo is young for an adult gathering?"

"Well yes. He's young for a symposium. But I hope you'll bring him because can keep company with Theous. My son needs someone his age to be with and talk with. It's a big favor I ask. Our sons are good friends you know."

"Oh! Yes. Yes, they are. Then, in that case, I'll bring both my sons. Thanks so much."

"See you in a few days, my friend. Bye."

"Goodbye."

That evening Theous's father picked up a wax tablet. Thereon he wrote the names of all the guests he invited to his symposium together with the day and hour. As was the custom, it would begin at the ninth hour. Then he handed the tablet to a slave who would make the rounds to the homes of the guests.

After talking with Theous's father, Nilo's father resumes wondering what he should say to Nilo.

Should I encourage my son to return to Lukos's class even if it gives him emotional pain? Would it be better if I let him do most of the talking or at least find out what he wants to do? Should I ask him if he wants a different teacher, even if the new one won't compare to Lukos? And now there's another concern. How would Nilo feel about attending a celebration for Theous's running performance that he lost in a big way?

Nilo's father remained confused as to what to do as he entered his house. As he wasn't sure what to do, he decided not to go immediately to Nilo's room but waited to see if his son would come down for the next meal.

When it was time for the next meal, Nilo's mother called him to come and eat.

No response.

The family commenced eating without Nilo.

Time passes.

Demetrius, who wasn't aware of the latest development with Nilo, stopped by his room to chat. He knocked on his door.

No answer.

Demetrius opened the door to see if his brother was okay. But he wasn't there. He rushed to tell his father.

"Nilo's not in his room; I don't think he's in the house."

His father was alarmed. Given all that happened in the past two days Nilo, from his view, was liable to do anything. But what could he do? He talked with his wife, he spoke with Demetrius, and he spoke with his friends. He even paid another visit to Lukos. No one knew what to do. He felt alone with his dilemma. He prayed. But Nilo's whereabouts remained a mystery.

It was two days before Nilo came home. He looked ruffled as he entered the door. He hadn't slept much and was exceedingly depressed.

His father was there. He didn't know what to say. All he could say was "Well...?"

Nilo wasn't in the mood for talking. He didn't respond. Instead, he went to where the food was kept to get something to eat. He found grapes, figs, and bread. He took it all to his room.

Nilo's father didn't follow him. Neither did anyone else.

Nilo was famished. He ate the fruit and bread rapidly and washed it down with water. That didn't satisfy his appetite. He went to sleep anyway.

Nilo's father was still unsure how to handle the situation though he decided to go slow. *Precipitous action might alienate the boy from the family or make it difficult to regain rapport with him*, he thought.

The next morning Nilo didn't want to go downstairs. He knew his father would question him. But he was hungry. He realized he'd have to leave his room sooner or later. So, he went downstairs and, as he imagined, his father was waiting for him.

Nilo's father decided things couldn't continue any longer without a confrontation with his son. When Nilo came down, he said, "Please listen. We've must stop ignoring each other. We're a family. We must live like one. You must tell me what's going on with you. And where were you the two nights you were gone?"

There was a silence before Nilo said, "Okay! I'll tell you what's going on. What's going on is I don't care anymore. I don't care about anything. I don't care about anyone, not my responsibilities, not my education, not even our gods. I curse them all because they don't care about me. And when you know what I did those two days and nights, you won't want me in your house. You'll treat me like a disfigured newborn infant whose parents leave it on the passageway to let it die of exposure because you'll be ashamed of me. You'll never want me in your house again."

"What did you do those two nights?"

"What did I do those two nights? Alright. I'll tell you. I went to a *stoa*. There were many people there—all kinds of people. As the evening wore on, the philosophers, those passing by, and others slowly left until all who were there were the undesirables."

"You mean...?"

"Yes. You're right. That's what I mean. I waited for the men, the ones looking for a *pornos* (hustler/male prostitute). At least they seemed happy to see me, and I eagerly went with one of them."

"Nilo!"

"I don't care. I don't give a damn anymore. Everything in Athens these days is about *agon*, the competitive quest for excellence they call it. Well, for years I played the *agon* game. And I failed. I failed at everything. Especially love. I thought I found a soul mate in Lukos. He only pretended to like me. So, go ahead. Throw me out of your house. Then maybe I can excel by myself. Maybe I can excel at being a *pornos*.

Maybe that's all I'm good for because those men who were looking to satisfy their lust, they all think I'm so beautiful. And besides, I need my freedom."

Nilo's outburst was followed by silence. It took a moment for Nilo's father to compose himself. Then he said slowly in as calm and steady a voice as he could muster, "I want you to go back to your room until your mother and I decide what to do. If you want something to eat, go right ahead."

Demetrius, who had been listening from the top of the stairs quickly returned to his room.

Nilo said nothing more, but he did get something to eat.

A few moments later, Nilo's father went upstairs to talk with Nilo's mother. She seemed surprised. "You look worn out dear. Is something wrong?"

"I had a confrontation with Nilo. He doesn't act like our son anymore. It's time you know what's going on. Our son isn't what he used to be. Not at all. He insists he's not good at anything, not being a student, not being a runner, not able to be like other citizen youths. He says he wants to be a *pornos* because that's all he's good for. What should I do? Do I let him continue to live in our house? Normally a father would send his son away under such conditions. But I love Nilo dearly. I've put a lot of time, energy and drachmas in educating him. I'd hate to lose him. I want to find out how you feel and what we might do. Please tell me your feelings. What do you think we should do?"

"Well, I'll tell you the truth. I'm not going to suggest a decision until I've talked with Nilo myself. I must hear first directly from him what he has to say."

"Fair enough. You can do that right now."

Nilo's mother goes to Nilo's room. She knocks on his door.

There was no answer.

She opens his door. Nilo's not there. She tells his father who checks downstairs.

"He's not down here. Nilo's gone."

When the impact of his disappearance subsided, Nilo's mother said, "What can we do now? What choices do we have?"

"Not many. We can wait and see if he returns as before. Or we can let him be. If he doesn't want to return, it's not our fault. We did the best we could bringing him up."

"We can look for him."

Nilo's father responded adamantly. "No! If he doesn't want to return, there's not much we can do. There may be nothing we can do. Anyway, I have other things to think about. There's a symposium tomorrow night and the day after that is Demetrius's trial."

"I'll think about this and pray to Athena, our goddess of wisdom. When I have some thoughts about this, I'll let you know, that is, if you want to hear them."

"Yes, I do. You're Nilo's mother. So yes. I want to hear them. Thank you for your interest."

CHAPTER 8

Nilo's Adventures I

*Your children are not your children. They are the
sons and daughters of Life's longing for itself.*

— **Khalil Gibran, author of The Prophet
1883–1931**

The moment Nilo learned Lukos already had his *eromenos*,
he bolted from the classroom. A slave let him out of Lukos's
house. He went directly home.

Nilo didn't feel he could have a meaningful talk with his
father. On arriving home, he avoided his father's attempts at
talking with him as best he could. After a brief confrontation
with his father, Nilo went to his room. Then, when his
father went to see Lukos, Nilo saw his chance. He left home.

He was somewhat in a daze. He didn't know where to
go or what to do. He was depressed. He didn't want to go
home again, neither would he return to Lukos's class. He
was confused. Not knowing what else to do, he decided to

walk towards the *agora,* the center of everything in Athens. That Lukos couldn't be a closer friend weighed on him. *Nothing in life works for me,* he thought. *The gods no longer care for me, nor do I care for them. I'll do as I please. I want to meet someone. Someone who cares for me even though I'm too young to have an* erastes. *Everyone says I'm attractive, so maybe I can find someone. I've been told men looking for boys can be found anywhere, so perhaps I can learn something by being on my own. Best of all, now I have my freedom. I don't need my father's control.*

As Nilo set out to do some exploring, he had concerns. He knew he had to wait at least two years before he might be an *eromenos* to a young man. Still, he had been pondering what a relationship with a mentor might be like. *How would that work for me?* He wanted to know. *How can I find an* erastes *who'll care for me and wouldn't take advantage of me? Could I learn from him how to be successful? Most of all, could I uphold my end of the bargain by being a good lover to him?* The whole idea of an e*rastes/eromenos* relationship gave him much to think about. Maybe he could learn something by living on the passageways. He wandered aimlessly for a few hours. By late afternoon, he knew he had to put more purpose in his wandering. The thought came to him again, *Could I find someone to care for me?* He didn't know but had to find out. *Where do I start looking? On the passageways? At the* agora? *At shrines to the gods and goddesses? Can men be found even there cruising boys? Where is it more likely?* Then he remembered what his father said about the Painted *Stoa.* He recalled his father said it was mostly frequented by elderly men, those beyond the age who could be an *erastes.* But he also said there are exceptions, he recalled his father saying.

He had passed by the Painted *Stoa* many times, but never ventured inside. *Stoas* are impressive buildings. They are narrow with a length sometimes approaching a city block. The front side is open without doors having only a colonnade. There were several in Athens. The Painted *Stoa* was unique because it wasn't used for public events, such as forums. It was mostly a drop-in place. Besides viewing impressive paintings on its back walls, there wasn't much point in being there, except, of course, to indulge in idle chatter with the others, usually older men. Most of the time it was meaningless chatter, though occasionally one could listen to philosophers expounding their ideas to anyone caring to listen. *Stoas* also served those in the passageways as a refuge from the rain or too bright a sun. Nilo knew of yet another reason. It offered a chance to see what a pick-up spot for a *pornos* is like. As the Painted *Stoa* was located within the *agora*, that's where he'd go.

The *agora* dominated downtown Athens. Its central focus, the marketplace, was mostly situated north of the busy Panathenaic Way. The road connected the Acropolis and the Parthenon to the City's outer Gate. Nilo couldn't help but notice how busy the Panathenaic Way had been spruced up for the Panathenaic Festival. The busy thoroughfare sliced through the middle of Athens. It also cut through the middle of the *agora* with its many shops, meetings places, law courts, baths, and *stoas*, all part of the greater complex, sprawling outward from its center, mostly haphazardly in many directions. The *agora* was indeed the heartbeat of the City.

It was a typically busy early evening as Nilo approached the *agora*. He found himself surrounded by crowds of

Athenians of all classes, ages, and sizes. Sellers hawking their wares yelling deafening promotions through the narrow, crowded passageways. But as he looked down the lanes mostly full of industries and businesses, he kept wondering whether he should venture to stop by the famed Painted *Stoa*. He knew his father wouldn't look kindly on his being there alone. But now, he could care less.

Pressing his way through the crowd, Nilo arrived at the Painted *Stoa*. This was a building he passed many times over the years, almost never giving it a thought. Now, for the first time, he was about to enter the long colonnade building he wanted to see and experience its ambiance. This *Stoa* was unique. It alone, among all the *stoas*, contained famous paintings. Here they were lined up end-to-end at eye level on wooden panels on the back wall. At the very least, he'd see some of these treasures. Standing in the passageway, in front of the *Stoa*, he could see paintings between many long floor to ceiling columns spaced from end-to-end of the building. He climbed the few steps leading up to the *Stoa*, passing a few men of various ages. He walked between the impressive Doric columns. He found himself inside where he passed between another set of stately columns, in this case, Ionic. From there, his gaze first went upward until it met the high ceiling with its wooden beams. Then his eyes swept around the long, but narrow room. The expanse was partially filled with small groups of men talking softly and a few others appeasing their curiosity. *Now what?* he thought. Then he made another sweeping glance, this time at the paintings. Nilo focused his eyes on a picture projecting an intense battle. It captured his attention. He wanted to see its intricate details. What caught his eyes were the expressions on some of the individuals. He was soon gazing at one poor soul who was about to die.

At that moment someone next to him said, "Do you know this is a masterpiece you're looking at?"

Nilo noticed the man standing to his right. He knew he was caught off guard. Nevertheless, he managed to say, "Uh, no. No—I didn't know that."

"The painting you're looking at is a depiction of the Battle of Marathon. Have you heard of it?"

"Well yes. All Athenians who went to school heard of that battle. But the truth is, I don't remember much of what was taught, except the Athenians won. It's been a while. Do you know something about it?"

"I don't know every detail either. But I can tell you this: it was fought about sixty years ago when King Darius of Persia sent his forces here to Attica. The Athenians were underdogs for having far fewer forces than the Persians. Moreover, many believed the Athenians couldn't win. But the truth is, our side sent the Persians running home. In the past, we relied too much on Sparta for our battles. They were the ones with superior forces. But Sparta didn't help us at that time. We did it nearly by ourselves. Only the small City-State of Plataea in Boeotia fought with us. Our military gained much prestige from that event. I'm glad you know something about this. Many who come here know nothing of our history."

"Having the paintings in this *Stoa* will let many know of our glorious past. Isn't it wonderful our City provides this space for its citizens?"

"Well, the truth is, it isn't our City that provides it. It came from the brother-in-law of the well-known military commander Cimon. He presented the *Stoa*, the building we're standing in, to the City of Athens. This was his gift to our *polis*. It was his way of showing his family's love for our City. Besides the *Stoa*, Cimon's brother-in-law also had shade trees and running tracks placed in open areas. In return, he and his family received much-deserved honor and respect from our citizens."

"My goodness! You know much about our past. Thank you for that. This is my first time inside the Painted *Stoa*. I never expected to learn much from coming here, historically speaking, that is."

"What's the reason you came here?"

"Uh, well, that's a long story. I don't want to bore you with that."

"That's okay. I have nothing else to do."

For the first time since he started talking with this man, Nilo took a good look at the stranger. A somewhat well-to-do man, he thought, though not necessarily from the aristocratic class. He was older than the average passerby in the *Stoa*—perhaps in his thirty's. But now he was confused. He wasn't sure what to say to the stranger. But after a pause, he managed to satisfy the man without giving his real reason for being there. "I've passed by here many times. Finally, I got curious and came in to look around."

"Well, that is fine. Fine indeed. But I'll give you a word of caution. Everything here looks innocent, and most of the time things are innocent. However, there are some who stay around here for reasons that aren't so innocent. The reason I'm saying this is you are young, some might say much too young to be here. Add to that, you're unusually good-looking, especially for a boy your age. And making things worse, you appear innocent—innocent of the world around you and innocent of your City of Athens. To some, you may appear like a babe-in-the-woods."

Having an idea of what the man was talking about, Nilo preferred to play up to what the stranger assumed was his innocence. "And what's so dangerous about some of those who stay around here? Might they want to rob me?"

"Yes, some may want to do that. But that's not what I was referring to. Boys your age are vulnerable. And you, dear one, an attractive boy like you appears susceptible to their ways. The truth is, they get their joys from corrupting boys. Boys like you must be careful. Such vultures may hang around here for hours looking for their prey."

"And what do they do when they find their prey?"

"I can't say their exact methods. They have many. But they'll likely try to befriend you. They'll try to be your friend, someone you'll trust. From there they may lead you on to temptations, physical temptations that is. I believe you know what I mean."

"Yes, yes I do." Now being more honest with the stranger, Nilo added, "My father warned me about such things."

"Well, that's good. You understand then. So, I'll advise you. Come back to the *Stoa* if you wish. Enjoy the paintings. Learn what you can from them. And all the while be careful."

"Thank you. Now it's getting late. I must hurry home."

Nilo didn't find what he was looking for at the Painted *Stoa*. But he believed he could find other *stoas*. That's what he decided to do. He was also hungry. He used one of his last drachmas to buy figs and juice. It took him a while to find another *stoa*. In time, he saw one. From a crowded passageway, he could see inside. Many were listening intently to one who might be a philosopher. He went inside to hear.

The speaker was an older man. He seemed like an odd person. Not one he thought people would pay attention to. He was short and stocky. He had a snub nose, bulging eyes with long hair and a long beard. How interesting everyone was listening intently. Nilo also began to listen. He soon became intrigued by the subject of beauty.

He's talking about real beauty, not the beauty one sees with one's eyes. He's talking about beauty in its purest form. What an incredible subject, thought Nilo. The young boy was compelled to listen. He pushed through the crowd to be near the speaker. Now at the front of the crowd, he sat on the floor with his legs crossed. He looked up with intensity. He heard the speaker summarizing his remarks.

> *Beginning from these beauties that is, the beautiful bodies which we perceive by the senses, to ascend continually in pursuit of that other Beauty going, as it were, by steps, from one to two and from two to all beautiful bodies, and from beautiful bodies to beautiful pursuits and from these to beautiful studies, and from studies to end in that study which is a study of nothing other than that but Beauty itself . . . If you ever see it, it will not seem to you beautiful in the sense that gold and clothes and beautiful boys and men are—though now you are excited when you see them, and you are ready, as many others are too, so long as you see your beloved and are always with him, to go without*

food and drink, if that were possible, simply gazing on him and being with him to think a man would feel if it were open to him to see Beauty itself, genuine, pure, uncontaminated, not infected with human flesh and color and all that mortal trash, but to see divine Beauty itself, in all its total pureness.

This was followed by a few questions and more discussion. After which the speaker fled from the *Stoa*.

Nilo, in his curiosity, questioned a bystander. "Excuse me, Sir," he said, "Could you tell me what's been going on?"

"Weren't you listening? Did you not listen at all? How could you not listen? If so, you would have heard some things are higher than earthly pleasures. We were given a taste of true Beauty, void of human banality. Our speaker discerned well the supremacy and eternality of true Beauty and pure goodness over that of 'mortal trash.' We were fed these truths by none other than the greatest philosopher of our time, possibly of all times. It was Socrates himself."

"Socrates! Oh, ye gods!" Nilo was stunned. He heard of Socrates many times but never imagined he might see him. He decided to stay and see others who may have reactions, maybe something profound to share. He walked around the *Stoa*, but no one seemed interested in talking with him. Nevertheless, he stayed in the *Stoa*. It took a while, but in time, Nilo was approached.

A gentleman in his late twenties walked up to Nilo. "Hello there. You seem quite young to be at the *Stoa* at this hour."

"I came to listen to the renowned philosopher, Socrates."

"I see. Well, that's interesting. Such a young fellow you are to desire philosophical diatribes. I thought you might have other reasons for being here. More profitable ones that is."

"I'm not sure what you mean, Sir."

"Boys like yourself hanging around the *Stoa* at this hour usually means one thing. I mean they're looking for business. Isn't that what you're doing?"

"Could you explain more exactly?"

The man was surprised at Nilo's seeming innocence. So, he explained in ways Nilo couldn't fail to understand. He finished by saying, "And wouldn't you like to come home with me tonight?"

Nilo fully understood the man and what he wanted. He also recalled being warned against such people. But he didn't want to return home. Nilo was also hungry. He had little money. He remained quiet.

The man continued, "It would make me happy if you come with me. I think you'll enjoy the evening also."

Nilo was conflicted with himself. He never imagined he'd go home with a stranger for paid sex. He was taught to think of such things as grotesque. But as their conversation continued, Nilo was more and more curious as to what such an encounter might be like. *Perhaps just this time. No one will ever know*, he thought. *And, as the man said, I might enjoy it.* After a few minutes of uncertainty, Nilo agreed to go home with the man. *Just this once*, he said again to himself.

The stranger said, "You'll never regret this night. I promise you that."

When they arrived at the stranger's home, the man invited Nilo to sit down. He lit candles to brighten the room. He took one long look at Nilo. "Ye gods, my lad. You're one of the most beautiful boys I've ever laid eyes on. Perhaps you are *the* most beautiful."

The stranger's words made Nilo uncomfortable. He also wondered if the man had listened to Socrates. *"If he had heard him, he might've learned about a Beauty higher than a mortal body."* The stranger's words also reminded him of his school days when hecklers yelled to him across the passageway to and from school. He was having second thoughts about his decision to be with this stranger. But there was nothing he could do about that now.

The stranger asked, "Would you like something to eat?"

Nilo was famished. He eagerly accepted the offer.

When the plate of food was placed on the table, Nilo ate it up quickly.

"Ye gods," said the stranger. "It's like you haven't eaten for a week. Don't other men pay you enough to buy food?"

"This is my first time," volunteered Nilo.

"Ay! I've encountered a virgin. If so, this night will be like no other for you. This is the night you'll recall for the rest of your life. And a happy night at that."

Nilo was wishing he had not said 'This is my first time,' was now expecting the worst. *Might tonight be like what happened to Demetrius when he was raped? How much might this man hurt me?*

When the stranger took Nilo by the hand and led him to his bedroom, the boy was frightened.

The stranger noting the boy's fears said, "You have nothing to worry about. Nothing at all." He asked Nilo to place his tunic over the bed as if it would serve as another blanket. He did the same for his own. He lifted all the bed covers and beckoned Nilo to climb under.

Nilo obeyed. Then the stranger climbed in as well.

What happened next was not what Nilo expected. "I'm not going to hurt you," the stranger said. "We're here to make each other happy. That's all."

Nilo wasn't ready to believe him. He was quivering with fear. But as he laid on the bed, the stranger kept talking.

"You never told me your name."

"I'm Nilo."

"Hello, Nilo. I'm Xavier."

Xavier sensed Nilo's fear. He did what he could to put Nilo at ease. Nothing worked.

Nilo continued shaking.

Nilo asked, "What are you going to do with me?"

"Nothing you don't want me to do. In fact, we don't have to do anything. That is, except sleep."

Nilo appreciated those words. But he did not yet trust Xavier. He was still a stranger to him.

Xavier asked the boy, "Why were you at the *Stoa* so late in the evening if you didn't want to be with a man in this way?"

Nilo tried to explain his situation at home. "I know this may be hard to understand. But this may be all I can do. I failed at everything else: school, athletics, even love."

"I'm sorry," said Xavier. "I wish I could do something to help you." Then noting the boy's continued nervousness, he said, "Why don't we go to sleep. We can talk more in the morning. Would you like that?"

"Why yes," said Nilo. "I'd like that."

"Okay, let's do it then." At that point, Xavier rolled over and closed his eyes.

For his part, Nilo couldn't sleep. He was trying to make sense from this unusual encounter. He lay there for hours while his bed partner slept, even snoring on occasion.

Trying to feel comfortable, Nilo tried laying on his stomach, then on his side and once more on his back.

Due to Nilo's motions, Xavier woke up. He looked at Nilo and asked, "How are you doing my friend?"

"I can't sleep."

"I'm sorry." To make Nilo feel more secure, he gently placed his arm over Nilo's thin body.

Nilo immediately thought, *Is he starting to do something with me? Is this how such things start?* But as he lay there, nothing more happened. Then, without thinking about it, Nilo slid closer to Xavier. The boy needed reassurance. Maybe he could find it here.

Feeling comfort from Xavier's warm body next to his, he instinctively placed his arm over Xavier. In the next moment, the two bodies were holding each other closely in their time of emotional need.

Nilo fell asleep.

Several hours later Xavier and Nilo woke up. The sun was high in the sky. Nilo looked at Xavier in a confused way. He immediately backed away. *Why did I choose to be here in this man's bed? On the other hand, why hasn't he had his way with me? Isn't that what men do with boys like me?*

Two persons, man, and boy were lying there on their sides looking at the other. Neither wanting to make the first move. But when they did, it was Nilo who began inching himself closer to Xavier.

Xavier, up to this point, had been the model of restraint. He knew all about platonic behavior and the philosophers' teaching that a man should love a boy's soul more than his body. But here they were, in the bedroom together. Xavier's ardor was getting the best of him. He whispered in the boy's ear, "It'll be alright my friend. There's nothing to fear."

For the first time since they met, Nilo began to believe him.

Xavier gently moved his face closer to Nilo and placed his lips over the boy's mouth. It was a brief kiss. When he saw his kiss did not perturb the boy, he did it again. This time their lips stayed joined together as they draped their arms over each other and were soon holding each other tight. It was a good feeling for Nilo, something he hadn't felt before.

He doesn't want to hurt me. He cares about me.

When their kiss came to an end, Xavier placed his hands and arms around Nilo's back.

His hands were now free to move around gently feeling his back and then to his stomach. Nilo didn't flinch. Xavier made him feel comfortable. So comfortable Xavier moved into a realm of activity that can't be described here, all with Nilo's consent.

Before Nilo left his house, Xavier said, "You may return anytime you wish."

Nilo said, "Thank you." But he didn't respond further.

As the young boy was going out the doorway, Xavier handed him a small leather pouch

"Please take this," he said.

Once on the passageway Nilo opened the pouch and looked inside. He was given enough Drachmas to buy food for several days.

Nilo continued walking on the passageway not knowing if what happened between he and Xavier was right or wrong.

If I take up this line of work, will it always be like this? he wondered. *I'll have to see.*

Nilo couldn't imagine where else to go. He decided to go home. He was hoping his family, and especially his father would leave him alone.

But they didn't. After a difficult confrontation with his father, Nilo left home again. He saw his chance when his father went to ask his mother what they might do regarding his behavior.

CHAPTER 9

The Symposium

Let lyre and pipes play on, voicing the holy song,
while we with due libation to the gods keep drinking,
making pleasant talk among ourselves.

— **Theognis of Megara**
570 – 485 BC

While preparing to attend the symposium, Demetrius's father realized, *I haven't been to a symposium for years. My socializing in recent years has always been with one other person—not a group. Maybe going to a celebration with others might help clear my thoughts. I can't continue being overwhelmed by Nilo's misadventures. I must also be concerned about Demetrius. His trial date is near.*

Demetrius's father didn't need much preparation. *I can hope the written words of a few songs and poems may be enough, that is, if I'm called on to recite or sing.* But he had no more time to reflect on this.

Demetrius was calling, "I'm ready to leave if you are."

It was dark when Demetrius and his father left their house together and walked to the nearby home of Theous's father. When they arrived, they were welcomed by a family slave.

The slave invited them in. He escorted them through the courtyard towards the *andron* (symposium room). Demetrius's father could spot the *andron* due to its off-center doorway. He pointed this out to his son. "As in our house, the doors are in a central place between the walls. But *androns* are different. Their doors are purposely off-center to allow space for more sofas."

As it was, they were impressed when the slave motioned them to enter the *andron*. Here they found sofas accommodating two persons reserved for each of them. The sofas were set against the walls facing the center of the room so the guests could easily see each other. Under each sofa was a low three-legged roundtable, to be pulled out to rest their food and drinking mugs.

Rooms in Athens' houses were usually simple, even in aristocratic homes. But again, *androns* are different. Looking down, Demetrius's father saw a tiled floor adorned with detailed mosaic designs. Looking up he saw elegant tapestries hanging from all four walls. *This is impressive,* thought Demetrius's father.

At that exact moment, his gaze was interrupted. He felt a hand from behind resting on his shoulder.

"I'd like to introduce you to a couple of my friends," said Theous's father.

Demetrius and his father turned to see two young men standing side-by-side. One of the men looked considerably older than the other.

"I'm Playtonus," said the older of the two.

"And I'm Adonis," said the younger.

Demetrius's father said, "Hello I'm pleased to make your acquaintance."

"Likewise," said the two men. They shook hands while maintaining direct eye contact.

Theous's father said, "These men are philosophers. We expect their presence will add much to our festivities."

Looking at Adonis and Playtonus, Demetrius's father said, "We'll look forward to that," said "And I'd like you to meet my eldest son, Demetrius. He'll soon begin his military service."

"How do you do young man? My name is Adonis; I'm happy to meet you. It's special when young men like you attend the festivities. I'm glad you're here. But tell me, why haven't I seen you before?"

"Well, to be honest, this is my first symposium. As for tonight, I'm not sure if I'm old enough to be in the presence of such distinguished men. They have lived in this world many more years than I have."

"Think nothing of it. Good looking young men like you are what makes symposiums more exciting and worth coming to."

"Well, I don't want to be the center of attention. I'm here to learn."

"Please know you're making everyone happy by being here."

Demetrius didn't know what to say. He was also nervous. He tried to end the conversation by saying, "Thank you."

Adonis stood out more than other guests. This was due in part to his longer than usual tunic. It was colored bright green. He reserved the tunic for symposiums. He would also prove himself to be assertive in the general conversation.

Soon, others came in.

Theous's father invited everyone to be seated on their respective sofas. Each found his place. One of the first things the men noticed were items resting on the low-lying three-legged roundtable in easy reach of each guest. These were hand-painted bronze drinking mugs. Designs on the mugs portrayed a high degree of refined craftsmanship showing birds, flowers, and animals. The mugs were specially reserved for symposium parties such as this one. (For everyday use, undecorated glazed mugs were kept in the cooking area.) Beside each mug was a small basket of poppy-seed rolls. The guests also saw garlands of flowers which they were asked to place over their heads to hang from their necks.

Their curiosity of these items was interrupted when Theous's father announced to everyone, "Good evening everyone. We're pleased you're here. I'm happy to say our special meal will soon begin. But first, there's something special to present." At that moment everyone's eyes turned to see a young boy, escorted by a slave, coming into the *andron*. They walked across the room until Theous was standing beside his father's sofa. Theous's father stood up as the slave left the *andron*. "My friends," Theous's father announced, "I wish to present my son. His name is Theous. He alone is the reason you were invited to my home.

"As you know, my son did exceedingly well at the recent Panathenaic races. We're meeting here to celebrate his performance. As you also know, most of the other runners were older and more experienced than Theous. Despite his tender age, Theous made a spectacular showing. He did it for the glory of our revered goddess Athena."

The others responded spontaneously:

"A new hero athlete for Athens is among us!"

"Hurrah for Theous!"

"Congratulations young man!"

And so, it went.

When congratulations winded down, Theous walked around the room. He shook hands with each guest. When he returned to his father's side, his father placed a laurel wreath around the top of his head. Again, the room erupted in cheers. Then Theous took a bow to onlookers after which he promptly left the *andron*. He would not return.

The entire scene wasn't without its effect on Demetrius's father. He imaged how Nilo might've been where Theous was. *How that might've changed everything,* he thought. *Perhaps it's better Nilo's not here tonight. This could have been too difficult for him. Maybe he couldn't have endured it. I'm sure he couldn't have. And now, tonight, where is Nilo? Where's my son? I wonder.*

As soon as Theous exited the *andron*, his father announced, "Our symposium-meal will now be served."

At this moment a slave entered the *andron* carrying a full tray. The tray carried a roasted pig, and the slave made the rounds allowing each guest a close-up view of the delicacy. The slave showed them the underside of the pig's belly where he could point out to the guests the stuffing of thrushes, duck meat, eggs, and oysters. The eggs came from quails and hens. In addition to sharing the visual delight, guests were encouraged to smell sizzling aromas from the well-cooked pork. Then the slave left the *andron* long enough to carve up the pig. He returned with the now cut-up pork and its inner contents. Added to his tray were green vegetables and bread. Honey, cheese and olive oil were also on-hand to go with the poppy-seed rolls. These delights were speedily distributed to the guests. When the guests began to eat, talking was subdued.

Adonis, sitting on the sofa next to Demetrius said, "To your good health," as the adolescent received his plate of roasted pig.

Instead of replying, Demetrius simply gave a nod and a smile to the man and proceeded to begin eating. All the guests commenced eating as soon as they received their plate.

When the main course was over, the slave returned to collect everyone's plate. Then another slave entered the *andron*. He was carrying a tray with an assortment of fruits including grapes, figs, apples, pears, and dates which were speedily passed out to each guest.

Now with finger food to consume, the guests resumed chatting. But the *andron* became quiet again as Theous's father, the host, was about to make another announcement.

"As everyone knows, this is the time when the wine is served. But before we do, we will recite a poem in honor of Dionysis, our god of wine. Those of you who will participate have learned your parts. I will start:

> *Hail, children of Zeus!*
> *Grant lovely song and celebrate the*
> *holy race of the deathless gods,*

Who are forever.
Those who were born of Earth and starry
Heaven and gloomy night,
And them that the briny sea did rear.

The epic poem was continued by the guest Playtonus:

Tell how the first gods and earth came to be,
And rivers, and the boundless sea with its raging swell,
And the gleaming stars, and the wide heaven above,
And the gods who were born of them, givers of good things,
And how they divided their wealth,
And how they shared their honors among them,
And also, how at the first they took many-folded Olympus.

When Playtonus sat down, the poem was continued by
Adonis:

These things declare to me from the beginning,
Ye Muses who dwell in the house of Olympus,
And tell me which of them first came to be.

Nilo's father concluded the poem:

Verily as the first chaos came to be, but
next the wide-bosomed Earth,
The ever-sure foundations of all,
The deathless ones who hold the peaks of snowy Olympus,
And dim Tartarus in the depth of the wide-pathed Earth,
And Eros, fairest among the deathless gods,
Who unnerves the limbs and overcomes the mind,
And wise counsels of all gods and all men within them.

When Nilo's father sat down, two slaves brought out three *kraters* to the center of the room. The large bowls full of wine were two-thirds diluted with water. Two slaves filled pitchers of the diluted wine from one of the *kraters*. They carried the pitchers to the small tables beside each sofa where the guests were reclining. Each guest filled his wide-brim mug with wine.

After the mugs were filled, Theous's father stood up again. He proclaimed a toast, quoting words from the renowned poet Eubulus to the guests:

Three bowls only do I mix for the temperate: one to health,
the second to love and pleasure and the third to sleep . . .

After that, the guests cheered loudly. When they quieted down, Theous's father continued his toast:

After the third one is drained, wise men go home.
The fourth krater is not mine any more - it belongs to
bad behavior; the fifth is for shouting; the sixth is for
rudeness and insults; the seventh is for fights; the eighth
is for breaking the furniture; the ninth to vomiting. The
tenth belongs to madness and throwing the furniture.

The guests again cheered wildly.

When the cheering subsided, Adonis held high his wine-filled mug again while saluting the young man on the sofa next to him, "To your good health Demetrius."

This time Demetrius responded smiling, "And also to yours."

The pause in activity encouraged Adonis to take advantage of the relatively quieter time to speak more to

Demetrius. He repeated his former question, "Why haven't I seen you at a symposium before? It's nice to see you here."

Demetrius responded, "This is my first time. I'm finally old enough to be out with the men. What do you think of that?"

Adonis wanted to say he hopes to see him at future symposiums. But at that moment a single woman entered the *andron* capturing the attention of the guests. She was playing a single reed instrument called an *aulos* (like the modern oboe). She was fully dressed. Her gown went down to her feet. The guests paid rapt attention to her as she sauntered through the *andron*. She walked perilously near a few of the sofas, flirting with her eyes. But when arms extended to touch her, she turned away.

When the *aulos* player exited the *andron*, Demetrius spoke up to Adonis saying, "What a surprise. I thought women had no place in symposiums."

"You're partially right," said Adonis. "Women and slaves are never guests. But it's a usual practice that some are present to entertain. The women who come here are usually *hetairai* (prostitutes). Their sole function is to entertain. Other than that, symposiums are strictly a male festivity."

"Thank you," said Demetrius. "I expect to have more surprises tonight."

"That could be," said Adonis. "But no doubt you'll like what you see. That is if things don't get too out of hand."

At this point, Demetrius began taking more notice of the young man sitting on the sofa next to him. Adonis appeared a few years older than himself. He was self-assured, not afraid to speak up if he had something to say. Demetrius felt him to be approachable.

Conversations died down again as the next entertainers entered the *andron*. This time it was a group of older scantily clad youths carrying various reed and stringed instruments. The following song was played that the guests would sing aloud. It was taken from The Bacchai, a tragic play by Euripides.

Where is home for me?
O Cyprus, set in the sea.
Aphrodite's home in the soft sea-foam
Would I lend to thee;
Where in the wings of the Lovers are furled,
And faint the heart of the world!

Y, or to Paphos' isle,
Where the rainless meadows smile
With riches rolled from the hundred-fold
Mouths of the far-off Nile,
Streaming beneath the waves
To the roots of the seaward caves!

After the singing, conversations started up again, Adonis told Demetrius the instrument players are all slaves.

"Slaves? That's incredible," said Demetrius. "What a magnificent job they do."

"Yes, indeed," said Adonis. "And there will be more surprises ahead."

At that point, Theous's father rose again. "There will be time for individual conversations. Now is your opportunity to share with everyone what's on your mind. For some, there may be philosophical concerns. For others it may be your concerns are personal. I'm sure some of you may have unsettled situations of your own. Please know, here you can seek advice, and hopefully, you can find help. We want individuals to stand up one at a time and share your concerns. We can discuss many things. Who's first?"

For a moment, no one moved. Each one looked around to see who would stand up. When no one rose, Theous's father called out, "Playtonus, you're a philosopher, why don't you begin?"

For his part, Playtonus didn't want to be overly noticeable. But being asked by Theous's father made it easier for him. He stood up. "Good evening my friends. And good evening to those who I hope will be my friends before our night is over. I was asked to stand up because I'm a philosopher. But I can tell you philosophy is not on my mind tonight. Tonight, I'm concerned about the state of affairs in our City-State of Athens along with our wider territory of Attica. Our Fatherland has problems. Many problems. You all know that. Is it possible we can discuss some of these things tonight? Some may have more expansive knowledge about the affairs of our City-State as it relates to other city-states. Perhaps you can amplify what we know." Playtonus then sat down.

On hearing these words, Nilo's father felt some relief. He now felt he would be able to express some concerns he had regarding Nilo and Demetrius. Both were much on his mind. But he didn't want to be the next to stand up. He was relieved when someone else took the floor.

A somber voice stood up from the far end of the *andron*. "Thank you Playtonus. Thank you for opening this discussion for us. You're right. Our dear City-State of Athens has problems—many problems. We felt that once the Persians were defeated decisively, which they were, then everything would be fine. But maybe that's not the case. We've had enough of war. So, in looking to maintain the peace, Athens was instrumental in forming the Delian League. But who would have imagined by forming such a defensive measure many problems were created?"

Playtonus shot back "And tell us, please. What kinds of problems could those be? As you all know, the League began with an astonishing one-hundred fifty city-state members. They all agreed an attack on any one of us would be considered as an attack on all of us. Many city-states saw the wisdom of this. Yes, they did. So, over the years, we've seen fifty or more city-states asking to join our League. For sure, they were welcomed in. And you must consider those waiting to join, and those who are debating if they want to be with us. Our League keeps growing. The way things stand, there's neither a nation nor a city-state wanting to attack Attica or any member of our League. Rest assured my friend. We're safe. Safe enough to live in peace. At peace with all city-states and at peace with the world."

"Thank you, my friend. I know you've always been patriotic. 'Athens first,' you often say. You care much for our City-State. That's commendable. But you may not be aware how many city-states outside the League don't view us as you described. As you said, there are one-hundred fifty city-states allied with Athens plus fifty more who may join. That leaves about one-thousand, two-hundred city-states in the Greek-speaking world that aren't allied. Believe me. There's much fear throughout the wider Greek world. They know Athens is getting strong. And they're frightened. In their eyes, we're too strong for them, and we're too strong for the world. They no longer see us as merely a League of allies. They're beginning to see Athens as an empire. They believe as our 'empire' continues to grow, we'll become increasingly belligerent towards them. That's what they fear. And don't even try to imagine they won't be doing something about it. Sparta had the larger Peloponnesian League for a much longer time before the Delian League was formed. They will make a formidable adversary if it comes to that. I'm truly worried my friends."

"I understand what you're trying to say. You want Athens to be ready for all eventualities. I applaud that. However, there are some things you must know. One reason Athens is strong is the tributes it receives from its allies, the less-powerful among the city-states. They can't afford their armies and navies. Athens uses that money to build up its fleet of ships. As you know, we in Athens have the most powerful navy among all Greeks and quite possibly in the world. That offsets the powerful army Sparta enjoys. That keeps our citizens free from outside control."

At that point, Theous's father stood up and said, "My friends, I know you are passionate about your political views. That, as we know, is a good thing. But let's continue with other matters." Looking over at Nilo's father, he said, "I know you have some concerns, my friend. Would you like to express them now?"

Nilo's father got up and said, "Thank you. Yes, I do. I have some concerns, and I'm speaking to learn your thoughts. I know what I'm going to say isn't the usual fare for a symposium. We're here to contemplate the meaning of life and love and other thoughtful issues. Then as the evening wears on, we're here to make merry. That is well.

That is good. But there's a problem in my family that's tearing me apart. I've got to have answers. I'd appreciate hearing from thoughtful persons such as yourselves.

"Some of you are fathers. Therefore, you may find it easiest to understand. But either way, it's a complex situation. I have two sons and one daughter. My daughter and my oldest son have been growing up without serious problems. My youngest son, who after many years of being loyal to our family decided to go out on his own at his tender age of twelve years. We were close, he and I. But after having difficulties, he believes he cannot compete in life like other boys. He talked endlessly of needing his freedom. He no longer lives at home. We do not know where he is, or what he does. Because we, that is, our close-knit family, have done much for him over the years and more so because we love him, we want him to succeed. We want him to return to our family. I talked with him many times before he left home. I placed him with an excellent tutor. That was in vain. Now I ask you my friends, has anyone had similar experiences? Or know of a similar experience? And even if you don't, might you have some thoughts about this? That's all I have to say."

Nilo's father sat down.

For a few moments, the *andron* was quiet. Some of the guests were looking at each other with puzzled looks on their faces. It seemed no one knew what to say. There was some low murmuring among a few of the guests. No one stood up.

Finally, it was Theous's father who again took to the floor. "My friend, we know of your pain. We wish we had an answer for you. But we don't. You probably know according to our laws, under such situations, you no longer must bear responsibility for your son. But I also know how much you care for your children. Nilo's welfare is foremost in your mind. That's for sure. But to tell you what you can do for Nilo, I'm not sure any of us can tell you what to do." Theous's father then sat down. He did not know what else to say.

For a few moments the *andron* was quiet. Then soft-spoken private conversations started again in various parts of the room. Among them were Adonis and Demetrius.

Adonis looked at Demetrius and said, "Was that your father speaking?"

"Yes," said Demetrius. "That was him. The course my brother has chosen pains us all. It hurts deeply."

Adonis was trying to form soothing words to say to Demetrius. But before he could, Playtonus took to the floor again.

Playtonus said, "My friends, there's an answer to the dilemma we heard. The former speaker is in deep emotional pain. He sees no way out. But there is an answer to his perplexity. We don't know what it is. None of us do. That doesn't mean it can't be found." Now directing his comments to Nilo's father, he continued. "You must've heard of the Oracle at Delphi. This is where Greeks and non-Greeks from all over the Mediterranean go to get answers to their most perplexing problems.

"I've heard of wonderful things coming from the mouth of the *Pythia* (priestess). Individuals, families, and governments have all benefited from the wisdom she bestows from messages she receives from our gods. Should we go to war? What's the best time for war? Should I marry? The questions go on and on. And your most difficult situation concerning your estranged son may be solved by talking with the *Pythia*. You might want to consider it."

Nilo's father then rose. He thanked Playtonus for his concern. "I appreciate what you say. I'll give it the consideration it deserves."

Then, before Nilo's father or Playtonus could continue, everyone's attention was directed toward the sounds they heard coming from the front of the house.

Most guests knew what was happening. The *ephebes* (older adolescents) were outside trying to talk their way in. It's usual for the symposium host to arrange for a small group of *ephebes* to arrive during the later hours of a symposium. Also, there were often others who wished to crash the party. Sometimes they're able to gain entrance, but this time Theous's father was adamant. He maintained only a specific number could enter based on spaces remaining on the two-person sofas.

Demetrius was confused. He hadn't attended a symposium before. So, he leaned over to ask Adonis on the next sofa. "What's happening outside?"

"Ah, don't you know? This is when our merriment picks up. From the sounds we hear, the *ephebes* have arrived. They're negotiating about who can come to the symposium. We'll see what happens."

Demetrius, still confused, said, "Why are the *ephebes* coming to be part of a men's party? Can you tell me more?"

"Sure, I'll tell you. The reason the *ephebes* are here is to provide 'companionship' for the original guests. That's why the sofas are built to hold two persons."

"Ye gods! I'm not sure I want to be part of this. I've heard of such things, but never imagined all guests have to take part."

"Oh yes. You said you're a novice to the symposiums and this is your first time. Tell you what. Since you're new at this, you may prefer to watch. If you come onto my sofa, no one will approach you, or if they do, you're being here will make it easier to rebuff their advances."

"Thank you, Adonis. I appreciate that."

"It seems the young men are coming in. You'd better climb onto my sofa now."

And Demetrius did.

In a moment they could overhear the loud voices of the *ephebes* coming through the courtyard. "Here they come," said Adonis. And within moments the *ephebes* were entering the *andron*.

Motions and calls to "come in, come in" came from the guests lying on sofas. Then music filled the air. A couple of *hetairai* began playing the flute-like *aulos* as the youths entered the *andron*.

The youths, flanked by Theous's father, the evening's host, slowly circled the room passing each of the sofas. The *ephebes* glanced at the men as each one passed the sofas individually. Smiles and motions came from both men and youth. Then during their second pass around the room, the *ephebes* selected the sofa (and adult) of their choice, usually with encouragement from the guests.

No sooner had the *ephebes* made their choices when a couple of slaves were seen bringing out yet another large *krater* full of water-diluted wine. Now, as before, the pitchers were filled and taken to the guests and their younger "friends." Again, all mugs were filled to the brim.

Theous's father rose to toast:

"I need your attention please. As you know, as in all symposiums, this is a night for love. Therefore, I wish this to be a happy time for all. Do remember the words of Plato, the great philosopher of our time:

> *...and when one of you meets your other half, the actual half of yourself, whether he be a lover of youth or a lover of another sort, you are both lost in an amazement of love and friendship and intimacy and you will not be out of his sight, as I may say, even for a moment.*

My wish is that you all enjoy the evening."

The room was again abuzz as conversations on each sofa began between the original guests and the newly arrived *ephebes*. Before long, the guests and their newly arrived "friends" were involved in various stages of intimacy.

Demetrius was more than a little startled and confused by it all.

Adonis assured him this is normal in a symposium. He also related what might happen as the evening proceeds. "At first it seems everyone has their partner for the night. But it only seems that way. After a little more wine, some of the *ephebes* will get up from their sofa and make ritualized rounds and thereby change partners. You may've noticed the gifts guests brought gifts for their *ephebes*. A hen or a hare is the usual gift." Adonis wanted to explain more. He stopped talking when he saw Demetrius's father coming towards their sofa.

When his father got close to Demetrius and Adonis, he said, "Demetrius. I dislike having to take you away from here as I'm sure you're enjoying yourself. But tomorrow you'll have your day in Court. You'll need to be well rested when you give your testimony."

"Ah yes. You' re so right. . ."

Before Demetrius could continue, Adonis interrupted with a request for his father. "I agree Demetrius should have a good rest tonight. But can you give us a few minutes before you leave?"

"Yes, I can. Please be brief."

"Will do."

After Demetrius's father stepped away, Adonis said to his sofa-mate. "I know we just met. But I think you and I might be kindred spirits. I'd like to see you again. What do you say?"

Demetrius said, hesitatingly, "Well—yes. Yes, I think we can."

"Oh good. I'll contact you in a few days. Goodnight Demetrius."

"Goodnight Adonis."

The men shared a warm embrace after which Demetrius got up from the sofa and left with his father.

CHAPTER 10

The Trial

*Justice in the life and conduct of the state is possible only
as first it resides in the hearts and souls of the citizens.*

— **Plato**
427 – 347 BC

Demetrius and his father were up earlier than usual. After a light morning meal, they headed out to the *agora*. But on arrival, they were told the trial wouldn't be held there.

An official told them, "Yes, most of the trials are held here in the *agora*. But due to so many jurors, its venue has to be the theater."

So, father and son walked the distance to the theater. As they approached the site, they were amazed at the large gathering.

"Ye gods!" said Demetrius. "We knew there was going to be many jurors. We also expected many observers. But I never expected anything like this."

"Trials mean much to the Greek people," Demetrius's father said. "Our trial system is unique. Unlike most other city-states and foreign nations, it is the people who make legal decisions in Attica. When people find out it is we who are the government, not a tyrant, they develop respect and interest in judicial proceedings. And now, here we are. We need to go to the registration area. They have to know you're here."

Demetrius, with his father beside him, walked to the registration area. Demetrius presented himself to the magistrate and introduced himself to some of the dignitaries. He was given a space on the bench near the dais to sit down until it was his turn to speak. He looked to see if he could spot anyone he knew. But the crowd's size was overwhelming.

Meanwhile, his father found a seat in the public viewing area.

Each juror had reached the age of thirty. They were chosen by lot among volunteers. Most jurors were farmers, the main occupation in Attica. Jurors were also paid for their service at three *obols* per trial. (The *obol's* value was one-sixth of a drachma.) The jurors were separated from the observers and the trial participants by a large railing.

Each juror was given a bronze disc on arrival to the arena. Later, following testimonies of the accuser and the defendants, each juror would cast his vote by putting his disk into one of two large urns. One urn was marked "guilty;" the other "not-guilty." All that was needed for a conviction was a simple majority.

When the time came to begin, the magistrate informed the vast gathering. The magistrate turned the meeting over to a Herald who would announce charges against the suspects.

The trial opened when the Herald spoke up.

"Good morning. We're here today to decide the charges against the suspects. The crime they are accused of is *hubris*. *Hubris* is a state of arrogance whereby someone does as he pleases towards another person without his permission. This is a serious crime in Athens. The jury is asked to be extremely conscious of what the accuser and the accused will say. Much rides on your verdict. I ask the jurors to rise and take their oath."

All five-hundred and one jurors stood up and raised their right hand. They repeated in unison the oath as told to them by the magistrate.

> *I will cast my vote in consonance with the laws and decrees passed by the Assembly and by the Council, but, if there is no law, in consonance with my sense of what is most just, without favor or enmity. I will vote only on the matters raised in the charge, and I will listen impartially to the accusers and defenders alike. I swear to this in the names of our gods Zeus, Apollo, and Demeter.*

A nervous Demetrius was called to the dais.

Before he began, he was told his testimony, together with the ones who support him, will be limited to three hours. Time would be kept by a water clock which uses the flow of water to measure time.

Demetrius began to speak.

Good morning fellow citizens of Athens. A small number of you know me; most of you do not. My name is Demetrius. I'm a citizen of our City-State of Athens. The name of my deme (neighborhood) is Kedoi. My father is also a fellow citizen of Athens and likewise his father before him, and along with the fact I'm now eighteen years of age, I'm legally qualified to present my testimony.

Although I'm legally qualified to be here, it's only fair I tell you that due to my tender age, this is my first time to address my fellow citizens. I'm awed as I look upon such a vast and noble gathering. I assure you I'm committed to telling the truth as best I see it. My desire in coming before you is to earn your confidence and respect. I know the decision you render today will be based on facts alone. My faith in you, the jurors, is such that I know you will deliver a fair and equitable verdict.

As mentioned before, I'm from Athens. I was born in Athens. I grew up in Athens. It's the only place I've ever lived. It's where I learned to love and honor our gods. I'm proud to be a free-born citizen of Athens. Soon it'll be my privilege to serve as a member of the military as a hoplite defending our City-State. And, should it ever be necessary, I'd be proud to give my life for our dear City of Athens.

I'd like to begin by explaining the reason I've called for this trial. It's to seek justice from an act of cruelty by a mostly unknown group of men. They committed their act of cruelty to satisfy their desires. This cruel and barbaric violation of my body was apparently an act of hubris, an arrogant, evil action.

The brutal act of hubris took place on the first day of the Panathenaic Festival. My family and I were up early that day, well before the rising of the sun. We desired to show homage to our gods and especially to our City's patroness, our goddess Athena. We walked from our home in the Deme *Kedoi through the darkness to be with the multitude of others who also wished to honor Athena. We waited a considerable time before the procession left the Dipylon Gate shortly after the sun's rising. When the procession began, we knew it was worth the wait. But there was a problem. I'm short of stature. I couldn't see over the dense crowd. I looked around. I saw someone leave a small mound of dirt. That was enough. I made my way through the crowd and stood on the pile of dirt. From there, I could see the procession. Unfortunately, I didn't inform my family I was moving to a new place. If I took*

*time to tell them, someone else might've taken
my new place.*

Demetrius had been warned public trials can be chaotic.
He knew observers are free to shout and heckle at those
testifying. Still, Demetrius was surprised when someone
screamed loudly. "I hope you learned your lesson" after he
mentioned he didn't inform his family of his new location.
Demetrius tried to appear unruffled. He continued.

> *For a while, all was fine. The procession was
> entertaining. It was exciting when the chariots
> appeared on the Panathenaic Way. What a
> thrill to see runners jumping off their chariots
> and keeping pace with them despite their fast
> speed. And unbelievably, they were able to
> climb up on them again, even at the speed
> they were going.*
>
> *It was then, the very moment I was enthralled
> by the spectacle of the chariots, I felt pressure
> behind me. I dismissed that. It was the press of
> the crowd, or so I thought until there was an
> arm around my neck. Immediately, a hand
> covered my mouth. The crowd around me
> was also engaged by the chariots. So much
> they didn't notice what was happening. They
> also were dealing with choking dust from the
> chariots' horses. It was then a group of men
> somehow dragged me through the crowd to
> a location many blocks away. I was taken
> through a door into a small room and from*

there into a larger room. There were a couple of symposium-like reclining sofas and a small platform. Nothing else was descriptive of the simple place. They took me up onto the platform and pulled away my tunic. They began to touch me and passed their hands over my body. I asked what they were going to do to me. A man appearing to be the leader told me not to talk unless asked.

Then the same man took me to the side of the room. He laid me on a sofa. They forced me to drink undiluted wine—lots of it. The leader climbed on the sofa. He had his way with me. I can't describe the horrible things they did to me. It was awful. It was clearly a case of hubris. That is, they were doing whatever they wished. Before long, two men had their way with me at the same time. By then, my body was racked with pain. Still, they wouldn't stop. The pain got worse and worse. It seemed a long time before they finished. I can't say how long it was. Fortunately, in time they became tired. The men had been up all night preparing for this event. They began to fall asleep.

I couldn't sleep. The pain was too much. Hours went by. I looked for a way out, but the room was secure. The men remained asleep. Finally, one woke up and was apparently hungry. He hurriedly found food. Then he came near. He sat next to me. He said he was sorry about what happened. That was the only way men of his age could find satisfaction, he said. He kissed me. He hugged me. And again, said he was sorry for what happened. I tried being nice to him. Then, very surprisingly, he asked if I'd like to leave. I said "of course." and he showed me a way out. By then it was dark again. I ran away as fast as I could, despite the pain. I asked strangers on the passageway how to find my way home. I arrived home. My family put me to bed.

That's the story of my abduction. It's not pleasant to repeat. But repeat it I did. After I had been home many days, I learned the authorities captured the men who they believe committed the crime. I went to the jail to identify them. The ones I recognized were the leader and the man who befriended me. The other faces remained a blur in my mind.

I wish to conclude my testimony by saying it's important these men be convicted. It wouldn't be right for another young man, a citizen such as myself, to encounter a similar situation. I plead with you, the jurors. Do your duty. Convict these men.

Thank you for your time.

After Demetrius stepped down from the elevated platform, his supporters were invited to testify. Demetrius knew who some of them would be, but anyone would be allowed to speak on his behalf. He had no idea if anyone else might add support for him. This gave a degree of mystery to the proceedings.

The first supporter to speak was Theous's father. He spoke passionately to the Assembly.

> *I come before you today in support of my friend Demetrius. I've known this young man for many years. I'm also a good friend of his father and all his family. I can in good conscience tell you Demetrius and his family are outstanding citizens. To the best of my knowledge, they've never cheated anyone or committed an untoward act. They act fairly and competently with their friends and all with whom they come in contact. They love our gods and goddesses. And as he told you, he and his family were there at the Panathenaic Festival, honoring, with sincere piety, our City's patron goddess, our dear Athena. He didn't deserve the horrific experience he was subjected to when he was taken from the ceremonies. So please, take it into your thought, take it into your hearts, the essential goodness of this man, Demetrius, soon to be a* hoplite, *protecting our City-State.*

Thank you for letting me speak on his behalf.
I bid you a good day.

As Theous's father stepped down from the platform, the next speaker, Lukos, took to the podium.

Good morning, my dear fellow citizens of Athens and Attica. We're here today to perform an essential service to our City-State. We're asked to see that justice is served. In that regard, I have important questions for you. What, may I ask, makes Athens a great City-State? What is it that separates Athens from other city-states and nations of the world? Take a moment to please consider this.

I wish we were a smaller group so we could dialogue about this. The reason is the answers to these questions are momentous. As citizens of our great City-State, we need to remember continually why our City-State is so uniquely special. We must keep this in our thought. Some of you may have different answers. But I doubt your answers are much different than mine.

There are, of course, many reasons for the greatness of our City-State. I'll bring out the most important. The first one I suggest to you is agon. *Agon, as I'm sure you know, is our motivational spirit to excel in every possible way. Agon is a gift from our gods. We see it most*

169

clearly in athletic competition, such as during the Panathenaic Games and our Olympics. The bodies of our athletes are models of muscular perfection. In many ways, the bodies of our athletes image our gods. But agon *also carries over into every endeavor our citizens engage in. Look at our art. Our sculptures and paintings are among the world's finest.*

We have the best debaters and philosophers anywhere. We have the best historians, those who chronicle our past. The drama in our theaters is like no other. Due to our naval prowess, we have the best military and defense the world has ever known. And to this list, I want to add our government. We all know our government is far from perfect. But, at the same time, it's the best the world has seen. But it's taken us years, indeed centuries, to bring us where we are. Athens stumbled in the past. We let ourselves be governed by awful tyrants who cared only about themselves. Of these, Draco comes to mind. Under Draco, our citizens suffered the death penalty for the pettiest crimes. Due to that tyrant, laws that were too harsh then and too harsh now are called "draconian." Later, our government improved under Salon. He's thought of as our first innovative lawmaker. His work made the birth of democracy possible. It was democracy, power to the people, that made Athens what it is today.

Today, our people are sovereign. All free adult males can participate in our Citizens' Assembly. It's also the same Citizens' Assembly that constitutes our supreme judicial authority. Good governments are fragile. We must be careful in our continual endeavor for a better government. This too comes from agon, our endeavor for excellence. Yes. Agon is the reason we've attained an advanced state of government. It's the reason we're here. And that's why you, the jurors, must be inspired by agon for this process to succeed. You must show total impartiality and base your decision on facts alone.

As a testifier for the accused, I believe the facts will show Demetrius to be a solid citizen. He doesn't tell lies. But please listen to all evidence and testimonies from both sides. If you do so impartially, you'll know Demetrius told the truth in his testimony.

Thank you for listening and have a good day.

The next speaker was Demetrius's friend Clymus.

Hello. My name is Clymus. I've known Demetrius for most of my life. Though I am a few years older than he is, we grew up together as close friends. We seek each other out when we need advice. I can tell you Demetrius is an excellent citizen. The welfare of Athens is paramount for him. Over many years I've seen

171

how he loves his family and they, along with our City-State, are the most essential things in his life. He's anxious to begin his service as a hoplite *to better serve his City-State. He didn't deserve what happened to him at the Panathenaic Festival. To be a warning against others who might want to violate other young men, I urge you, the jurors, do your job. Convict the men who brought harm to Demetrius. Let justice reign in Athens! That is all.*

The next several speakers included Demetrius's tutor during many of his teen years. Other speakers were friends who came to voice support. When they were finished, all the registered list of speakers for Demetrius had testified. The magistrate then spoke to the crowd.

"May I have your attention, please? All who registered to speak on behalf of the accuser have completed their testimony. Together, they were allotted three hours to speak. The water clock shows time remaining if others wish to testify on behalf of the accuser. If anyone wants to give supportive evidence for Demetrius, you may come to the dais at this time."

Demetrius was nervous. He knew the meeting was open to anyone who wished to testify could put the trial on an unpredictable course. *Maybe no one will come forth,* he thought. *Let's see what happens.*

For a few moments, nothing happened. Many turned their heads to see if anyone was heading for the podium. The magistrate was about to return to the dais to announce testimonies for the accuser have been completed. Then at that moment, a citizen rose from his seat. He went to the dais. A surprised Demetrius strained to see him. Unfortunately, he was on the far side of the arena. Demetrius could not make out who he was.

As the man walked briskly towards the dais, the buzz in the crowd grew louder. Everyone was curious as to who he was. Demetrius and his supporters understandably wondered: *Is this man friend or foe?*

When the man reached the dais, he turned toward his audience and looked into the assembled crowd.

With the man who would be the next speaker now closer to him, Demetrius saw him clearly. *Oh, ye gods! I know that man. He's Bacchides, the man who befriended me.* He wanted to signal his father and supporters who he is. But they were too far removed from him.

For his part, Demetrius didn't know what to think. *What will happen now?* Demetrius knew the man had clearly been loyal to the group's leader, even though he was befriended by him.

Bacchides cleared his throat and was about to speak. The crowd went silent as Bacchides began to address the Assembly.

> *Good afternoon everyone. I wish to thank the magistrate and other officials present for allowing me to speak. Almost all of you do not know who I am. My name is Bacchides. I was one of the men who took part in the violent gang-rape of Demetrius, who is now my accuser. . .*

He tried to continue, but the assembled crowd drowned him out. Their voices were too much. Many were yelling:

"You're out of order."

"Not your turn yet!"

"Sit down!"

"Shut up!"

"You're going to jail."

The magistrate went to the dais to speak with Bacchides. The magistrate asked him, "If you wish to speak against your accuser, why don't you wait until the period for the defenders?"

"I understand what you're saying. But the truth is, I do not wish to speak *against* my accuser. It's my wish to speak in *favor* of the accuser. What we did to Demetrius was wrong. We're all guilty."

The normally well-composed magistrate was startled by Bacchides's remarks. *This has never happened before. I'm not sure how to handle this,* he thought. But he had to decide. What he decided to do was call for the crowd's attention. The magistrate pleaded with the audience, "Please listen to the speaker. He has something important to say."

Bacchides waited for the crowd to settle down. When they did, he tried again to speak.

> *Please listen. I'm here to speak in favor of my accuser, Demetrius. I wish to tell you we were wrong in what we did. I want you to know I'm prepared to suffer my punishment, whatever that may be. As to the others who also violated Demetrius, I don't know their wishes. But let me tell you what happened*

from my point of view. We had been planning many days to find a youth or young man to satisfy our lustful yearnings. We felt the easiest way to accomplish this would be at the Panathenaic Festival during the parade on the Panathenaic Way. As it turned out, that's precisely what we did. Oh, what joy! We were happy when Demetrius, such a beautiful lad, was brought into the room where we could enjoy him to the fullest. And enjoy him we did. We drank undiluted wine and did whatever we wished with him. What a fine specimen of youthful manhood we had! As I told Demetrius, the men in our group are too old to find ourselves an eromenos. No good-looking youth in Athens would want to be lovers with us. So, we did what we believed was the only way to fulfill our desires.

I know the other men in our group will be unhappy with what I say. Let that be. I'm talking for myself. They'll have their turn to try to defend themselves if that's at all possible. There's also the question of identity. It's my understanding some, many, or maybe all the defendants plan to testify they were not the ones who committed this brutal crime. Therefore, I want to testify that I know all these men. They are the ones who were with me on the day of the Panathenaic Festival when Demetrius was captured. They are the

*ones who, like me, inflicted pain on him to
satisfy our desires. I have no good reason to
lie about this. We are all guilty of committing
hubris against Demetrius. That's all I have to
say. Thank you for listening.*

The entire arena broke out into a frenzy of many voices.
They were startled by hearing straight talk from one of the
accused. No one could remember a defender of an illegal
act ever addressing the Assembly that way. One of the most
surprised was Demetrius. This was not how he expected the
proceedings to go. After a few moments of contemplation,
Demetrius asked if he could speak with the magistrate.

The magistrate agreed to listen to his concern.

Demetrius asked if it would be possible for him to
address the Assembly again. He had something important
to say.

Again, the magistrate was confused. It wasn't standard
procedure for an accuser to speak a second time and
especially before the defenders had their chance to testify.
After consideration of the unusual circumstances, Demetrius
could speak again.

The crowd was surprised when Demetrius appeared on
the dais to speak again. They wondered what he might say.
They would listen carefully.

Demetrius proceeded with his second testimony of
the day.

*My fellow citizens, I wish to thank the magistrate
for allowing me to address you again. I know
this will be a long day for you, so I'll be brief.*

I was startled, as were all of you, when the last speaker, Bacchides, gave his testimony in favor of myself. It was a selfless gesture on his part. The reason I need to address you again is that Bacchides didn't tell you everything. If you recall my earlier address to you, I mentioned one of the men in the group befriended me. I want you to know he was Bacchides. He woke up before the others. He found food. He sat down next to me. He offered me food. I wasn't interested in eating more than a little bit which he shared. He explained why he and the others did what they did. Then he repented. He expressed sorrow for what he did. At his request, I kissed him and allowed him to embrace me. He was truly sorry. To try to make up for what he did, he offered to set me free. I didn't know how he could do that. He took me to another room. There he pulled aside a tapestry on the wall. This revealed a small door. He opened the door as we heard stirrings from the others. Seemingly not worried about the danger to himself, he told me to go and go fast. I did as he said. I returned to my family.

I have a request for the jurors. It is this. If you find this group of men guilty, please make an exception for Bacchides. For sure, he lapsed in his thinking—so excited he was in having a sexual adventure. But in my opinion, he atoned for his misguided behavior. He took a risk to himself by setting me free as this was obviously contrary to the will of the others. We can't imagine how much more pain I would've endured by remaining with those men. But if you feel Bacchides must be punished with the others, then please treat him with more leniency. That's all I ask.

Demetrius sat down as the magistrate stepped up to the dais.

He told the Assembly, "The testimony period for supporters of the accuser is over. There will be a recess before we continue."

During the recess, the defendants huddled with themselves. This was necessary considering the damaging testimony given by Bacchides which identified all of them as guilty.

When the crowd reassembled, the magistrate announced the defense can begin its testimony. The first speakers would be from the accused men themselves, followed by their supporters.

The leader of the defendants asked to speak with the magistrate before giving their testimonies. Their entire defense had been that they were not the ones who committed the crime. This position was weakened by Bacchides's testimony. The leader said to the magistrate, "We no longer believe we can convince the jurors we are not guilty. Would there be leniency towards us if we admit our guilt and forgo our testimonies?"

The magistrate told the men "That's not my decision. The jurors can decide that."

So, the defendants huddled once more. After much discussion, they decided they had no choice but to sorrowfully plead guilty. They hoped the jurors would feel their remorse and let them off lightly. They decided just the leader of the defendants would present testimony. The leader went to the dais. He was ready to make his remarks before a hostile, but also a hushed Assembly.

> *Good day fellow citizens of Athens. We know it's been a long day for you. You'll be pleased to know my brief testimony will be the only one coming from the defense. We thank you for your participation as jurors. We know your non-biased participation is a big reason our democracy works as well as it does. We're grateful to you for that. In the interest of brevity, the defense studied our peculiar situation. We know we committed a horrible act of hubris against a fellow citizen. We want you and our accusers to know we're deeply sorry. We wish it hadn't happened. But it did. We were overcome with lust and sexual appetite for one of the most enticing and attractive young men in our City-State. We hoped he'd enjoy the experience as much as we did. But he did not.*
>
> *If there's anything we can do for the defendant and/or his family, we would be pleased to comply. We hope our admittance of guilt will*

facilitate today's proceedings and help everyone get on with their lives. But we cannot, and we will not forget the pain the defendant had to endure. We send our best wishes to him and his family. But we beg you: try to feel the intensity of our remorse and our desire to atone for the injustice committed to a fellow citizen. We pray to the gods, especially Zeus, Apollo, and Demeter, that they too will see and truly know how remorseful we are. That's all I have to say. Thank you for your kind attention.

The leader of the defendants returned to his seat.

Because the defendants pleaded guilty, there was no need for the jurors to vote. The proceedings then went to the next phase which was to determine punishment for the guilty party.

According to Athenian law, each side would propose a form of punishment. Generally, the types of penalties included: death, jail, loss of citizenship, exile, and/or fines. The jury would then vote on which of the two punishments the guilty party should receive. There was a pause in the proceedings to allow each side time to decide the form of punishment they wished to propose.

Demetrius huddled briefly with his father, Theous's father, and Lukos. After a brief discussion, they decided to propose exile from Attica for everyone for life. An exception was made for Bacchides. He would receive exile for ten years, after which he would regain citizenship on returning to Attica.

As to the defendants, they found determining a punishment especially tricky. If they were to choose too light a punishment, the jurors would be more likely to vote in favor of the accuser's proposal. What they decided was exile from Attica for all of them for ten years.

The two urns used for receiving the votes (bronze disks) were placed on a table next to the dais. One was labeled "accusers;" the other "defendants." If the accusers' urn received the most votes, the defendants would be exiled from Attica for life. If the defendants' urn received the most votes, they would be exiled for ten years.

Per Athenian law, no discussion was allowed among the jurors. It took a while for all five-hundred and one jurors to cast their vote. A simple majority was needed. Six jurors were appointed to count the votes. When votes were counted, the accusers won by a margin of more than two to one. The group of men who repeatedly raped Demetrius was banished for life from Athens/Attica, except for Bacchides. Bacchides would be sent away for ten years, after which he could reclaim his Athenian citizenship.

Soon a crowd of supporters gathered around Demetrius. All his supporters wanted to congratulate him. "Perhaps we should celebrate with a symposium," said Demetrius's father.

CHAPTER 11

Nilo's Adventures – II

Day by day, what you choose, what you think and what you do is who you become.

— **Heraclitus of Ephesus**
535–475 BC

Nilo found himself alone again on the passageway, not knowing where to go. But this time he had more money than he remembered having in a long time, thanks to Xavier. The money gave him confidence. Confidence he'll be alright. At least for many days. *But what to do?* he wondered. *Where should I go? And how am I ever going to meet the right man to take care of me?*

Nilo's immediate problem was that it was still morning. The places he could think of to go were evening and late-night venues, a time when he might find men cruising for boys. But morning? Where to go in the morning? What would he do now? As it was, he wandered aimlessly through the passageways with no destination in mind. As he continued walking, his thoughts turned to his home and family. *What are they doing now? Might they be thinking about me? Might they miss me? Demetrius will be in the military soon. There will be no sons in the home. How will they feel then?* Nilo had no answers for his questions. Of one thing he was sure. He was not ready to go home. Not yet. He needed to explore his freedom.

Thinking about his family reminded him again of the conversations his father had with him. Sometimes his father talked about older adolescents and young men who would hang around public places like the *palaestra* (wrestling school) and the *gymnasias. They're interested in boys like me.* Thereupon Nilo decided to visit the *palaestra*, a place he could visit in the middle of the day. He wouldn't have to go inside. The vultures are always outdoors. It took him a while to recall where it is, but eventually, found its location.

The sun was nearly at its high point when the *palaestra* was in sight. He knew then, there may be opportunities waiting for him.

As he approached the *palaestra*, he could spot the vultures. They were obvious. They were there harassing those entering and leaving the building. Nilo wasn't sure how to engage these young men. He simply decided to draw closer to see what might happen.

As it was, it didn't take long for Nilo to be noticed.

"Hey there little boy. Wanna have some fun?"

For the first time in his life, Nilo would answer the heckler. No matter it had been drilled into him first by his parents, then by his schoolmaster, also his friends and even by his slave Chamus, that he should never, ever, pay attention to such people. But now, he was living by different standards: his own rules.

"What are you talking about?" Nilo asked the heckler.

Pleased with receiving a response, the heckler said, "I'm talking about a good time. Would you like that?"

"Tell me more," responded Nilo.

When the two of them had drawn closer, the heckler explained precisely what he wanted to do. "And would you like to come with me?" he asked as he reached his hand inside the boy's tunic for a friendly fondle.

"Maybe for a little while," said Nilo cautiously.

"Whatever you say," said the heckler. "Shall we go?"

Nilo followed him.

The young man didn't take Nilo to a house, but to a room. To Nilo, this brought thoughts of what happened to Demetrius. Once they had entered, the young man pointed to a cot at the end of the room. "That's where we'll have our fun," he said.

"And tell me, what would you like to do, pretty boy?"

"I'm not very experienced," said Nilo. "What don't you suggest something?"

"Come here. I will show you." When Nilo came closer, the young man pushed Nilo onto the cot all the while holding onto his tunic leaving the boy stripped of his garment. Then he got on top of Nilo. He had his way with him. While the experience seemed to last a while for Nilo, it didn't take long. Then Nilo was ordered back onto the passageway.

Nilo was not in as much physical pain as emotional. He began to cry. He also realized the young man took all his money. What hurt him most was the total lack of affection he was given as the young man cared only for his body. Nilo was distraught. And again, he had no idea of where to go or what to do.

For a while, he walked around the City without a destination in mind. This took a few hours.

Oddly enough, he finally decided to return to the *palaestra. Maybe I can find someone nicer there,* he thought. But when he arrived, he couldn't bring himself to respond to the hecklers' taunts. Neither a greeting nor a retort was suitable. Instead, he ignored them. Nilo lost his appetite for following hecklers home or even saying a word to them. He was hoping there might be a kinder person around. That wasn't to be. He was hungry. He was tired. He was void of ideas. He left the *palaestra* and searched for a soft place to lie down. When darkness came, he craved to find a decent spot. Eventually, after walking to the edge of the City where there were fewer houses, Nilo came to a depression by the side of the passageway. He put himself down. His thoughts again turned to home, his warm bed and loving family. *Maybe I should return home sometime,* he thought, *but not now. I must live my freedom.* In time, he fell asleep. He slept many hours.

When the sun's rays first touched his face, Nilo opened his eyes. *I'm cold; I'm hungry.* He clutched his hands over the sides of his loosely hanging tunic. He pulled the sides tightly together until he felt his tattered garment stretching more securely around him. *So, is this what freedom is?* he asked himself. He had no new ideas of what he might do or where he could go. All he could think of was to return to the *palaestra,* which he wasn't sure he wanted to do. But he could think of no other place. This was despite his renewed aversion to the ever-present hecklers. He would walk slower than usual this morning. He knew the *palaestra* wouldn't open until the sun was higher in the sky.

When he reached the *palaestra*, it was quiet. Not even the hecklers had arrived. But the door was open. He decided to go in. *At least it might be a bit warmer,* he surmised.

Following the custom, Nilo left his tunic with the others near the doorway. He went out from the colonnade and into the open court. He saw a pair of men doing their wrestling routines.

He felt, m*aybe if I do my wrestling routines, I'll be left alone.* So, he did. He found the routines coming back to him. He performed them automatically, not needing to think about them. Exercising seemed to make him feel better. *It's been a long time since I did this,* thought Nilo.

As he was doing his routines, others came into the court area. A few of them were watching Nilo. It was strange for them seeing someone so young in the *palaestra*.

Eventually, Nilo needed to rest. He looked around the large space as he sat down on a spectators' bench. He stayed there for some time. As he began to think about what he might do next, someone who watched him doing his routines came by.

"May I sit here next to you?" he asked.

"Certainly," said Nilo.

"I saw you working out. You know your routines well. I wonder if you'd like to join me in a friendly wrestling match."

Nilo was surprised by the offer. The adolescent seemed to be a few years older than him. He was thin, not as muscle-bound as the others. But he was larger than himself. As it was, Nilo agreed to "a friendly match."

The two wrestlers began from a standing position in the center of the wrestling pit. They immediately extended their arms to gain a holding position over their opponents' shoulders. They continued by pushing hard with their arms and at the same time trying to trip the other with their legs with the aim of knocking their opponent down. Nilo soon learned his opponent was stronger. But he was able to hold his ground for some time before he was forced down. Shortly his back touched the ground, scoring a point for his opponent. The match continued for some time before Nilo's opponent won. The final score was three to one, enough to win the match.

Nilo and his opponent shook hands as they walked off the wrestling pit. They congratulated each other for their performance. "Nice work," said Nilo. "You deserved to win."

"Ahh, but you made me work hard. You're quite good for your age and size. By the way, I'm Cilon."

"I'm Nilo."

At that point, they noticed they had been watched during their match. One of the spectators called out, "Hey Cilon, who's your friend?"

Cilon called back, "His name is Nilo. We just met."

Cilon and Nilo then walked over to the spectators' bench.

"Hello, Nilo. I'm happy to meet you."

"Likewise," said Nilo.

Cilon said, "He's the supervisor here. He coordinates all the activities here in the *palaestra*."

"It's a pleasure to know you," said Nilo.

The supervisor suggested the three of them retire to the social room where they might talk. "It's quieter and more comfortable there," he said.

And they did.

After everyone sat down, the supervisor opened the conversation by speaking to Nilo. "I watched your match with Cilon. I was surprised to see someone of your stature holding your own so well against someone who was larger and obviously stronger. We don't see that every day. You even forced his shoulder to touch the ground on one occasion. That scored a point for you. You're quite agile. You seem to maneuver yourself well."

"The reason I could do all that is because wrestling was a major activity in my school. Our trainer was demanding. I learned a lot. Also, I love it. It's my favorite activity next to running."

"That's interesting. I don't think I've seen you're here before. Is this your first time here at the *palaestra?*"

"Uh, no it isn't. I came here once with my father not long ago."

"It's nice you felt comfortable enough to return by yourself."

"I didn't have much choice, Sir. I couldn't think of another place to go."

"Could you explain that?"

Nilo then told the supervisor and Cilon the reasons why he left home and what he has been doing since, omitting he had been a *pornos.*

"That's some story," said the supervisor. "Do you have plans for the future?"

"No Sir. I have no plans. But I do have to find a place to stay. I don't enjoy sleeping without shelter."

"Why can't he stay here at the *palaestra*?" asked Cilon.

"The *palaestra's* set up for athletics. It's never used for lodging."

"I know. But the *palaestra* is a large place. There's plenty of room here."

"We can set him a place to stay for one night. Beyond that, I'm not sure we can continue. Even if he could remain, this isn't a safe place for him. There are too many here who would love to corrupt a young boy like Nilo. He'd be a prime target. That doesn't mean I don't want to help him. There may be better ways to do that."

Nilo was getting nervous as they discussed what they might do for him. "I don't want to be a bother for you," he said. "I can survive on the passageways."

"The passageways can be a cruel place for a boy like you," said the supervisor. "I don't want to see a boy like you subject to that kind of life. But we need some time to see what we can do."

"Thank you," said Nilo. "I'll try not to be a problem for you."

"Have you had anything to eat today?" asked the supervisor.

"No Sir. I haven't."

"Okay. We have a small cooking area where we keep food for our staff. I'll ask that something be prepared for you and show you where you can sleep tonight."

"Thank you very much," said Nilo.

Nilo passed the rest of the day mostly talking with some of the men and adolescents who came into the *palaestra*.

He also had an afternoon nap as he didn't sleep well the previous nights.

For his part, the supervisor was kept busy trying to find a way to help Nilo. He couldn't take Nilo into his home. But he thought maybe someone among his contacts could. He spent the rest of the day visiting them.

Evening came soon for Nilo. The *palaestra* shut down at sunset. After that, it was he and the caretaker on the premises. Nilo spent a few hours contemplating his situation. At times the thought of leaving the *palaestra* crossed his mind. But he decided to wait to see the outcome of events and then decide.

Nilo had his best sleep in several days. He woke up when the sun's rays broke into his little room. It would be a few hours before the staff, and the users would come to the *palaestra*.

Nilo got out of his little cot when he heard the staff coming into the *palaestra*. Before long he was called to the cooking area for a light morning meal. He was grateful for this meal. Now his main worry was what might happen to him. *Will the supervisor be able to help me?*

After the morning meal, Nilo returned to the wrestling area. He took a seat on the spectators' bench. He remained there for some time. He enjoyed watching the routines of others and the occasional matches among wrestlers. But he'd be a spectator. *I'm not going to take part in any matches. Getting hurt could cause problems with the supervisor's efforts to help me.* He hoped the reason the supervisor wasn't around was due to his looking for someone to help.

Not until late afternoon was there was a sign of hope. The supervisor approached Nilo. "I have news for you."

On hearing this, Nilo sat up straight while looking directly at the supervisor. His heart was beating faster.

"I'm not sure where we are in finding a situation for you. You should know, I've seen many persons. Most of them couldn't help. They had problems of their own. A few said, 'Can you ask me later?' But there were also some who said they wanted to think about it. Then there was an interesting contact. He's an important citizen active in the theater. I've known him a while. He trusts me to the point of believing I wouldn't ask him to help someone I feel is a poor risk. Then he asked how long I've known you. I had to tell him the truth. I've known you only for the brief time we talked yesterday. His answer was he'd like to get to know you and could he see you today. I said yes, hoping you'd be willing to meet him. His name is Horus."

Such uncertainty made Nilo nervous. He didn't know what to say.

The supervisor remained patient. He let Nilo take his time.

Finally, the boy said, "I'm afraid. I've met some good people in my life and some not-so-good people. Then there were those who seemed wonderful. But they turned out to be only interested in themselves. The same thing might happen here. Maybe I should fend for myself."

"Well, you know we can't continue keeping you here at the *palaestra*."

"Yes. I know that."

"If you want help, you have to look at opportunities when they come up."

"But maybe I don't need help. Maybe living on the passageways is what the gods want me to do."

"Nilo. You weren't happy on the passageways. Remember how hungry you were when you arrived here? Remember the cold night when you slept in a ditch? Remember how unhappy you were? You don't have to arrange anything with Horus right away. You can take your time. Why not agree to talk with him?"

Nilo was speechless again. He couldn't think of a reason why he shouldn't at least meet Horus. After a few moments he said, "Okay, I'll see him."

Waiting for Horus to arrive made Nilo nervous again. It wasn't until nearly closing time when he showed up.

When Horus arrived at the *palaestra*, he went directly to the supervisor's room.

"Sorry for being late," said Horus. "Can you tell me the situation?"

"Yes. First, I'm glad you were able to come. Nilo arrived here yesterday. He was living a short time on the passageways. After he came here, he did his wrestling routines followed by a match with one of the regulars. He did well with that. He scored a point from a larger, more experienced wrestler. I talked to him a little while. Nilo apparently comes from a good home. Therefore, he's probably an honest boy. He says he was a failure at many things. He couldn't live up to his father's standards. So, he prefers to live on the passageways rather than home."

"I see. Well, I'd like to talk with him and go from there."

"Thanks for being here and taking an interest. I'm sure the boy is someone who would respond positively to the right person."

"Okay. I'll talk to him. Thanks again."

"Hello. You must be Nilo."

"Yeah. And you must be Horus."

"That's right. I'm happy to meet you."

"So, what do you want with me?"

"Nilo, we haven't much time. The *palaestra* is about to close. That means we have little time to talk. I came here to ask if you want to come with me."

Nilo was taking a long look at the man. *He's a good-looking person. Maybe in his 30's.*

But why does he want to know me and perhaps take me to live with him? What did the supervisor say about me? I'm not sure what to think. "I don't know how to answer you," said Nilo. "I don't know you at all."

"You're right. So, if you would like us to get to know each other why don't you come with me and we'll see how we feel?"

At that moment, one of the *palaestra's* attendants came by. He told Horus and Nilo, "We're closing now. You'll have to leave."

Horus repeated his question to Nilo, "Will you come with me?"

Nilo, now understanding the difficulty of the situation, said, "May I come back to the *palaestra* in the morning if I want?"

"Of course, you may."

The two of them left, pausing to say "Goodbye" to the supervisor at the entrance.

As they left the *palaestra,* Nilo was happy to see the hecklers were gone.

As they were walking together on the passageway now in total darkness, Nilo asked Horus, "Why do you want me to go home with you?"

"It was a sudden request, I know. But the *palaestra* was about to close. I had no choice. There wasn't time to explain why I wanted you to come with me. There are different reasons. One, you're too young to live on the passageways. You need a good home. The *palaestra* was unable to keep you another day. I'm also doing a favor for the supervisor.

And I hope I'm doing a favor for you."

"But why do you want to do me a favor?"

"According to the supervisor, you're a deserving young boy. He told me you're intelligent. He thinks you've had bad breaks and you're a good wrestler. He also believes you have the potential for many things."

"Ha! How can he say that? He barely knows me. Is the real reason you're taking me home is you fancy young boys like me?"

"If I'm to be honest, I think we have to say nearly all men in the Greek world are attracted to either young men or adolescents or boys or a combination of them. But men don't get all their satisfaction from being a physical lover alone. You've heard of the philosophers' talk of loving a boy's soul, being a good mentor to them and the joys of caring for them. That's different from lust."

"That's what the philosophers say. But I bet even they've had their share of young men and boys as well."

Horus was becoming impressed by how well Nilo could discuss mature topics in a grown-up way.

"You may be right about the philosophers. Nevertheless, each couple has to work out their own situation and how they want to handle it."

Nilo and Horus continued their give and take conversation about such things until they reached Horus's home. When they arrived, he said, "Well, here's my home. Please come inside."

Nilo went inside with trepidation, not knowing what to expect.

Horus showed discretion to Nilo doing all he could to make him comfortable and not threatened. He lit candles allowing Nilo to see what his home looks like. When he saw Nilo gazing in every direction out of curiosity, he asked, "Would you like a quick tour of the house? Later we can talk about the rooms in detail."

"Sure."

The boy was led to the rooms connected to the courtyard. The first was the cooking area. "As you may know, this area is normally the province of women, at least in Athens. But I'm not married, so there aren't any women in the house. The slaves do the cooking and cleaning up. I stop by now and then to see if everything's okay."

Next to the cooking area, Nilo's attention was diverted to the bathing room. He saw a large tub for bathing. On the other side of the room was a chamber pot for relieving oneself.

As in most homes of aristocrats, the most elegant room in the house was the *andron.*

Here, Nilo saw the usual sofas with a small low table beside it. He loved the mosaic tiled floor and wall tapestries.

The other downstairs room was used for storage.

Upstairs, Nilo was first taken to visit the women's sitting area. "This is where women would be weaving and doing other feminine chores," explained Horus. "But no women live in the house. At least not now."

Horus then took the boy to see the bedrooms. The first one was used by Horus. "This is where I sleep," he told Nilo.

Nilo winced. *Ye gods!* he thought. *Is this where I'm going to sleep too? That bed looks too narrow for both Horus and I.* Nilo was feeling uneasy.

Horus continued to the next bedroom with Nilo following. "This room isn't used by anyone. At least not for sleeping."

As Nilo glanced around the room, he happened to see a collection of unusual masks. *What could those be about?* he wondered. *They look strange.* Some had exaggerated smiles while others portrayed frowns. He asked Horus, "Do you collect masks?"

"Oh yes, the masks. Those are from my work."

"Your work? You mean you make masks?"

"No. I work in the theater. All our actors wear masks during plays. You may have seen them if you've ever watched a play."

"Yes," said Nilo. "When I was younger, my father took his children there. I remember the actors wearing masks. But tell me, if you don't make masks, then what do you do at the theater?"

"I have many roles. It's like the actors who play more than one role. I do different jobs.

"Now let's go to the next room."

Horus showed Nilo the remaining bedroom. "This is where you will sleep," said Horus.

The room consisted of a simple bed and a wooden chest for clothing.

Nilo was relieved. He didn't expect this. *If we're going to have separate bedrooms,* he wondered, *then why am I here? What does he want from me? I don't understand. I don't understand at all. What could he possibly want from me?*

Not wanting to share his anxiety, Nilo said, "Thank you for showing me your home."

Finished with the tour, they went downstairs.

Nilo still had trouble understanding Horus's motivation in wanting to bring him home.

He decided to ask in as polite a way as he could. "You're being kind to me is appreciated, but I don't understand. Why do you want me here?" he asked.

"There may be no easy explanation. Why don't you enjoy it?"

Before anything more could be said, a slave brought them some bread and cheese, along with mugs of diluted wine.

"You should have something in your stomach before you go to sleep," said Horus.

"Thank you," said Nilo. "There's something else I was wondering."

"What may that be?"

"I was wondering how we'll spend our day tomorrow."

"Sure. I'll be glad to answer that. The supervisor at the *palaestra* said you had been sleeping outside."

"Yes."

"He also said there were times when you had very little or no food to eat."

"Yes."

"Well, wouldn't it be best if you were to get more sleep and put food in your stomach?"

"Thank you for thinking about me like that. But I'll be alright no matter what happens. Also, I don't want to take advantage of your kindness."

"You're not taking advantage of me. I don't want to see a boy like you living in the passageways, that's all. Having you here isn't difficult."

Nilo, helping himself to the bread and cheese on his plate, said, "Well, thank you for everything."

"You're welcome. By the way, I'll be getting up with the sun in the morning. You may stay in bed if you wish. A slave will make your morning meal. Also feel free to take a bath if you'd like. I'll be at the theater tomorrow. We can talk again when I return."

Horus then suggested they turn in for the night. And they did.

Nilo found his new bed comfortable compared to the cot at the *palaestra* and much more than sleeping outdoors. His chief concern remained wanting to know Horus's motivations in wanting to look after him. *Why am I here? Is this something the gods planned? What's going to happen now?*

Nilo soon fell asleep.

CHAPTER 12

Going to Delphi

*We were given two ears and one mouth so that
we might listen twice as much as we speak.*

— **Epictetus, Greek Stoic Philosopher
55-135 AD**

Following the trial, a lot of the stress disappeared for Demetrius's father. He told his family, "Much weight has been lifted. We can relax now." So intense was the preparation for the trial and then going through with it was an unusual ordeal. They deserved to relax. But that could only last so long.

The conclusion of Demetrius's trial brought the family's thoughts back to its youngest member, Nilo. There was much conjecture. "Where might he be?" thought Nilo's mother out loud.

"Wherever he is, I hope he's well and happy," said Demetrius. "But what should we do?"

No one knew.

Not much happened for a few days following the trial. Life changed somewhat for Demetrius following a knock on the front door. Chamus went to see who's there. He called to Demetrius, "Someone wants to see you."

A surprise when Demetrius came to the door. The startled young man said, "Adonis. How nice you came by."

"Well, you know I wanted to see you again. Did you all have a good rest from the trial?"

"Yes. But we've been lethargic since then. Anyway, please come in."

Demetrius led him through the courtyard to where they could sit down.

Adonis began their conversation, "When I heard the good news of the trial, I was so excited and happy for you."

"Thank you. We're glad that's behind us. That's something we never want to go through again."

"Who would've thought one of the guilty men would come out so strong in support of your position? So surprising that was."

"Yes indeed. It made the jury's job much easier."

"Tell me, Demetrius. What's been going on since the trial ended?"

"I wish I could say something positive. The trial was stressful. So naturally, when it was over, we wanted to rest. Instead, our thoughts went back to my brother Nilo. He left home on his own. We're depressed about that. No one knows where he is. The boy is only twelve-years-old."

"Oh, yes, yes. I remember your father standing up at the symposium to talk about him. Do you want to tell me more?"

"Well, Nilo's had a few bad breaks. He never took to school very well. What I mean is the formal schooling he had from age seven to twelve. He couldn't grasp what the teacher said. Out of frustration, he allowed his mind to wander. He was sometimes caught singing to himself in a low voice. Many times, he felt the scourge from the teacher's whip. But it wasn't all bad.

"He loved his time in the *gymnasia*. He's a gifted runner. So gifted he decided to run in the Panathenaic Games. But during his race, he had an accident. He fell as he rounded the first bend. That devastated him. He never recovered. He neither wanted to continue with his running nor with school. My father found him an excellent tutor. After some coercion, Nilo agreed to the arrangement. As it turned out, the tutor was too good. Nilo developed a passion for him. Then, when he learned his tutor already had his *eromenos*, he was devastated again. He turned against everything. He left home. He became a *pornos*. Can you imagine that? My little brother, a *pornos*! When he's not in someone's bed, he lives in the passageway. Normally, a family would disown their child at that point. But my father's different. He loves everyone in our family. He'd do anything to have Nilo back. What he won't do is look for him. We want to believe Nilo will return. At the same time, we know that's unlikely. Meanwhile, my father stays depressed."

"Wow. That's quite a story. I feel sorry for you and your family. I do."

"Thank you. But we can't stay frozen in this mood. We've got to move on. As to my father, I don't know how or when he'll be himself again."

"Yes. I can understand that. On the other hand, it's nice to see a father with such concern for his son. As you said, most families would disown their child and get on with life."

"I don't know what we're going to do. I don't even know if there's anything we could do."

"Do you remember at the symposium, after your father spoke? There was another gentleman. I think he was the host. He stood up to offer condolences to your father. But he too was sorry he didn't know what to do. And after him, Playtonus stood up. Do you remember that?"

"Vaguely. Could you remind me what he said?"

"From what I recall, he brought up the Oracle at Delphi. He spoke of marvelous things the *Pythia* does. Individuals, families, even governments have been helped by the wisdom she gives from the messages she receives from Apollo. 'Should we go to war? What's the best time for war? Should I marry?' The questions go on and on. And then he said to your father, 'Your difficult situation may be solved by talking with the *Pythia*. Maybe she can tell you what to do.'"

"Your memory is good. And you're right. It's coming back to me. But I have no idea if that's something my father would want to do or not."

"You could talk to him. Maybe he can speak with others who have already seen the *Pythia*."

"That's a good point. But our problem is father wants Nilo to make the first move. He doesn't want to look for Nilo and beg him to return. From his view, Nilo must make the first move."

"Well, alright. The *Pythia* will consider that. Or perhaps she'd say your father has to initiate contact with Nilo.

Otherwise nothing will happen. And we can always hope the *Pythia* is someone with whom your father might listen."

"You're right, Adonis," said a happier Demetrius with a smile. "You convinced me. I'll see what I can do."

Adonis returns the smile as he put his arm around his friend's shoulder. "I hope it works out for you, Demetrius."

Demetrius looks into his friend's eyes as Adonis bends down to kiss him on the lips.

"I'm grateful for your help, Adonis."

"That's what friends are for. But I'm going to be honest. I hope we can be more than friends."

"I'd like that too, but as you know, I'm entering military service soon. They may not let me out to see you very often. I'll also have to visit my family."

"I understand. I also know you'll be out someday. Meanwhile, I may be able to see you. I've recently completed my service. Some of the officers know me. They might let me enter the Post sometimes and spend time with you."

"That would be wonderful. Thank you for befriending me."

"I knew from the outset you were someone I wanted to know. Knowing you hasn't disappointed me. I believe the gods are looking favorably towards us."

The men embraced together with a lingering deep kiss.

"Goodbye."

"Goodbye."

Demetrius knew his father would have to decide to visit the *Pythia* soon to complete the trip before his military service begins.

When his father returned from a round of errands, Demetrius was ready. After a few pleasantries, Demetrius asked, "Father have you decided what to do about Nilo?"

"No, I haven't. It's something I can't figure out. We may have to accept the fact he'll never return. Maybe that's what the gods want. If that's the case, we have to accept it."

"But maybe that's not the case. The gods have no reason to punish us. We've always been devout in glorifying them. They shouldn't do that to us."

"It is not for us to say, Demetrius. We must live by the way the gods wish."

"You're right. But shouldn't we at least try to learn what the gods want?"

"And how can we do that?"

"We can go to Delphi. The *Pythia* is endowed with the ability to communicate with our gods. We can receive their answer from her."

"Demetrius, don't you know what a trip to Delphi entails?"

"No. Not actually."

"Well, I can tell you, it's no easy matter."

"Having the gods to speak to us. Isn't that worth everything?"

"That's easy to ask but going through the experience can test the endurance of the strongest inquirer. Let me explain.

"First there's a brief period when the *Pythia* communicates revelations to those seeking them. One must be ready for the *Pythia* when she's ready, not the other way around.

"Second, it's a long, arduous trip lasting three or more days. It's a journey fraught with danger. One must take his security with him.

"Third, we can't tell how many will be lined up to see the *Pythia*. She can stop working whenever she feels the gods aren't answering. No one knows how many days you'll need to wait at Delphi. Longer stays result in more expense. Then there are wealthy aristocrats and military leaders. They can donate large sums, so they don't have to wait in line. As the Oracle only serves the public a small number of days over nine months of the year, vast sums are paid by the well-to-do so they can get to the front of the line. You might wait three days. You're about to meet the *Pythia,* and one of those rich dudes comes along, and you must fall in behind him.

"Then after all that, you get to see the *Pythia,* and there are more problems. Answers, when they come, aren't easy to decipher. Oracles are open to different meanings. They can signify dual and opposite meanings. Many were those who misinterpreted what the *Pythia* said. This can result in grave consequences for them.

"So, I'm asking you, how do we know if we'll understand an Oracle about how we handle Nilo?"

"I don't have an exact answer. But we can get opinions from other priests, and other experts. They can help interpret the *Pythia's* Oracle."

"Maybe they can. Maybe they can't. And don't forget the risk factors. The high costs together with awkward inconveniences could be too much for us. And knowing our security is at stake. All that makes going to Delphi questionable at best."

"You've raised concerns. They need to be sorted out. But I still believe you should consider it. There's no other option on what to do, if anything, about Nilo."

"Yes, you may be right. Let me think about it some more."

"You might want to talk with Adonis, the young man we met at the symposium. He seems to know much about the *Pythia* and how to interpret oracles. I know he'd be happy to share with you whatever he knows."

"I can't see him right now. But if you're correct about his knowledge of the Delphi and the *Pythia*, I'm willing to see him. Can you ask him to stop by in a few days?"

"I will. Thanks for your willingness."

A few days later Adonis dropped by.

"So good to see both of you again. I'm glad you're looking at the possibility of consulting the *Pythia* at Delphi."

"Well, there are problems with that. We want to do as the gods wish. And, I want what's best for Nilo."

"Yes. I can understand that."

"Well, let's get started. You believe it's worth the trip despite the pitfalls?"

"You mean receiving an Oracle from the *Pythia*? Yes, I do. I've seen it helpful to many. They're not sorry for the inconveniences they endured."

"But you must also have heard about fatalities when pilgrims were attacked on the roads going to Delphi, haven't you?"

"Yes, I have. Everyone must arrange for their security. But I encourage you to go despite possible perils. If the gods wish it, you must go."

"The terrain's not friendly for us. We'd have to cross rugged mountains, ravines, rivers. How long would that take?"

"Good question. And yes, you're right, it's difficult. It would take a long time. But you know what? We wouldn't have to go only by land. We Greeks are a seafaring people. We can go by sea for most of the trip. It would take less time."

"Hmm. You've got a point. I see how that can be done."

Demetrius entered the conversation. "Father, do you have other concerns?"

"Well, yes. We may be gone from ten days to two weeks. We can't take all the food we'll need for that much time. Nor do we know about accommodations."

"That can be worked out," said Adonis. "It isn't a problem. Many people go to Delphi. They find lodging and can purchase food. The main problem often is keeping the food vendors away. That can be a real nuisance. As to finding a place to sleep, the offering of lodging has become a big business in Delphi."

"Okay, Adonis. You've become a big help in all this. Maybe we can work this out. Now I have a favor to ask."

"Sure. Go ahead."

"Well, as you've no doubt come to see, my main concern is security. Going to Delphi by ourselves can be dangerous. You Adonis, you're a veteran of military service. You've learned to deal with security concerns. And perhaps you still possess the weapons you had during your service. So, I want to ask if we were to go, is there any possibility you might want to come with us?"

"Go with you? Why yes, if you'd like to have me. I'd be happy to be a part of the adventure with you."

Now feeling much better about travelling, Demetrius's father said, "Well, it's settled then. It will be you, Demetrius, Chamus, and myself. What do you think of that?"

"That seems fine. But we'd have to leave soon to return in time for Demetrius's scheduled date to enter his military service. Let's remember the *Pythia* only gives oracles on the seventh day of the month, and then just during the warmer months of the year."

Demetrius wanted to know, "Is there a reason why the *Pythia* only gives oracles on the seventh day?"

"Good question. It's because the Temple's god Apollo was born that day. Oracles were originally given on the seventh day of the same month Apollo was born. But as its popularity grew, its number of days had to increase. So now the seventh day of other months are included as well."

Demetrius said, "You know so much Adonis. You're like a tutor for us. You're so intelligent in these matters."

"No, I'm no more intelligent than the rest of you. I happen to owe everything I know to a certain teacher. I was blessed with an incredibly good tutor in my earlier years. It's to him I owe everything."

"Is he one of Athen's famous philosophers?" asked Demetrius.

"Oh no. He's a common man, someone like you and me. His name is Lukos. He's from the *Deme* Kolonai."

"Lukos, *oh ye gods!*" exclaimed Demetrius's father. All his concern for his son Nilo returned to his thought. "That's amazing. He was my son's tutor for a short while. Nilo thought the world of him."

"So did I," said Adonis. "Lukos is that kind of man."

Remembering his son this way reinforced Nilo's father's need to go to Delphi. *The gods know how I need to handle Nilo. I must have their thoughts.*

The seventh day of the month was fast approaching as the men prepared for their journey. They would leave four days before the seventh day to give them enough time. The arduous journey would have to begin soon.

Demetrius's father was able to obtain four mules to carry them from Athens to Delphi, a three-day trip.

On the day of departure, Demetrius's father and Chamus were loading their provisions onto the mules when Adonis arrived.

Adonis called out, "Good morning, my friends. How nice to see preparations are going well." He and Demetrius greeted each other with a warm embrace.

"Yes," said Demetrius's father. "Now that you're here, we can leave soon."

As the men were climbing onto their respective mules, Theous's father arrived in time to bid them "Farewell and a safe journey. And may the gods of Zeus, Athena and Apollo watch over you and care for you," he said.

"And may all be well with you," responded Demetrius's father.

They left as the morning sun was coming up. The mules carrying the four men fell into a single file as they began their trek through the City going towards the Port town of Piraeus. They would make Piraeus their first overnight stop.

They would be in the Port town well before the sun was high in the sky. It would be a relatively short journey to Piraeus. Their mules would take them all the way to the Port town trekking between the high defensive walls, one on each side of them. Each wall was given a name: Cimon and Pericles. Cimon was a prominent Athenian general who was instrumental in taking Athens to glory after leading his City-State to victories in the Persian wars. He was also a leading statesman. Another statesman, Pericles, had much to do with advancing democracy and the building up of Athens in its golden years. Pericles had argued persuasively before the Athens Assembly to allocate funds for constructing the eight miles of 'Long Walls,' as they were to be called, to connect Athens with Piraeus. His idea was to make the City and its Port one fortified enclosure. The walls were to be open during wars and then just open to the sea. It was there on the sea that the Athenian ships would be the dominant force among all Grecian city-states.

Most of the trip to the Port town was routine. But when they got close to the Port, they were bogged down by slippery mud, a reminder of recent heavy rains.

As they entered the town, there were no surprises. The men, even their slave Chamus, had been there before. They knew well the bustling Port town with its main industry, shipping. The town had its share of shipping offices, warehouses, shops, and brothels. Looking towards the sea, they could view a shoreline with its vast complex of ship sheds in each of the town's three harbors.

Their first activity was the need to find passage by ship to their next destination, the City of Corinth.

After settling in their modest, but adequate lodging, they made their way to the nearest harbor, Munichia. While each of them had been to Piraeus, this was the first time they went to the moorings where the ships were docked. "My gosh!" said Adonis, "The ship stalls go on forever. For the *triremes* alone, there must be a hundred or more." But as excited as they were, their first order of business was to find passage to their next destination. They went directly to the first shipping office they spotted to ask about getting on a ship to the Corinth Isthmus.

The shipping manager told them, "Ha! You've come to the wrong place. The Munichia Harbor is for military use. The same is true for the Zea Harbor. You must go to the farthest harbor, Kantharos. There you'll find what you're looking for."

They set off again.

When they arrived at the Kantharos Harbor, the amount of activity was startling. Every kind of trade, it seemed, was going on with ships coming and going. They discovered no central office where they could inquire about a sea voyage. They had to speak to each shipping enterprise individually. As passenger vessels didn't exist, they had to find a commercial ship going to the Isthmus of Corinth the next day. They needed a boat with enough space to carry four passengers and four mules. Most ships try to carry a full load. They don't take kindly to passengers. Nilo's father and the others began looking for boats with light loads where space was more evident.

They soon passed a fisherman's boat that was nearly empty except for a small cargo of *amphora* jugs full of olive oil, the most exported commodity from Attica. "Good day," Nilo's father called out to an elderly man working on the ship. When he answered, "Good day to you too," they drew nearer the ship and hollered, "We're looking for passage to the Corinth Isthmus. There are four of us, plus four mules. Can you help us?"

"I have no idea," said the man. "We're not leaving until we have more cargo. We also need to save space for the loads of fish we hope to catch. It's not likely we'll leave till tomorrow sometime."

"That's alright with us. When would you like us to check back with you? We're willing to pay our way."

"In that case, there might be space for you. Why don't you check back in the morning, a short while after the sun rises? We may know something by then. By the way, what's the reason for your voyage?"

"We're going to the Temple of Apollo in Delphi. We're going to receive an oracle from the *Pythia.*"

"Ah well then, good luck with that. She isn't always available when they say she is. Or at times she has more visitors than she can handle."

"Yes. We know all that. But we must try."

"Okay then, see you tomorrow. Perhaps I'll have news for you."

The men continued checking with commercial ships, but it seemed useless.

"I don't think we're going to find anything more today," said Demetrius's father. "None of the ship owners seem to know what tomorrow will bring. But if at least one of them doesn't have much cargo, we might find a spot. We need to return early in the morning if we're to have a chance."

The others concurred.

"So how do you want to spend the rest of the day?" Asked Demetrius. "The sun is still high."

"If no one has another preference," said Adonis. "I'd love to go back to the military ships. They're exciting to see."

The others agreed with Adonis while Chamus took figs from his bag and passed them around.

"Let's go there then," said Adonis. And they all began walking again toward the Munichia Harbor.

On arrival, their awe was again apparent on seeing the seemingly infinite number of ship sheds lined up one by one along the shore. "This is fascinating," said Adonis. "I wonder if we can get closer or perhaps even enter one of the many sheds."

"We can try," said Demetrius.

The men proceeded down toward the waterline. They were about to enter the alleyway that runs along the back side of the ship sheds when they heard a voice.

"Who goes there? What are you doing here?"

They cast their eyes on a man in full military uniform. He was holding a spear in his hand.

"We wish you no harm," said Demetrius's father. "We're visitors to Piraeus. We're here to admire Attica's great ships. Nothing more."

"Can you explain yourselves more fully?"

"Yes. We're on our way to Delphi. We need to visit the *Pythia*. But no ships are leaving for the Isthmus of Corinth until tomorrow. So, we decided to pass our time here, getting to know the great ships of our City-State Athens and Attica."

The man drew closer. He was looking for weapons. He didn't see any. After looking them over carefully, he asked the visitors, "What kind of ship do you want to see?"

"Any of the great warships would be fine, but our main interest is the *trireme,* the mightiest ship of all."

"Ah yes. That seems to be everyone's favorite. Follow me please."

They were led down a narrow corridor until they were in the back alley of the sheds for the *triremes*. As they were about to enter one of the ship sheds, the man said, "Now you're going to see one of the *triremes* up close."

As they entered the shed, the king of Athens naval might was before their eyes. Never had they had the chance to see a *trireme* at such close range.

"This is what you wanted to see: our Athenian *trireme*," said their guide. "It's perhaps the greatest warship in the world. It's the real thing. It's exceeded our best expectations."

"I'm awe-struck," said Adonis. "I never expected to be so near a *trireme*. It's amazing. But tell me, what's it about the *trireme* that's it's so special?"

"Oh, that's easy. First, these ships are called *triremes* because each of them has three levels or rows of oarsmen. The *trireme* may not be as strong as some of our enemy's vessels. Not at all. But most of theirs, while they're strong, they're usually clumsy at sea. The *trireme*, on the other hand, was built for speed. It is also incredibly maneuverable in the water. The strength it gets, instead of coming from the ship itself, comes from the muscle power of all one-hundred seventy rowers. And don't forget its ramming power. Such power has devastating effects. That was shown to be especially true during the battle of Salamis.

"Athens lost forty *triremes* at Salamis while the Persians lost three-hundred ships.

"The front of the *trireme* is built to look like the head of a bird. You'll notice the front of the ship is covered with a brass plate. It's not only there to appear like a bird's beak but to give the *trireme* the strength to ram through enemies' ships.

"Now, in addition to the rowers, there can be as many as thirty *hoplite* soldiers on the top deck of our ship. When the *trireme* comes up to an enemy ship, sometimes that's by ramming into it or merely sliding up beside it, the *hoplites* try to get onto the other ship's deck. That's when hand-to-hand combat begins. That's where *hoplites* are trained to excel. Now, would you like to board the vessel?"

"Board the vessel? You mean we can?" asked Demetrius.

"Well, wouldn't that be the best way to see the *trireme*?"

"It certainly would!" exclaimed Adonis.

And they all followed the man onto the deck of the *trireme*.

"In the name of our gods, I can feel the power standing here," said Demetrius. "I can try to imagine how difficult it must be taking this ship out of the water."

"That's always a challenge. The truth is, it takes a hundred and forty men to pull one *trireme* from the water."

Then Demetrius's father spoke up. "Might this experience be an omen that our venture to see the *Pythia* will be positive?"

"Yes," said Adonis. "That's what gods do. They send omens."

The men walked around the deck of the *trireme*. They also went below to see the ship from the rowers' view.

"Does this ship get much service?" asked Adonis.

"Yes. It was one of the ships taking part in the battle of Salamis. Also, it goes out regularly for exercises. It will be going out in the morning to the other side of the Gulf for exercises. All the way to Corinth, I believe."

"Did you say Corinth? That's where we're headed," exclaimed Demetrius's father. "Is it possible there might be space for us on this *trireme*?"

"I don't know. We don't normally take civilians on military ships, especially not when doing exercises. But I don't make those decisions. You can check in the morning if you care to and are up early enough."

"Thank you," replied Adonis. "Might it help I've finished my two-year military service? And my friend here begins his duty when we return to Athens."

"Well again, I'm not the one who makes those decisions. Regardless, this is a military ship and not normally used for ferrying civilians. But you can check tomorrow."

"Will do. In any case, we're glad you allowed us to come on board. It's an exciting experience. Thank you for letting us look at the *triremes*."

"No problem. I wish you well in seeing the *Pythia*."

"Thank you."

The men were excited having seen a *trireme*. But they paid little attention to the ship sheds until they stepped off the ship. It was then they noticed the sheds were not separated by walls, but by columns of pillars. And they were again awestruck as they looked out at the seemingly never-ending number of ship sheds going off in the distance.

Voicing the thoughts of everyone, Demetrius said, "What an incredible afternoon!"

The men walked back to their lodging. After getting refreshment, they turned in to get a good night's sleep.

CHAPTER 13

Getting to Know Horus

Be slow to fall into friendship; but when thou art in, continue firm and constant.

— **Socrates**
470–399 BC

The sun was high in the sky when Nilo woke up. It was his best sleep in many nights. But he was confused. *Where am I? What am I doing here?* Then he remembered. *Ah yes. This is Horus's house. That's where I am.* He rubbed his eyes, sat up on the bed and wondered, *What am I supposed to do today?* At first, he had no answer. Then he remembered. *Horus said he'd be at work today. I could sleep if I wish. He said I can take a bath. His slave will make my morning meal.* This was unexpected for the young boy. *It's been a while since someone thought of me like this.* Nilo got up from the bed, wrapped his simple one-piece tunic around his thin body and went downstairs.

Now in the daylight, Horus's house seemed different. *Wow! What* a *big house.* He went to the cooking area. He saw a slave maintaining a cooking fire.

"Good morning Nilo," said the slave.

"Good morning," said Nilo. "How did you know my name?"

"Horus asked me to prepare your morning meal. He told me your name is Nilo."

The boy still surprised someone was caring for him. He could only say, "Oh, I see."

With his simple, but adequate morning meal before him, Nilo sat down. The slave felt he had to get busy on his chores. Before he did, Nilo asked, "Could I ask you some questions?"

"Of course, you can," said the slave.

"I'm new here. I don't know why I'm here. I wondered if you know anything about that."

"That's complicated. Have you known Horus very long?"

"No. We met yesterday. He learned I had no place to go and he invited me to come home with him."

"Well, that's Horus."

"What do you mean, 'that's Horus?'"

"That's what he does."

"I don't understand."

"Well, I can see you don't. But Horus does that."

"Can you explain?"

"Of course. Horus has special feelings for aristocratic boys like you who have fallen on hard times."

"You mean he's done this before?"

"Yes. Many times."

"Can you tell me about that?"

"Certainly. But first, you must understand something. Horus is different. He does care for himself like everyone else. But he also wants the world to be a different place. A place where concern for others is at least as important for everyone as it is for themselves. At times he seems to have *more* concern for others than he does for himself. Their concerns are his concerns. And when it's a boy like you, he has more than concern. He shows it by acting on his concern. That's why you're here."

"I thought he brought me here to satisfy his sexual needs."

"His sexual needs? Well, let's be honest. Everyone has sexual needs. That includes Horus. I am sure he's been attracted to some of the boys he's brought home. But I doubt if he's ever acted on his attraction. I think he hasn't. But if I did know, I couldn't tell you. Horus wouldn't want me to do that."

"What makes him feel like he does, valuing others so much?"

"I don't know for sure. But I can tell you this. Horus studied under the philosopher Plato."

"Plato?"

"Yes. I say this because what he learned there has much to do with his beliefs and behavior."

"How does that have anything to do with bringing boys home like me?"

"That's not easy to answer. And as you know, I don't have an education because I'm a slave. To Horus's credit, he believes everyone should be educated. That includes *metics* (foreigners), girls, and women. Even slaves like me. So,

Horus doesn't mind if I listen to him when he's educating boys or guests about his philosophy. I've learned much from him. Like Plato, Horus accepts the theory of Forms. That relates to the qualities we observe with our senses such as love, beauty, and goodness. Such qualities when expressed by humans are nothing more than imitations of the pure, eternal, and unchanging world of Forms. Love, for example, can never reach its absolute when consummated by two persons. That's true. It is. That's why Plato admonishes his students who want to experience *agape* (absolute love) to forego love that's physically expressed (*eros*). What we know as platonic love is void of a physical element. That's the love Horus expresses when he's involved with a boy like you. It's that Horus doesn't expect others to take it as far as he does. He knows men and youth have a strong need for sexual gratification. He knows such needs can only be quenched by physical expressions of love. Therefore, Horus is neutral when it comes to fulfilling physical needs. He never judges anyone who sees this differently than he does. 'We can't all be Platos,' he often says. 'Let's be truthful about this,' he says, 'Not even our gods abstain from sex.' Therefore, he doesn't see sexual contact by others as lewd behavior. He also knows we won't reach absolute goodness and love while we remain in our human condition. But that doesn't prevent him from working toward that goal. That's why he relates the way he does with boys like you. He delights in seeing their improvement while they're living with him. For him, it's pure joy when he sees their progress."

"Isn't that unusual for someone to be so unselfish?"

"Yes, it is. But I tell you again, that's Horus."

"Could it be that someday I'll get to know Horus well? If so, all this might make sense. I should also say you talk like an educated person. Not only that. You make a good morning meal."

"Well thank you. But the credit goes to Horus. Educating those around him is one of the ways he expresses goodness and love."

"By the way, what am I supposed to do today?"

"Horus gave me no instructions about that. He only said you can take a bath. I'll fill the tub for you."

"Thank you."

The tub was already filled when Nilo finished his morning meal. He discarded his tunic and lowered himself into the tub until the water line was up to his neck. He was now feeling satisfied. He recalled the peaceful days when he would lie in the stream by his *gymnasia* during his school days. He enjoyed examining himself from his toes up to his head as he did before. *It's special feeling clean and refreshed,* he thought.

The slave was waiting for him when he got out of the tub. The slave dried him off and gave him a brief body rub.

Nilo wrapped himself again with his tunic while the slave went downstairs to resume his chores.

While Nilo slept well last night, he still needed to compensate for many days without much repose. His next few hours were taken with more sleep.

He woke up after the sun reached its high point for the day. The house was still quiet. Horus hadn't yet returned. For a few moments, Nilo found himself not knowing what to do.

Then he remembered the masks. He was soon entertaining himself by looking at them again, this time in daylight. In a short time, he was laughing at himself. Each mask was different. Looking at one with a pained expression he thought: *That's strange. Why would they have a mask so grotesque? I can't imagine anyone having an expression like that!* He was also intrigued the masks could indicate, not only happiness or sadness, but also gender, approximate age and even whether one is rich or poor—all kinds of people. *Maybe they can't find an actor for every type of person, so they use masks.* Then a childish idea came to him. *Hey! Maybe I can have fun with these.* He took hold of one of the more grotesque-looking masks and placed it over his face. Then he went downstairs to see the slave. He soon found him cutting wood in the cooking area. He crept up slowly behind him. When he was close enough, he tapped him on the back shoulder.

The slave turned around.

Nilo, still wearing the mask, let out with a loud blood-curdling animal sound, "**Gaagga!**"

The slave jumped. But in the next moment, he started laughing. "Ah! You've found Horus's mask collection."

"Yes. He showed them to me last night. It's an incredible collection."

"Yes, it is. Horus likes to keep his masks at home. It takes him a long time to decide which masks are the most appropriate for each actor."

"I'm going back to look at the rest of them. I know you have work to do."

Nilo had already looked through one set of masks and was now reaching for another group of them. As he was about to pick them up, he heard a voice.

"Nilo! You're enjoying the masks."

"Horus, you're home!"

Horus said, "Yes I am," as he gave Nilo a brief hug. "And how nice to see you again."

"You have many masks. They're all different. Some are hysterical."

"I'm glad you enjoy them. They're important to our productions."

"You must have interesting plays if these are the masks you use."

"Yes, they're interesting. But we choose our plays first. It's after that we look for the best masks for our plays. I have work to do now. I'll see you at the evening meal."

Nilo went back to rest. He laid in bed until the slave called him for the evening meal.

Nilo thought it unusual there were only Horus and himself for the evening meal in such a big house. He was beginning to feel important. He climbed onto the sofa the slave pointed him to. Then he pulled out the small three-legged table from underneath the sofa, where his evening meal would be served.

Horus soon joined him on an adjoining sofa. The thought came to him to ask Nilo to share his sofa. But he rejected the idea almost as soon as it came to him.

"I think you had a hard day," said Nilo opening the conversation.

"Well, yes and no. There was plenty of work to do at the theater, but the truth is, I like being there. The work means much to me."

"Why do you like it so much?"

"Well, there are reasons. Would you like to hear a few?"

"Of course. My father occasionally took my brother and me to the theater. So, I know a little about it."

"Basically, our theater is the bringing together of our communities. In our Greek culture, there's no better way to share ideas with so many people. The stories in our plays allow everyone to get a good laugh at ourselves. That's what our comedy plays are about. They're different from the tragic plays. Theater helps develop a unity of thought among our people. It helps us love ourselves more. And it's good for our team, that is, everyone who works with us producing the plays. Not just the actors, but all those who help in any way. But above all else, the theater exists to honor our god Dionysus. Perhaps I should share with you something about Dionysus. Would you like to hear about that?"

"Oh please!"

"Okay. I'll make it brief.

"Dionysus is our god of wine, theater, ecstasy, and merriment. All those things. You may hear Dionysus compared sometimes with his half-brother Apollo. These two gods couldn't be more different. Apollo represents our intellectual side. Dionysus, on the other hand, is identified with our libido and sexual gratification. He's identified entirely with merriment and fulfillment. That's why our comedy plays are all about that.

"The development of Greek Theater came out of our worship of Dionysus. It evolved from our intense devotion to him. The devotion increased greatly over the centuries. And we don't fail to remember Dionysus in every aspect of theater work we do."

"That's amazing. It seems special knowing about that."

"It sure is. By the way, would you like to go to the theater with me tomorrow?"

"If you want me to go with you, I'd be happy to."

"Okay, we'll leave early in the morning."

CHAPTER 14

On to the Oracle

The Lord whose oracle is a Delphi neither
reveals nor conceals but gives a sign.

— Heraclitus of Ephesus
535 BC – 475 BC

Demetrius, his father, Adonis, and Chamus woke up early as planned. They were determined to find a ship to take them to Corinth.

"Two possibilities came up yesterday," said Demetrius's father, "going to Corinth on the *trireme* or the commercial ship. Which should we try first?"

"Ah, we all want to go on the *trireme*, don't we?" asked Adonis.

The others agreed.

They made their way to the *trireme* sheds along with their four mules and their belongings. They arrived shortly before sunrise. The men were surprised at how many were already there waiting to board the war vessel. They soon learned most of them were oarsmen for the *trireme*. It took a while to find the man in charge. When they did, Adonis asked, "Is there a possibility we can get to Corinth with you on the *trireme*?"

"No. Not at all. We're doing naval exercises and many maneuvers today. We're unable to take on passengers. And frankly, the *Trireme* isn't a passenger ship."

Frustrated, the men left. They proceeded to the Kartharos Harbor to see the commercial ships. They went first to the loading dock where they were told yesterday there might be a spot for them.

Finally seeing the man, they talked with the day before, Adonis said, "We've returned as you asked. Is it possible we can go with you to Corinth? We're willing to pay for our voyage."

"Well, we don't know yet. We're still loading cargo. We'll know if we have room when the sun is higher."

"Thank you. We'll check back."

Meanwhile, they went to other loading docks to see if they might have better luck. They were frustrated again when they saw workers at the other loading docks too busy to talk.

"If we can't leave for Corinth today?" asked a worried Demetrius. "There's only a short time when the *Pythia* will be available. Should we return to Athens if we can't go to Corinth today?" he asked.

"We've come this far. We've got to keep going," said his father.

The men spent the next few hours walking the docks, still looking for an opportunity to talk to a worker or official on one of the ships. But to no avail. They returned to the dock where the one person they spoke with gave a ray of hope. The man in charge saw them coming. He asked as they drew closer, "Do you still want to go with us?"

"Yes, we'll be happy to go." said Demetrius's father.

"There's a little room left. It'll be tight. I'm sorry, but it's all the space we have."

"That's alright," said Demetrius's father.

"Okay. That'll be twenty obols for each of you and the same for each mule."

That was more than they had bargained for. But the men accepted it. They climbed aboard and found their spot.

As soon as they boarded, they noticed two of the ship's workers were bringing a ram to the boat. The Captain and a few others met them on the dock. One of them was dripping water over the ram's head. This caused the ram to shake his head, permitting his death. Then the Captain slit the ram's throat as a sacrificial offering to their sea god Poseidon for a safe journey. Then the Captain and the others returned to their ship.

It wasn't long after the sacrifice before their ship sailed out of Piraeus and out onto the open sea.

"We're on our way again," said Adonis. "Depending on the wind and how the weather holds up, we may arrive at the port settlement for Delphi before sunset."

"The wind is mild today. I hope it lasts or maybe gets a little stronger," said Demetrius.

"I know the gods want us to arrive in time to see the *Pythia*, so I'm sure we'll arrive in good time," said Demetrius's father.

With little to see on the open water, Adonis and Demetrius decided to nap. Despite cramped conditions, they found a way to be comfortable as they curled up together. As for Demetrius's father and Chamus, they would keep their eyes on the direction their boat was taking them.

Time passed slowly.

When the sun traversed most of its journey across the sky their ship landed at Corinth.

Immediately, workers on the boat, as well as those from the shore, began unloading cargo. Demetrius and his father, along with Adonis, Chamus, and the four mules, climbed out of the ship and onto dry land.

"It feels good to walk again," said Adonis. "The ship was confining. We could hardly move."

"We'll spend the night here," said Demetrius's father. "We need to cross the Isthmus early in the morning and find a ship to take us to the port town for Delphi. It's important we get a good night's sleep. We'll need energy and a clear thought for our preparations before I meet the *Pythia.*"

Everyone agreed. The men soon found accommodations and after an evening meal, went to sleep.

They woke up earlier than usual, as planned. After a light morning meal, they again mounted their mules and crossed the narrow Isthmus.

On the other side of the Isthmus, they were able to find passage by ship to the port town for Delphi. This second trip on the sea took the rest of the day. They had to spend the night at the port settlement and would leave early in the morning.

They left extra early in the morning to have a better chance of arriving in the sacred town the same day.

The remaining part of the trip was uneventful until they drew close to Delphi.

As they came near the sacred town, a noticeable change was sensed by all in their consciousness. The men took notice once more of their trip's purpose. This was reflected in their thoughts and feelings. While this was sensed by all four of them, it was felt most by Demetrius's father. It was he who would commune with the *Pythia*. As they approached the sacred town, they were overcome with awe. There was a reverenced silence among them as they sensed they were drawing near a holy place.

As for Demetrius's father, his concerns about Nilo returned. His thoughts were many. Primarily, he wondered, *Could my being here somehow change my experience with Nilo? Might Apollo's words show me how to better relate to him?*

This weighed heavily on Nilo's father. Soon, they caught sight of the small mountain town, Delphi, in the distance. It spread out in front of them, tucked well into the base of the towering mountains.

Demetrius was happier than ever he persuaded his father to make the pilgrimage. He certainly fulfilled the requirements to make the journey. First, he was highly motivated out of a need to embark on a long and arduous trip. Second, his desire to make the trip had to be spiritually motivated, which it was. Third, he had to mentally entertain a sense of the Oracle's actual existence and purpose, which he did. Finally, he had to have learned about the Oracle as an experience that could yield answers to perplexing questions. This he also did to the extent he felt in awe now that meeting with the *Pythia* was imminent.

Despite being tired from their trek, they were overcome with genuine euphoria as they entered Delphi. There was a sense that they arrived at *the* place where gods and mortals come together in spirit, if not in person. But first, there were earthly considerations to consider.

They wondered if finding lodging might be a problem. Such thinking was quickly dismissed. Hawkers approached them on all sides. They accepted the offerings of one and were speedily directed to its location. Once there, they were able to learn where they must go to prepare themselves for the Oracle experience.

As it turned out, there was more involved in preparation to meet the *Pythia* than they thought. They learned Nilo's father had to meet with an attending priest for a preliminary interview. This was to see if they were genuinely in need of meeting with the *Pythia*. And they would learn of other obligations.

They immediately went to the house of the priesthood. As they entered, a young man attended them "You may sit here," he said. "A priest will attend you shortly."

They waited. Soon a priest wearing a hooded garment came and sat down next to them. "Which of you will meet the *Pythia*?" he asked.

Demetrius's father acknowledged it was him.

The priest looked him over carefully. Then he said, "I need to know the nature of your question to the *Pythia*. What is it she needs to tell you from Apollo?"

"It's about my son," said Nilo's father. "My youngest son."

"Yes. Go on."

"I love my youngest son as I do all my children of whom I have three. He was brought up as he should with a father's love and close attention. I complimented his schooling. I did it with the best education I could give. But he failed in different ways. First, it was with his school work; then with athletics; and finally, with love. He came to believe he's a failure in life at the tender age of twelve. He left home. His days have been filled with riotous living. He doesn't care anymore.

"I need to ask the *Pythia* if it's right to want him to return home? If so, what must I do to make that happen?"

The priest asked, "How do you want to make the question for the *Pythia*?"

"I'm not sure."

"It should be simple, not include many words."

"Yes, I know. Can you help?"

"The gods are observant. They may know what's happened regarding yourself and more importantly, with your son. If they know this, and I think they do, your question can be brief."

"Alright. How about this? Would it be correct for Nilo to return home? If so, how can that happen?"

"Yes. I think that will work."

"What else must I do?"

"You will see the *Pythia* tomorrow as it's the seventh day of the month of *Bysios*, which is Apollo's birthday. You and those who accompanied you will make a procession along the Sacred Way. You are to carry laurel leaves."

"Why must we carry the leaves?"

"There are two reasons for carrying the laurel leaves. First, the leaves are symbolic of the journey you took to arrive in Delphi. Second, we once believed that the god giving the Oracle lived within laurel leaves which is his holy plant. The god spoke his messages through the rustling of the leaves when the wind blows. The priests then interpreted what the messages were. We don't do that anymore, but the gods still understand the symbolism of respect when you carry the leaves.

"When you arrive at Apollo's Temple you are to present your gifts (payment) to the Oracle."

It wasn't just Nilo's father who had to engage in ritualistic procedures before he petitioned for an Oracle. The *Pythia* herself had much to do.

On the day before giving pronouncements from the Oracle, the *Pythia* had to take her purification rites. This was to prepare herself for communications with Apollo. A dark purple veil kept her face unseen. Two oracular priests led her to the foot of the rocky crag called Phleboukos. This was inside a ravine separating two prominent cliffs called the Phaedriades (meaning "the shining ones"). The cliffs rose high above the Oracle site over the lower slope of Mount Parnassos. Between the two Phaedriades cliffs lies the Castalian Spring. It was here an oracular priest intoned forcefully what next occurs:

Servant of the Delphian Apollo,
Go to the Castalian Spring.
Wash in its silvery eddies,
And return cleansed to the temple.

Guard your lips from offense
To those who ask for oracles.
Let the god's answer come
Pure from all private fault.

Then, the *Pythia* removed her clothing. She entered the holy spring. She bathed herself in the sacred waters. Before leaving, she drank from the holy streams. From there, she and the priests returned to the Temple awaiting those wanting to receive her oracles.

All those consulting the *Pythia* on this day, including Nilo's father, also came to Apollo's Temple. They were piously carrying laurel branches, sacred to Apollo, following the upward course of the Sacred Way leading to the Temple. They also brought a kid goat. The goat was for sacrificing in the forecourt of the Temple where they would donate their monetary fees. All consultants drew lots to decide their order of admission. Those representing a city-state or anyone willing to pay a larger donation to Apollo would secure a higher place in line.

When his turn came, Nilo's father made his sacrifice and paid his donation to see the *Pythia*. Now he was free to enter Apollo's sacred Temple. He climbed the few steps leading to the entrance. He walked slowly and reverently. As he approached the portal, two vivid inscriptions caught his eyes. They were burned deep into the wall above the entrance-way:

γνῶθι σεαυτόν ("know thyself")
μηδὲν ἄγαν ("nothing in excess")

A priest was standing at the entrance-way to usher him inside. Once inside, Nilo's father had to continue alone. He would soon meet the *Pythia*. It was humbling for him to recall that numerous military leaders, wealthy aristocrats, even heads of state also made their way to this exact spot in

Apollo's' Temple. He was also aware he was standing at the center of the earth. Beside him was the *omphalos* (Greek for "navel" or "bellybutton"). It was flanked by two solid gold eagles, each about a meter high. The eagles represented the authority of Zeus. This reminded Nilo's father that Zeus, King of the gods, at one time wanted to know where the exact center of the earth was located. To find out, he released eagles from the two ends of the world. The spot where the birds crossed flight paths was directly over Delphi, which is why it is called it the *omphalos*, the navel or center of the earth.

The time arrived to see the *Pythia*. Nilo's father was emotionally animated, as well as humbled. He was about to learn how to better relate to his son. Before going into the dark chamber called the *adyton*, where the *Pythia* would await him, he would give his question to a *Prophetai*. He, in turn, would pass it on to the *Pythia*.

Nilo's father entered the *adyton*. Seeing was difficult. As his eyes got used to the darkness, he made out the outline of the *Pythia*. There she was, sitting high atop a covered tripod. Her purple veil now removed. The tripod was positioned directly over a deep chasm in the ground. Coming from the abyss he saw vapors rising. *The smell from the vapors are sweet, sort of like perfume*, thought Nilo's father. He began to see the mists slowly putting the *Pythia* into a trance. The moment had a disorienting hallucinatory effect over her, like a dream. What he saw was unlike anything he ever experienced. As he watched the *Pythia* inhale the vapors, her body gained stature. He saw her hair unwind until it stood on end. Her complexion changed. Her heart panted, and her bosom swelled. Even her voice had changed. In a way, she became more than human. In a deep trance, the *Pythia* began to receive her inspiration. This is the moment she attained the state of mind allowing her to "hear" messages from Apollo or possibly a surrogate god. When she understood the message, she would relay what she heard.

Nilo's father listened to the utterances from the *Pythia*. He could not make sense from them. He recalled many of those who awaited important information from the *Pythia* were disappointed. The actual responses she gave were almost always incomprehensible. Only the *Prophetai* could understand them.

The *Prophetai* transcribed what he learned from the *Pythia*. He then passed it on to the pilgrim or envoy. Again, to the disappointment of many, the given responses were often ambiguous, and obscure. They could not be understood. Therefore, many took their message to a priest to clarify.

As soon as Nilo's father received the *Pythia's* message, he stepped out of the *adyton*. Like many others, he too didn't understand the *Pythia's* words. He also had to wait for the *Prophetai* to share what she told him.

Nilo's father didn't wait long. The *Prophetai* came to him and invited him to sit down. The *Prophetai* received the message.

The words were clear. He was able to understand the *Pythia's* message which he translated. He then passed it on to Nilo's father.

Let him be, and you will see.

"'Let him be, and you will see!'" exclaimed Nilo's father. "Ye gods! Is that all she said?"

"I'm afraid so," said the *Prophetai*. "It's her custom to make messages short when she can."

Nilo's father was astonished.

"I came all the way from Athens. And after having had a long, arduous journey over land and sea and paying the oracular fees, that's all she's going to tell me?"

"I'm sorry if you don't find it satisfactory. But think about it. Maybe the message does answer your concerns."

Feeling unsatisfied, Nilo's father left Apollo's Temple and went to look for Demetrius and Adonis. He didn't have to look far. They were waiting on a bench outside the Temple.

On seeing his father, Demetrius cried out: "Hey! How was it? Did the *Pythia* give you a good message? Tell us about it."

His father didn't want to talk. But he felt he had to. "No. It wasn't a good message. She hardly said anything at all."

"I'm sorry father. I am. But please tell us what she said."

"She said, 'Let him be and you will see.' And nothing more."

"Wow! That's all?"

"Yes. And I don't think the *Pythia* will let us have another question. Not this time. So, all we can do is go home."

Adonis and Chamus added condolences.

As it was late in the day, the men decided to spend another night in Delphi. They would prepare to leave before sunrise.

While having their evening meal, Adonis mentioned the *Pythia's* message directing his words at Demetrius's father. "Is it possible the statement the *Pythia* made about Nilo might hold importance for you?"

"I don't think so," said Demetrius's father. "It appears she took a quick look at the question and came up with the first thought that came to her."

"But the message only passes through the *Pythia*." said Adonis, "Don't we all know it comes from Apollo?"

"Yes, but . . ."

"Apollo isn't any deity. He's one of the most important gods on Olympus. He's the god of music, truth, prophecy, healing, and more than I remember. He's also the son of the mighty god Zeus, King of all our gods."

"Then why did he send a meaningless message?"

"Let's take a closer look at it," said Adonis.

"'Let him be, and you will see.' That's all he said unless the *Pythia* didn't give us all that Apollo told us."

"I'm sure she did."

"Then why?"

Demetrius entered the conversation. "Is it possible you concluded that Apollo via the *Pythia* wanted to tell us something important? I hope so. Might the message mean, don't worry about Nilo? And if so, would a god say such a thing unless he knows Nilo will be okay? What do you think?"

His father said, "I don't know."

Adonis said, "You may have a point, Demetrius. We don't know exactly how much the gods, especially Apollo, know about Nilo's whereabouts and what he's doing. But the reality is, our gods know many things. They predict the future. We all know that." Now looking directly into the eyes of Demetrius's father he said, "Apollo has a special gift of prophecy."

Demetrius's father, now getting more interested in the conversation said, "Yes. That's all true. But it's hard to imagine the gods can know about everyone all the time. Don't the gods need first to have the desire to know about someone and then go about getting to know their situation?"

"Could be," said Adonis. "But it's not our privilege to know how the gods operate. The *Pythia* has an excellent reputation. We should go with what she seems to be telling us. Might she mean, if we don't interfere with Nilo's life, the day will come when we'll see how he is? If Nilo was going to have a negative experience, then I doubt Apollo would have advised us to 'let him be.' But I'm not trying to dictate what anyone should think. Those are just my thoughts."

"Well-spoken Adonis," said Nilo's father. "I understand you better now. What you said takes us back to the very purpose of oracles. The truth of the *Pythia's* pronouncement can only be realized if the supplicant complies with her explicit orders. So, you're right. We must comply with her wishes. We'll let Nilo be. Now perhaps we should all get some sleep. A long trip awaits us tomorrow."

CHAPTER 15

Demetrius Joins the Military

Yesterday we obeyed kings and bent our necks
before emperors. But today we kneel only to truth,
follow only beauty, and obey only love.

— **Kahil Gibran**
1883–1931

Having returned safely from Delphi, Demetrius's thoughts were centered squarely on entering the Military. He was getting nervous.

"Could it be it's the unknown we fear the most," Demetrius's father said, trying to console his son.

"I think you're right," said Demetrius. "In spite of all the information I found about military service, I'm still wondering what it'll be like. Living quarters are crowded. It could be difficult living with so many. And there's the question of physical fitness. That's where I'm lacking. But whatever's in store, I report tomorrow."

Demetrius rose earlier than usual the next morning. After having a larger than usual morning meal, he gathered his uniform and the few belongings he'd take with him. The family and slaves gathered inside the front door to wish him well. "We'll miss you," said his mother, "but we know you'll be back to see us."

The others responded with similar words.

Following a warm embrace with each one, Demetrius left his home and made his way to the Military Post.

It was still early when Demetrius arrived at the Post. He was waved in and taken to his new quarters. He was shown his sleeping cot and the chest where he would keep his belongings. He noticed he wasn't the only one reporting for duty. *There seem to be many new enlistees arriving. I won't be the only one needing to know everything.* He saw many gazing around their new surroundings. He also learned the new arrivals were placed in the same area of the sleeping quarters.

One who had made eye contact with Demetrius extended his hand. "I see you just arrived. My name is Zeno."

"Hello, Zeno. I'm Demetrius."

This simple gesture seemed to open the way for the others to introduce themselves. In a short while, in addition to Zeno, Demetrius was meeting Leto, Artemus, Nikios, Philon, and Sophos. He was about to greet a few more when an officer came in their quarters.

"Good morning. I want to let you know there will be a meeting of all new recruits in the early afternoon. At that time, you're to go to the Assembly Hall. A bell will ring letting you know it's time to report. That is all."

Before time came to go to the Assembly Hall new recruits who hadn't seen the army facility were invited to take an organized tour of the Military Post. Others were getting uniforms and weapons. Each *hoplite* needed to be equipped with a bronze helmet, a bronze and leather chest plate, shin guards, a thirty-inch shield and an eight to ten-foot spear.

Demetrius felt pleased he procured his uniform before reporting for duty.

In due time, the bell rang. This informed recruits it was time to report to the Assembly Hall. When they were seated, the Post Commander stood up and spoke.

> *Hello everyone. On behalf of Attica's government and its General Assembly, I'm happy to welcome you as you begin your military service. You're here for a glorious purpose. That is to serve your City-State of Athens. You may be required to defend it from enemies near and far. It's an honorable duty. We're pleased you're here. You'll be expected to take your job seriously. You're expected to keep yourself in top physical condition. We'll begin the day, every day, the moment the sun rises. You'll report to our athletic field where we'll go through our daily routine of physical conditioning. This includes calisthenics and running. It will last for two hours. We'll then have our morning meal. The morning meal will be followed by weapons training. Our principle weapons training programs*

focus on using bows and arrows, spears, and the catapult. In time other weapons will be introduced. Also, you will learn hand-to-hand combat and our battlefield strategies. They include fighting from the phalanx formation which was devised by our military organization. Of that, we are proud. Our overall objective will be to turn each of you into a one-man military machine as well as a member of a robust, united fighting force.

Next, I'd like to talk about the rules. There are many rules pertaining to your jobs. The ones relating to your duties in the mess hall and cooking area will be explained following the midday meal. For that reason, you're to remain in the mess hall following our next midday meal. You may have already heard you have a free period every afternoon. This is for the many personal things you may have to do. There will also be rules announced regarding your personal areas and how you're to relate to your fellow hoplites and the officers. You'll be advised of your training schedule soon. Everyone must adhere to that. There have been questions as to leaving the Post for personal reasons. This is not a usual practice, especially in your beginning months. If anyone needs to leave the Post for any reason, you must have my permission. Additional rules may be announced from time-to-time.

The next part of my remarks relates to Attica's position in the world and the dangers we face militarily. As you may know, we've developed relations at the allied level with one hundred fifty other city-states. This alliance is known as the Delian League. As many as fifty other city-states are now poised to join. The Delian League has been headquartered on the island of Delos. We're now in the process of bringing its headquarters to Athens. This will give us more flexibility by having easier access to its treasury. It also gives us more flexibility in preparing to fight whatever enemy may attack us. You need to know there's another side to this. Sparta is uncomfortable that we in Athens and our allies in the Delian League are getting stronger and more unified. Furthermore, bringing the headquarters of the Delian League to Athens is making them furious.

As a counterweight to the Delian League, Sparta and its allies are re-invigorating their centuries-old Peloponnesian League. It's getting stronger. Their members now include Corinth, Thebes, Elis, and Megara. Both Corinth and Thebes have strong armies, and they along with Sparta are stockpiling weapons at an alarming rate. This is due to their uneasiness about Athens and the Delian League. They also see us rebuilding our City walls that were destroyed during the Persian conflicts. As the

Persian threat diminished, they see no reason for the walls from their point of view, unless rebuilding suggests a conflict with them. All this creates tension. We don't yet know yet what this means for us. But we must be ready.

This is an evolving situation. We're monitoring it carefully. You'll be advised from time-to-time as new information arrives. Now, are there any questions? Yes, the gentleman over there.

"If the time comes when war seems likely, will the recruits have to remain in the army more than two years?"

Good question. There's no present policy regarding a change in the length of service. If the course of events warrants, that's something that will be discussed. Other questions?

"Might the army be employed to help rebuild the walls around Athens?"

Probably not. Our City is blessed with many mason and construction workers. It may happen work will be slowed down on some temples being constructed in our City to give us manpower to reconstruct our walls. Our primary concern is safety.

In conclusion, in addition to increasing our army's strength, we're confident of Athen's superiority. Why is that? The answer lies with our navy. Our naval force is the strongest the world has seen. We have the best ships, the largest number of ships along with talented manpower to defeat any power on the sea.

Now, as my last comment, please note: whenever you hear the bell, you're to report to the Assembly Hall. Usually, you're being summoned because there's relevant information you need to know. For those who haven't been shown our Military Post, one of the officers will give you a tour. The rest of you are free until the evening meal.

That's all gentlemen. Thank you for listening.

As Demetrius had already taken his tour of the Post, he went to lie down. Here he finally had time to reflect for himself. He was feeling uneasy about his military experience. Demetrius wondered, *how is it going to work out?* He was nervous about the beginning of physical training that would start tomorrow. *What will it be like when everyone sees how poorly I run? What happens then? I'll try hard to be as good as the rest. That may not be enough. What a disgrace if I'm discharged as being unfit. What will my family and friends say?* Demetrius tried hard to get such thoughts out of his head. He wasn't successful.

In time, the call came to go to the mess hall. Soon the new recruits wandered in along with the others. There was no assigned seating arrangement, but the newest *hoplites* felt comfortable sitting together. And they did. Demetrius found a seat between Zeno and Leto and across from Nikios.

The others were animated about having received their uniform and weapons. They were also excited about their full daily routine that would begin the next day. "I can't wait until we begin simulated combat conditions. We'll get a feel of what battlefield conflict is like," said Zeno.

"I agree," added Leto. "That will be exciting for me too."

"I worked hard to be in good shape for our military service. Now the army's going to push us even harder than we did to ourselves," said Nikios.

All the while Demetrius was quiet, even depressed.

"What's wrong?" Zeno asked Demetrius.

"I may not be ready to take on military service."

"Why?"

"Don't get me wrong. I'd love to help Attica if we were attacked. That's why I'm here. It's my duty. But I haven't got into good physical condition like you and the others. I worry I might be eliminated from the program when they see how poorly I run and do calisthenics. I might not qualify."

"Oh, we understand," said Zeno. "That would make you feel uncomfortable. But why didn't you work out harder?"

"Apathy, I guess. My little brother's an excellent runner. I never felt I could do as well as he could. I couldn't get the ambition. I never got touched by *agon*, it seems."

"Well, maybe the army will have patience with you. We can hope for that. I'm sure you have potential."

"I think so too," chimed in Nikios.

Demetrius closed this part of the conversation as their food was being served, "We'll have to wait and see."

Demetrius had a difficult time going to sleep that night. He was worried about his likely poor performance. But he finally got to sleep for a few hours.

As the earliest predawn light was visible, the *hoplites* were waking up, getting out of their cots and wrapping themselves with their tunics. Demetrius wasn't accustomed to being around so many at this early hour. This was when he was used to being alone in his bedroom. But he got up. He followed other recruits to the outdoor exercise area. When they arrived, the instructor invited them to sit down in a grassy area. He explained the rules and procedures for morning drills that would be an everyday occurrence. "We'll meet here every morning until further notice. Punctuality is a must. When we do our drills, you're expected to give your utmost. *Agon* is part of your routine. You must always do your best. And never forget, our gods are watching you. You don't want them to see you as disinterested." The instructor then asked everyone to "Stand up. Shed your tunics and maintain yourselves in row formations."

At that moment, without their tunics, Demetrius could see developed bodies of the recruits. He saw their muscular tone: their biceps, their pectoral, abdominal and thigh muscles. *These men worked out hard. The must've spent much time in the gym. I could never be like them.*

With the recruits now in formation, the Instructor continued. "Extend your arms sideways. At the point where you can touch the fingertips of those on either side of you, that's the distance we'll have between each *hoplite*. Now turn sideways in the direction of the rising sun. Keep your arms extended. The distance between rows will also be determined where you can touch the fingertips of those on either side of you. Now return to your original formation."

The instructor explained the first exercise drill. He then demonstrated it in front of the recruits. "Now we'll begin: *Alpha, beta, gamma,* **start!**"

All recruits followed the example.

When they finished, the instructor bellowed, "**Again!**"

He continued the drill until he could tell the recruits were tiring.

When they were ready again, the instructor asked all to get up and return to their formation. He then explained the next drill. The recruits followed suit.

The instructor was watching the recruits one-by-one. In time, his eyes fell on Demetrius.

Demetrius wasn't practicing the drill as were the others. He was sweating profusely. His body bent forward. His hands rested on his knees.

The Instructor, not knowing Demetrius's name walked up to him. "What's going on?" he asked. "Why aren't you doing the drill?"

"I did it as long as I could. Then I had no energy left. I'm sorry."

"You'll have to come out of formation. One of my aides will work with you."

Demetrius retreated to the grassy area and waited for the Instructor's Aide to come to him. Meanwhile, he watched others continue with their drills. *Will I ever be like them?* Demetrius wondered.

After a short wait, the Instructor's Aide came out to see Demetrius. "Hello, young man. What seems to be the problem?"

"The problem is I don't have enough energy to keep up with the others."

"Weren't you told about being in condition before arriving at the Post?"

"Yes, Sir. But apparently, I didn't work at it hard enough."

"Apparently not. And why not?"

Demetrius explained he was kidnapped at the Panathenaic Festival and repeatedly raped, "I got ill in the process and lost much weight. I couldn't work out and run for many days. Later, I had to help my father go to Delphi to meet with the Pythia and receive her Oracle. That also took many days."

"I see. Well, I don't know what to do with you. Our Commander will make that decision. It may depend on how long it would take for you to be in condition."

"Yes. I understand."

"As for today, you can relax until you feel you're able to run. Then we'll see how far you can go."

"Agreed."

Demetrius continued watching the drills until he felt he was rested enough to run. He stood up. He did several muscle movements to loosen his arms and legs. Then he said, "Okay. I'm ready."

"Very well," said the Aide. "Follow the parameter of the court. Do as many laps as you can."

Demetrius did as he was told. He commenced with a slow jog and rounded the yard several times. He thought he was doing well, even pushing himself near the end to get in as many laps as possible. Finally, when he couldn't go any farther, he stopped. He went to lie down.

"Is that all?" asked the Aide. "You couldn't do more than that?"

"I thought I did pretty well," said Demetrius.

"You watch the recruits when they run. You'll see what I mean."

Demetrius was discouraged. He didn't know what to do.

When the time came for the recruits to run, Demetrius would watch them carefully. He listened as the Instructor called out the familiar words, *"Alpha, beta, gamma—***GO***!"* He watched the hoard of well-developed bare bodies take off forcefully from the start. *"Ye gods! They're starting at full speed. They can't keep that up.* Demetrius watched, and he watched the runners zoom by. Round and round they went, never tiring, or at least not seeming to. *How can this be?* He wondered to himself. *I've never seen anything like this.*

When the running was over, Demetrius remained despondent. He didn't know if he could ever fit in the program. *It's too much for me,* he felt.

Nevertheless, the Aide continued helping him. Every day Demetrius came out and practiced the drills and running apart from the main group. At the same time, Demetrius with the Aide beside him did the grueling exercises prescribed for him. This was always followed by running.

Demetrius felt he wasn't making progress. *I'll never be like the others,* he thought. Still, the drills and the running continued day after tiring day.

One day, the Aide was pushing Demetrius especially hard.

Finally, Demetrius said, "I can't continue. I have no energy left."

"You must drive yourself. No one can force yourself but you. You must go on."

"But I can't."

"Okay, that's all for today. Get a good rest tonight because tomorrow we must go further than today."

Demetrius was wondering when this nightmare would end. He tried hard but felt he wasn't making progress. He could leave the program, of course, but that would disgrace him with his family and friends. He didn't know what to do. But he would do as the Aide asked. He'd try to get a good rest that night. With the help of the Aide, he was able to turn in earlier that evening. Almost immediately he fell asleep. He went into a deep sleep. But he was soon awakened.

Demetrius woke up startled. "Uh, uh what's happened? Why did you wake me? Are we being invaded?"

"No, no, nothing like that. You have a visitor."

A visitor! Who might that be? My father perhaps. But why would he come here? Demetrius picked up his tunic and headed for the reception area to meet his guest. Through the darkness, he could make out the image of a young man. *But who?* He wondered.

Before he could identify him, it was the guest who spoke first.

"Demetrius. How good to see you."

"Adonis, my friend. It's you! How wonderful to see you."

The two men entwined themselves in a long embrace.

"I'm thrilled to see you," said Adonis.

"And likewise," said Demetrius. "But why did you wait so long?"

"I came here many times. They didn't know who I was. I had to return when someone on duty remembered me."

Again, the men embraced. Then Demetrius led Adonis away from the reception area to a place they could talk in private.

"How's it going my friend?" asked Adonis.

"I wish I could say everything's well, but it's not that way at all."

"Tell me. What's going on?"

"Well, as we discussed before, I don't have the level of proficiency like the other recruits. They're much stronger. They're able to do drills and run much further than me. I tried hard. That wasn't enough."

"I see. But to be honest, I thought it might be this way. So, what would you like to do?"

"That's the difficult part. I don't know. I could quit the program and be in disgrace by everyone, especially the other recruits, my family, and my friends."

"You'll never be disgraced by me."

"Adonis, you're special. I don't think I could live if it had to be without you."

"Thank you, Demetrius. As you know, I've always been overjoyed in being your friend. But let me say this." Adonis became serious as he looked into Demetrius's eyes and spoke slowly. "I believe you can make the grade. You *can* meet the standards of the program. With your permission, I'd like to speak to the Commander. I don't know him well. But he's the one who makes decisions here. I'll ask him if I can return to military life on the Post. My job would be to bring you, and perhaps others, up to standards. It won't be easy. But again, I believe in you, Demetrius."

For his part, Demetrius felt overwhelmed. "I don't know what to say, Adonis. Sometimes I feel with your support, your love and understanding I can do anything. Anything at all."

"Think nothing of it. I'll learn when I can speak to the Commander. After he gives us his decision, I'll come back and let you know."

Before Adonis left, the men let their tunics drop to the floor. They pressed their bodies together in a warm embrace. Following the long embrace with a lingering kiss, the men said their goodbyes. Adonis left the Post.

Demetrius had never been happier since he arrived at the Post. He returned to his cot and fell into another deep sleep.

The next day Adonis returned to the Post to see if he could meet with the Commander. On arrival, he explained his situation. He was told to wait. And he waited. He was there most of the morning. Finally, he got to see the Commander. When they were together, the Commander asked Adonis to explain the purpose of his visit.

"It's like this. My friend, a recruit named Demetrius is having a difficult time. He's unable to meet standards for either the physical drills or the running exercises. An Aide was assigned to help him. But Demetrius has made little progress. Demetrius doesn't want to leave the program and face the disgrace that would give him. It'd be awful for him if he were rejected from the program."

The Commander responded, "And what makes you think you can make him perform better than the Aide has done?"

"Good question Sir. I cannot say exactly how, but I believe I can. I know Demetrius well. I know he wants to do well. I know he's willing to make sacrifices needed to be successful. I can help him find his *agon,* the will to do whatever it takes to be a good *hoplite.* I also believe Athen's army will be better by keeping Demetrius."

"You seem to be sure of yourself young man. But it would be a shame if we go to the trouble of trying to make him into a decent soldier and learn he can't meet the standards."

"I understand that Sir. Believe me, I do. But I wouldn't be here taking your time if I didn't believe Demetrius is worth the effort."

"Tell me this. When more new recruits come into our program and if there are some who are far behind the others, in their physical abilities, would you work with them as hard as you seem to want to help Demetrius?"

"Absolutely Sir. I absolutely would."

"If you can feel as much concern for the others as you do for Demetrius, it might be worth it. But I want to talk with a few of the officers before deciding. I'll let you know. You may go now."

"Yes, Sir."

Before leaving the Post, Adonis decided he would watch Demetrius during his exercise program. He didn't want Demetrius to see him. He found a position allowing him to observe his friend going through his routines.

Again, as Adonis was watching, Demetrius couldn't keep up with the demands from the Aide. He tired easily. Weeks had gone by. He wasn't improving.

Adonis was disappointed. *Perhaps I overstated to the Commander my ability to help Demetrius,* he thought. Now he wasn't sure if he could help his friend improve or not.

At that moment Demetrius's Aide ended their session. He was free to leave.

Adonis decided to join him.

"How nice to see you so soon," said a surprised Demetrius.

"Likewise," said Adonis. "I finished meeting with the Commander. He said he wants to talk with some of the officers before deciding. That might take a while."

"Thanks for getting the ball rolling. I'm sorry to say my improvement is slow. I think the Aide is getting tired of working with me."

"You mustn't give up on yourself. It is a question of knowing you can do it and having the desire to do it."

"Yes, yes, I know all that. But up to now, it hasn't been working."

"Maybe you can't do it yourself, and maybe I can't get you to do it myself either. But maybe the two of us working together, we can reach the high standards of the program."

Adonis then pulled Demetrius into a small recess in the wall of the courtyard. Once again, they pressed their naked bodies into each other. There they cherished the intimate warmth coming from the other's skin with the genital arousals that incurred. They lingered that way with long, deep kisses. The men separated when they heard the call for the midday meal.

"Won't you stay and join us for the midday meal?" asked Demetrius. "I'm sure they'll let you dine with the rest of us."

Adonis agreed.

They went into the mess hall and found their seats. Demetrius and his new recruits had continued sitting in the same area at their table. In this way, they were getting to know each other. Demetrius explained, "Adonis was a former *hoplite* at the Post and is looking at the possibility of returning."

They were chit-chatting for some time until the wine was poured. At that moment someone from the Commander's office came to their table. He told Adonis the Commander wants to see him immediately.

Adonis left the table.

Could it be that the Commander feels I shouldn't have stayed? Adonis thought. *My reason for coming here was to see him. I should have left right after our meeting.*

The Commander was waiting when Adonis arrived to see him.

"I have news for you Adonis. I've made my decision."

"I apologize for extending my visit, Sir. I wanted to watch Demetrius do his drills. After that, he invited me to stay for the midday meal."

"That's alright. I am glad you stayed. My decision's been made. I've decided to let you return to the Post as an active *hoplite*. Your primary duties will be to help Demetrius. You are to work with Demetrius alone."

Adonis was astonished.

"I don't know what to say, Sir. I'm extremely thankful. I'll do all I can to measure up to expectations. I'm surprised you decided so soon."

"There was something I didn't know about you. When I learned that, there was no need to consult with the officers."

"Oh!" said a surprised Adonis. "May I ask what that something was, Sir?"

"Yes, of course. I happened to spot you and Demetrius after his drills. I could see both of you from across the courtyard. What I learned is, you are lovers."

"Yes, Sir. We are very much so."

"That's the point. Lovers can do for each other what no other teacher can. There was a time when such an idea seemed ridiculous. That's how I felt. Stupid sentimentalities have no place in the military. But then we learned from other armies, primarily Sparta, but others as well. They taught us how truly effective lovers work together. That was beyond our wildest beliefs. But its truth can't be denied. We now embrace the idea throughout our City-State. Male-to-male love enriches the *agon* of partners like nothing else. That's one of the secrets about the prosperity and greatness of the Greek people."

"I'm impressed by what you say, Sir."

"Well, no need to be. It is just a fact. Nothing more. Now, as soon as you can, bring your uniform and whatever personal belongings you may need to the Post. You're to begin training Demetrius right away. Both of you are assigned to the alternate dormitory."

"You mean the room with the extra wide beds?"

"Yes. Those are reserved for couples."

"I'm at a loss for words. Indeed. I'm extremely grateful for your help, Sir. I'll do all I can to be worthy of your kind support."

"Thank you. You may go now."

Adonis returned to the mess hall. The new recruits were deep in conversation. That didn't deter Adonis from sharing the news. "Demetrius, we have our decision. The Commander said I can stay and help you."

"That's wonderful. I'm happy for both of us." The men embraced at the table. The others were confused.

Sensing their confusion, Demetrius said, "Adonis is returning to the Post. He'll be with us. We'll be working together with the morning drills."

Everyone shared in the excitement as Adonis sat down to have his meal. When he was finished, he said, "I have to leave now. I'll return in the morning, but not as a visitor."

Demetrius walked out of the mess hall with Adonis. As they neared the main gate, Adonis said, "Oh! I forgot to tell you what else the Commander said. You'll be moving upstairs to be with me in the dormitory for couples."

Again, a burst of emotional excitement as the men realized they'll be living together as lovers for the first time. The intensity of their delight was palpable.

Demetrius returned to his area feeling happier perhaps than he ever had been. That night as he prepared to go to sleep, he realized it would be his last night in the narrow cot and his last night without Adonis. *This military experience will be the best part of my life,* he thought.

CHAPTER 16

Nilo Arrives at the Theater

Begin doing what you want to do now. We are not living in eternity. We have only this moment, sparkling like a star in our hand and melting like a snowflake.

— **Francis Bacon**
1561 – 1626

Nilo woke up early. He was anticipating visiting the theater with Horus. It was too early to rise. So, he laid there imagining what the day's experience might be like.

Unbeknownst to Nilo, Horus was already up. In time, Nilo could hear him washing and walking around. Soon, Horus came by to "wake" Nilo. As he entered the boy's room, Nilo feigned sleeping. As he quietly drew closer to Nilo's bed, he held a grotesque mask over his face. He then leaned over the boy and in a loud voice said, "**Nilo!**"

Even though Nilo was awake, the sight of the mask startled the boy, and he jumped. "Ye gods! What are you doing Horus?"

"I'm having fun with you, my friend. But please get up now so we can have our morning meal and get out to the theater."

"Yes, yes. I want to go with you."

Nilo was soon out of bed. He wrapped his one-piece tunic around him, and they were soon sitting down for their morning meal.

"We have a busy day ahead," said Horus, softening his hard barley bread by dipping it in wine. "We're trying out new people for our chorus and even a few actors. Keeping our cast intact always present challenges. Having the best is the way to go."

Nilo hadn't considered all the activity needed to go into a play production. This made him know it can't happen without hard work. "How do you know when you have the best?" asked Nilo.

"We don't always know. It's sort of like having a hunch, especially after comparing my feelings with others. Here, have some *teganites*."

Nilo took a few.

"I see," said Nilo while spreading honey on his *teganites*, a pancake-like substance made from wheat flour. "The *teganites* are tasty this morning."

"I'm glad you like them. Now, when we get to the theater, I'll take you around to see the different areas. That way you'll get a feel for the operation."

"I'd like that," said Nilo. "Do you sometimes use children in any part of your theater's operation?"

"Uh, no. Well—I take that back. We occasionally use children. They've helped us off-stage. When we use them, they're a small part of our operation. I think you'll like knowing about the theater. Take your last *teganite* with you. We have to go."

When they arrived at the theater, several persons came up to Horus. "Are we going practice in costumes today?" asked one of the actors. Another wanted to know about the use of special effects. And there were more questions.

It appeared to Nilo that Horus is the man in charge. *He won't have much time for me today, it seems.*

Then, almost as if Horus was reading Nilo's mind, he asked someone to find Clio and tell him he wanted to see him.

When Clio appeared, Horus said, "This is Nilo, a good friend of mine. Please show him around. Explain to him how our theater operates. I'd do it myself, but there's too much demanding my time."

To Nilo, Horus said, "You'll be in good hands with Clio. He knows the operations here perfectly, better than almost anyone."

"Thank you, Horus."

Then Clio and Nilo were gone.

Clio was a young man with an even more youthful appearance. His beard was starting to grow. His hair was cropped short. Nilo thought him to be attractive. As Nilo would soon learn, he's a talkative person who knows much, not only about the theater, but life itself. After they walked into the theater arena together, Clio suggested, "Let's sit here, at the front of the seating area. We can get a good look from where the audience sits for performances. You notice the seating here in the spectator section is built in stone. This is recent—well, relatively so. Since shortly before you were born, I'd guess. Before then everyone sat on wooden benches."

"How come the rows in the front are different from the others?" asked Nilo.

"The front rows are for dignitaries. As you see, the seats are more comfortable for having backs to them. They look like thrones. There are sixty-seven such seats. Priests take up fifty of the sixty-seven front row seats. Then come officials and guests of honor. The remainder are for ordinary citizens. The theater audience holds about seventeen-thousand when it's full. You may have noticed how the theater is tucked into the backside of the Acropolis. An advantage the builders had was a preexisting hollow the theater fits into naturally."

Nilo was captivated by the way Clio was animated when describing the theater. He thought his excitation was more delightful than the descriptions he gave.

"And who's the large statue in the front row?"

"Good question. The statue is Dionysus. He was put here to see the plays. We were sure he'd want to watch them. All our plays are done in his name. This is the Theater of Dionysus. The purpose of every aspect of the Theater is to honor him. You must have heard of him?"

"Oh yes. He's the god of wine and merriment."

"Yes. But he's a lot more than that. He's the god of the vine, the grape harvest, ritual madness, fertility, religious ecstasy, and of course, the theater. All that you see around you is because of him. Now take a good look at all you see. This isn't just another theater. Let me tell you something of great importance."

"I'm all ears," said Nilo holding his open hands behind his ears.

"The entire seating area you see was constructed in the most phenomenal way. Let me tell you what was done. The theater was built so *everyone* in the audience can hear what's said on the stage. It's true. They can. Even at the highest and furthest corner of the seating area, those in the audience can hear what's said from the stage."

"How could they do that?" asked Nilo.

"Well, people say I know a lot about the theater. But the truth is, I don't know that much.

And I don't know how the builders accomplished all they did including the way sound is carried. But I'm glad they did."

"Well, if it's true what you say about the sound, I want to hear it."

"Certainly Nilo. You can come here to see a play and sit in the farthest upper corner. There you'll hear all the stage dialogue."

"Oh! But I don't want to wait until there's a performance. I want to hear it now."

Although Nilo is a visitor, all at once, he takes command. "I'm going to the highest and farthest spot in the seating area. And you, Clio, would you run up onto the stage? When I'm at the highest and farthest spot, talk to me with the same level of sound actors use in a play. I'll listen for your voice."

"Okay Nilo, if you want to go to that much trouble, we can do that."

At that moment, Nilo takes off and runs up to the top of the seating area. Then he turns and goes to the farthest corner. He waves his arms to Clio, who's now on the stage, to signal he's ready to hear his voice.

Clio, looking up to Nilo from the stage says loudly, "Hello Nilo. Can you hear me?"

As soon as Clio finished saying those words, Nilo came running down to be with him.

"It works! It works!" said a jubilant Nilo. "It's true. You said, 'Hello Nilo. Can you hear me?'"

"Yes. That's what I said. Isn't it amazing?"

They shared a brief hug.

"Oh no!"

"What is it?"

"We forgot to try to see if you could hear me too."

"That's a good point."

"And what if someone in the audience has to sneeze or cough during a performance? Would everyone hear him too? Even the actors?"

"Yes, you've got a point. Those are things we need to know about. Okay, now let's go on the stage.

"As you can see its shape is somewhat like half a circle. The rounded portion extends out into the audience. Here's where plays, dances, religious rites, and acting all take place. The stage is the focal point of the theater. The back of the stage has a building painted to look like the front of a temple or a palace. Here, actors retire when they're not needed on stage or use when they need to change costumes. We call it the *skene*. Let's go there now. We can enter the *skene* (root word for 'scene') through this set of doors. If you look up, you'll notice there's also an access door to the roof."

"Why is that?"

"Well, there are times when the play requires an actor to be at a significantly higher elevation than the others on the stage. He'd then be on the roof of the *skene*.

"The *skene* has many uses. It's a storeroom for costumes, boots, and masks. It's also where the actors change costumes and sometimes masks."

Nilo picks up a mask. "Horus keeps a collection of these at home. But why do they have to be so big? They're larger than anyone's face."

"They do that so those who are far from the stage can see expressions on the masks. The expressions are essential ways we portray each actor. Now if you look carefully into the mouth of each mask, you'll see it has unusual formations around the edges. What this does is help expand the distance of the actor's voice which is another way to enable those far from the stage to hear every actor's voice. Now let's look at the costumes.

"You see the costumes are made well and elaborate. They're also expensive. As you may know, the maximum number of actors used in a play is three. Therefore, every actor takes on different roles. So, when an actor's role changes, so does his mask, his costume, his voice, even his gestures are different. Sometimes his shoes are different. One might wear thick soled shoes to make him look taller. This is important in theatrical settings. Raised platform shoes in tragic plays symbolize superior status. Comic actors, on the other hand, wear plain socks. As to costumes, they're sometimes padded. This makes them look fatter or stronger. On occasion, actors may even have to wear animal costumes. Now, let's look closer at some of the costumes.

"Over here you'll see some with long fitted sleeves. Some also reach down the legs to the knees, or like this one, all the way to the ankles. And look at the patterns, how elaborate are the motifs. They weave the recurring patterns into the cloth by using a loom.

"So, you see a major function of the costumes is to support the props and masks in helping define an actor's social status and gender."

"But it must all be expensive," said Nilo.

"Oh yes. The costumes, masks and keeping the theater going, yes, that's all expensive."

"But why do they have to spend so many drachmas for a costume? Does the audience care?"

"It's called narcissism. That's why they do it."

"But what's narcissism?"

"You must've heard of the god Narcissus who fell in love with his reflection in a pool of water?"

"Ah, yes. I do remember."

"Okay. Well, Athens is like Narcissus. We all love ourselves. The people of Athens have a great desire for everyone in the Greek world to notice us. Everything done in the theater is to impress the audience and the world on our wealth and the greatness of our City-State. That makes sense. If we appear powerful on the stage, they must know the same is true in real life. Then maybe they'll leave us alone, militarily, at least."

Clio had been taking note of Nilo's reactions. *The boy is genuinely interested. He not only takes note of what I'm saying, but he thinks all it though and asks interesting questions. He's inquisitive. He wants to know the why of everything. I'm impressed.*

"Well Nilo, there's more we can talk about. You might want to know about the plays. The one being worked on now and the mechanics of how plays are put together. But maybe we should save that for another day."

Remembering he's a guest at the theater, Nilo said, "Whatever you say is fine. I learned a lot today. Thank you for that."

"Perhaps Horus will bring you to the theater tomorrow. It'd be good for you to be here. The chorus will be rehearsing on stage. It takes a big effort to choreograph their presentation. It's part of the overall performance. I think you'll like it."

"That would be splendid. I look forward to the possibility. Perhaps we'll see each other then."

Nilo went to look for Horus as Clio returned to his regular work. When Nilo found him, Horus said, "It's nearly time for us to return home for our midday meal."

Nilo waited until Horus was ready to leave.

When the two of them were having their midday meal, Horus brought up the question of Nilo's education.

"There's one thing we haven't yet talked about, my friend."

"There are lots of things we haven't talked about," said Nilo.

"Well yes, but of important things, maybe not so many. I want to talk about your education. What are we going to do about that?"

"Oh, that! I wish I didn't have to be educated."

"But Nilo, you're going to want to take your place in our City-State. That requires a strong education."

"Yes, but whenever I get into an educational experience, there are problems with it. I don't want to do it."

"Well let's both give it some thought. We can try to discover what's best for you."

Nilo had been fearful Horus would bring this up. Now that he did, he wasn't sure how to handle the situation. *I'm here at Horus's pleasure. If I become too defiant about my education, Horus may ask me to leave, and I like it here.*

Then Horus said, "Apart from your academic studies, there's your physical education training. You're too young to go to the *gymnasia*, but you can do physical training on your own. Have you done much running?"

Nilo was glad Horus brought up his running. "Yes, but not recently."

"Well, as for this afternoon, it may be better for you not to return to the theater with me. There's not much you can do. I can't take Clio away from his work. He has much to do to catch up on what he missed this morning. Why don't you use the afternoon for getting back to your physical training? There are many good places to run near my home. The passageways are excellent for running. Maybe you'll want to return to the theater in the morning. I understand there will be a dress rehearsal of the choral group."

"Ah yes. Clio also suggested I see them practice."

"Okay then, we'll leave it at that. And please consider what you want to do about your education."

"Yes, I will."

After Horus left, Nilo decided to rest awhile before getting back into his physical routine. As he lay in his bed, he wondered about many things. His thoughts went back to his family. *How're they doing? I hope they're well. Demetrius is in the military now. I wonder if they kept him, even though he wasn't physically fit.* Nilo's ambivalence toward his family remained conflicted. *I'd love to see them, but I don't dare return.* He soon drifted off to sleep. When he awoke, he was worried. It was getting late. He hadn't done his physical training. He went outside and quickly discovered the passageways near the house are good for running, as Horus said.

His love for running was returning to him. The breeze slapping against his bare body was a delight he welcomed back to his life. *Why did I ever stop running?* he wondered. But he didn't push himself to run as far as he once did. Some of his stamina had been lost.

When he returned to the house, he discovered delightfully the slave filled the tub for him. He quickly immersed himself. After washing, followed by his usual contemplation of his body, he dried himself. As he reached for his tunic, he heard voices downstairs. *I hear Horus, but there's also another voice. Who could that be?* He quickly wrapped himself in his tunic and descended the staircase. "Horus, you're home! Oh! And I see Clio. What a nice surprise. Hello Clio."

"Hello, Nilo. Yes. I invited Clio home for our evening meal. We got busy this afternoon and didn't have a chance to discuss many things of the theater we need to resolve."

Clio added, "Hello Nilo. It's nice to see you again."

"I'm happy to see you too," said Nilo.

Nilo was thinking; *Perhaps I'll also get a chance to chat with Clio.*

But before he could say anything, Horus said, "Well, let's get busy Clio, we have much to go over. We'll see you at the evening meal, Nilo."

"Oh! Yes, of course," said Nilo, "See you at the evening meal."

Nilo went to lie down until he was called for the evening meal. But the evening meal wouldn't be the exciting time he wanted. Horus and Clio monopolized the conversation by continuing discussions on the operation of the theater. They didn't seem to realize they were keeping Nilo out of their conversation until near the end.

"Will you pardon us Nilo? We didn't mean to leave you out of our talk. We had some serious business problems we had to resolve. I hope you'll forgive us."

"I understand," said Nilo, though it was painful for him to be sitting there without being involved.

"Tomorrow, we can watch the chorus rehearsal together," said Clio. "I'm looking forward to that."

"Me too," said Nilo.

Despite their concern for Nilo, the two men resumed talking about the theater, leaving Nilo out of their discussion. When the evening meal was finished, and the men kept talking, Nilo excused himself and went to his room.

As he lay on his bed, he thought, *What I need is to have friends of my own. I can't depend on Horus to spend time with me. He's a busy man. Maybe I'll get to know more people at the theater. And what am I going to say to Horus about my education? Is it fair if I ask him to find a tutor for me because he would have to pay for him? I don't know what to do.*

Eventually, Nilo fell asleep.

The next day, Horus and Nilo met at the morning meal. After pleasantries, Nilo opened the conversation. "Were you and Clio able to finish your discussions last night?"

"Oh no. Those types of discussions never finish. Theater work goes on and on. There's much involved. We never run out of the concerns we need to handle. Last night as you could tell, wasn't a social visit. We had to work. I don't like bringing work home, but occasionally it has to happen. Perhaps Clio and others from the theater can come over some time on a social visit alone."

"I'd like that," said Nilo.

"Okay, my dear. It's time we leave for the theater. We should have an interesting morning."

When they arrived at the theater, their attention was taken by the activity. Everyone, it seemed, was moving here and there in preparation for the choral rehearsal. As before, several came up to Horus with questions about what they were to do. In time, they spotted Clio. Nilo asked if he could go and talk with the young man. Horus agreed. When they met, Clio, while briefly hugging Nilo, said, "Welcome my new friend. I'm happy you came today."

"So am I," said Nilo.

"Tell me please, would you like to sit with me today, so we can watch the rehearsal together?"

"I'd love to," said Nilo.

"Tell you what. I have a few things to do. When the rehearsal is about to start, why don't we meet at the front of the seating area? I doubt Horus will join us because his job takes him everywhere. We can find a place to sit together."

"I'd like that," said Nilo.

Shortly before the rehearsal began, Clio and Nilo found seats.

"Normally in a play, we wouldn't be able to have seats as close to the stage as these. Let's enjoy what we have while we can."

"I'm excited about seeing it all," said Nilo.

Clio began by explaining the role of the chorus. "If this were a real play, it would start with an actor coming on the stage. That's called the prologue. Usually, the audience doesn't have enough background information to grasp the meaning of the events portrayed in the play. It's the actor's duty during the prologue to give the audience what they need to know.

"In a play, as soon as the prologue is over, the chorus comes on the stage. Currently, our Dionysus Theater uses fifteen men for the chorus. All of them wear identical masks and costumes. This creates a sense of unity and uniformity in the group. As you've already seen, their costumes can be elaborate. They'll be singing as they enter the stage. Accompanying the singing will be musical instruments. The ones most used for our theater are the lyre, the kithara and the aulos (flute). It was our god Hermes who invented the lyre, while it was the goddess of our City, Athena who gave us the aulos.

"If you're around the theater very long, you'll hear about these things over and over. That way, you'll know them well. And who knows? Maybe someday, if you're interested, you can have an important job here at the Theater."

"Ha-ha. I don't think so. It's a lot of work to put on a play. Maybe it's too much for me."

Clio didn't put much stock in what Nilo expressed. He continued explaining how things operate. "Did you know everything involved with the chorus is handled by a chorus director? That includes training for each chorus member. He's called the *choragus*. The *choragus* also must provide or select all the equipment, costumes, props, even the trainers. We have at present twenty-four chorus members, but only fifteen are on the stage at any one time. The training period for each play can be up to six months."

Despite Nilo's feeling of being overwhelmed by this information, Clio felt the boy was taking in everything more than most others he tried to enthuse. He kept thinking, *Nilo is special.*

The music began. It was emotional. Nilo sat up straight, knowing this is the beginning.

The chorus dancers came out on the stage.

"Wow!" said Nilo. "The costumes are bright; so vivid they are. And look at them dance!" Nilo was enthralled. He saw the chorus was not just singing and dancing. There was commentary. Nilo was learning the chorus could provide a broader interpretation of what, in a real play, would transpire with the actors. It was more than their reflection of the plot. The chorus gave meaning to the audience in ways the actors couldn't do through dialogues. They also prepared the audience for crucial periods in the plot. The chorus was especially adept at being supportive of the actors by helping build up interest. The chorus could express uniquely what the main characters were unable to do, even as to their hidden fears or secrets. Nilo was fascinated. As he continued watching, he saw before each act, the chorus reciting a lyric poem. This wasn't a separate activity. The verses served to keep the play's momentum moving along.

Finally came the time for the *exodos,* the play's conclusion. The chorus sang a processional song. This included profound statements that mimicked not only the plot but also the play's meaning.

When it was over, the small audience consisting of theater personnel with a small number of guests, stamped their feet loudly, showing approval.

"Wow! That was something," said Nilo as he stomped his feet with the others. Before leaving the theater, Nilo and Clio shared an embrace. "Thank you, my friend, for explaining all this to me. I'm beginning to love the theater."

The next several days were uneventful. Nilo sometimes went to the theater in the morning. Horus would put Nilo in the hands of different workers, so he could have a broader feel for the overall operations. Nilo was doing his physical training in the afternoon. He was getting back to his former self in running. Clio sometimes came over to the house in the evening, but only to work with Horus. Nilo was getting restless. Horus didn't have much time for him except during meals. Most of all, Nilo saw his time with Horus as not getting anywhere. Life again seemed without purpose.

One evening, Nilo was near the front door when he heard a knocking. So instead of asking the slave to see who's there, Nilo opened the door.

"Clio, what a nice surprise."

"Good evening Nilo."

"I'll get Horus. He'll be glad to see you."

"Oh no. I didn't come to see Horus."

"You didn't?" asked a confused Nilo.

"No. I came to see you."

"You came to see me? Well, anyway, come in," said Nilo. *What might he want to see me about?* Nilo wondered.

Sensing Nilo's confusion, Clio said, "I wanted to talk with you. Nothing more. I hope I'm not disturbing you."

"No. Not at all." Nilo took Clio to the *andron* where they could talk.

On the way, Clio, putting his arm over Nilo's shoulder, said, "I'm sorry for not having had time for you on your visits to the theater. It's been a busy time."

"I understand Clio. Work always comes first. I was surprised you were able to stop working long enough to help me learn about the theater during my early visits. Well, here we are. Find a sofa you like."

"Thank you."

Nilo said, "This is a big surprise. Is there something special you came to see me about?"

"Well, yes. Yes, there is. But I didn't want to bring it up right away."

"Now you've got me wondering. But don't worry. Take your time on whatever you want to say."

"Thanks, but I might as well bring it up now. Else you may keep on wondering and wondering."

"Ha-ha. It's okay. Whatever you like."

Clio became serious. "I will tell you. Ever since we met, I've been intrigued by you. Your inquisitive mind and your excitement in learning new things were unexpected. You have a jest for life. I thoroughly enjoy being with you." *I can't tell him how beautiful he is. This isn't the right time.*

"You were helpful teaching me about the theater. I liked that."

Not wanting to delay further, Clio decided to give the reason for his visit.

"Nilo you're special to me. Would you like to be my *eromenos*?"

"Your *eromenos*! Ye gods, I had no idea you were thinking anything like that."

"As I said, you are special. I've never met a boy like you."

Many things flooded into Nilo's mind. His father told him, n*ever appear too interested with someone who wants to be your erastes. Never make them think you're easy prey.* Nilo's demeanor changed at that moment. He stopped making eye contact with Clio. Not that night. He began to stare at the floor.

"Oh, I'm sorry Nilo. I was too sudden. You weren't expecting this. I should leave now. But I hope we'll see each other soon."

Nilo stood up without saying a word. They walked to the door in silence. Clio tried to embrace Nilo at the door, but the boy paid him no attention. Then Clio was gone.

For Clio, this was difficult. But he wasn't surprised. He knows how the game is played. He also knows he'd have to be patient if Nilo was going to continue in his life.

As for Nilo, he went to bed. While he laid there recalling Clio's offer, he didn't know what to think. The idea of having an *erastes* hadn't been in his plans.

Morning came as it always does. Horus was already on his sofa in the eating area, as Nilo came to join him.

"Good morning."

"Good morning."

"I'm sorry for not being more attentive to you. There's much we need to do at the theater. But there's also much we need to do about you. I'll have some free time during the day. Would you like to come with me to the theater today?"

"No, I'd rather not go."

"Oh!" cried Horus, surprised at the rejection of his offer. He couldn't imagine why Nilo would reject his offer. "Do you have something planned today? Something I don't know about?"

"No, nothing like that."

"Well then, what is it, my friend? You've always enjoyed your visits to the theater."

"Yes, you're right. But today I don't want to go."

"Is everything okay?"

"I don't know. There are things I don't understand."

"What is it, my friend?"

"I don't know if it's right to tell you. But I will. Our friend Clio was here last night. He asked if he could be my *erastes*."

"Ye gods! How amazing. I'm glad you told me. What did you say to him?"

"I said nothing. You know how young boys have to be."

"Well, yes. I do. But what do you want to do about that?"

"I don't know."

"Let me say something about this. I know from experience from myself and others, the *erastes/eromenos* relationship, if it lasts, can be the finest time in a persons' life. But while that's true, it wouldn't be good for you to be involved like that with Clio."

"But why? Is he a bad person for some reason?"

"No. Clio is one of the most intelligent, friendly and worthwhile persons I know. Under the right circumstances, he'd make an excellent *erastes*. I'd have a difficult time thinking of someone better than he is."

"Then what's the problem?"

"The problem, my dear, is your age. You're way too young to be in a relationship like that."

"I don't know if I'd want to be involved with Clio that way. But I can say this: we get along well. We like each other. He's smart. I like being taught by him."

"You're right. He's smart, and he would be a good teacher for you. But being an *eromenos* means more than having a good teacher. He'd be not only a mentor for you in every facet of life, but you'd have to be his lover. You're not ready for that. You're only twelve years old. You're not physically mature. You haven't had your growth spurt yet. It's far too early for you to have an *erastes*."

"I'll soon be thirteen and people say I'm mature for my age."

"That's not enough."

"I see." *It's futile for me to keep talking with Horus about this. I won't argue anymore.*

"I have to leave for the theater now. If you're not coming with me, I'll either see you at our midday meal or possibly not till tonight."

"Thank you, Horus. Thank you for caring about me."

Horus left for the theater while Nilo retreated to his bedroom.

On his way to the theater, Horus remained concerned about Nilo. *I hope he won't accept Clio's offer to be his* erastes *and expect me to go along with it. It's not right.* But when Horus arrived at the theater, he was again overwhelmed by decisions he had to make. He also had to give his staff their instructions for the day. One of those who approached him was Clio. Everything they talked about was theater business. As Clio was about to leave, Horus asked: "Would you mind stopping by after you get your work done?"

"Certainly," replied Clio.

It was near the end of the workday when Clio came by to see Horus.

"I was thinking maybe you weren't going to come by."

"Well, here I am. I sensed your concern was important."

"It is. Nilo told me you want to be his *erastes.*"

"Well—yes. It's true. It seems perfect. Don't you think?"

"In some ways, it might be. You're a good man. Nilo could learn much from you. But he's way too young to be your lover. You know that. I'm sure you do."

"Yes. Most *eromenoi* are older than Nilo. That's for sure. But Nilo isn't an ordinary child. He's endured many things boys older than him were never exposed to. That includes living on his own and having sexual experiences."

"The public won't see it that way. And Nilo isn't ready to have a lover. That's the way it is. And as you said, he's a child."

"Our gods may approve. What about the boy Ganymede who Zeus, King of the gods, brought home to Mount Olympus to be his beloved?"

"Yes. But his stay with Zeus was brief. Zeus, although he made the boy immortal, he still had to protect him from the rage of his ultra-jealous wife. Zeus had to send the boy far away. So, he sent Ganymede to the constellation Aquarius to be water-bearer for the gods in the sky. That doesn't relate at all with what we can do with Nilo."

"I'm sorry Horus. I thought it might be best for both of us. That's all. Nilo needs someone in his life who can help him. You've done much by taking him into your home. But you don't have time to give him the guidance he desperately needs."

"Yes, you're right. I wish I knew what to do about that. Much of his time is wasted. I'm unable to fill his time constructively. But for him to have a lover/mentor? No. That's not the answer. Now, you tell me something."

"Certainly."

"I have a proposal for you—and Nilo. I want you to tell me if this would work for you.

"You're correct. Nilo needs a teacher. He needs a teacher who's not only proficient in the academics but also able to teach him about life. In many ways, I think you could fill that void in his life. What do you say to that?"

"On the surface, it seems fine. But we'd have to define the exact duties further."

"That can be done. But let me make one thing clear. Physical intimacies are *not* to be part of whatever arrangement you may have. Do you understand?"

"Yes. That shouldn't be a problem."

"I'm not his father. But if he lives with me, I'm responsible for him. He will not have an *erastes* until he's older. Do you understand that?"

"Why yes. I understand you."

"But you can fulfill most of the duties of an *erastes* up to a point. The main rule will be that the two of you can never be alone. If you are teaching him in my home, my house slave will monitor you. If you decide to take him hunting or go anywhere together, one of my slaves must follow you.

281

These are hard rules. I know that. But we must follow them. Do you understand?"

"Yes, I do. But how do you think Nilo will react to this? I'm sure you'll let him make the final decision."

"Yes, the final decision is up to Nilo. That's the way it must be. And I think he'll accept it. I also think he would agree to be your *eromenos* if I were to allow it. But, regardless, I think he'll accept this. His life is purposeless right now. He's getting nowhere."

"Yes. You're right about that."

CHAPTER 17

Trouble on the Battlefield

Only the dead have seen the end of war.

— **Plato**
427 – 347 BC

The bell sounded at an unexpected time. That meant everyone in the Post knew it wasn't for a routine meeting. It had to be something important.

Adonis and Demetrius were working out with their physical training program when they heard the call. They immediately stopped and went to the Assembly Hall. On their way, Demetrius opined, "Maybe there's something to the rumors we've heard about war being imminent. Could that be?" asked Demetrius.

"Yes, and it could be anything. Anyway, we'll know soon," said Adonis.

From all over the Post, men were coming into the Assembly Hall. When Adonis and Demetrius arrived, the

Post Commander was approaching the podium. As he did, a pronounced hush came over the *hoplites*.

"He looks serious. This could be something big," whispered Adonis.

"Shh. He's about to speak," whispered Demetrius.

Good day everyone.

It's been a while since updating you on dangers facing Attica. We were hoping the dangers would go away. But they've become worse. Some historical background may be helpful. Most of you are between eighteen and twenty-one years old. That means, you have no memory of our wars with Persia. You may have learned from your parents about those wars. While the Greeks were eventually able to drive the Persians away from our shores, the toll taken on our city-states was great. We saw enough of the horrors of war to want to do all we could to avoid them in the future. Build our Army and Navy, of course. We felt the surest way to avoid war was to build up our defenses. We planned to concentrate more on defensive tactics than offensive ones. But the result was that it made our potential enemies nervous. What unfortunately developed is a multiplicity of states are now bitterly hostile to each other. Out of concern for our safety, we decided to build a wall. A wall long enough it encompasses both Athens and our Port town of Piraeus. The "long walls" of Athens are around four and a half miles each. The entire length of the walls around the City and the Port is around twenty-two miles.

For reasons we don't entirely understand, this infuriated Sparta and its allies. They knew Persia was no longer a threat to us. So, from their point of view, it must indicate we're planning an attack on their city-states. But that's not true. Everything we know about Sparta tells us it lives for war. Their whole society is organized for war. Everything they do is to enable them to have the best fighting force possible. They start training their young boys as early as age seven to be soldiers. So why should they be upset with Athens building a protective wall? Sparta also felt disturbed about the growing strength of our Delian League. Our League now has nearly three hundred city-state members and is still growing. Our alliance is thought of as an empire. It includes most of the islands and coastal states around the northern and eastern shores of the Aegean Sea. All its members pay tribute to the League. That's in exchange for mutual protection. This alliance with other city-states is our answer to the Peloponnesian League which Sparta sponsors. What outraged Sparta was the relocation of the Delian League's treasury from the island of Delos to

Athens. This gives us easier access to funds for military purposes. But that's our business, not Sparta's. Nevertheless, tensions have reached an all-time high. Our sources tell us Sparta's King is strongly considering an invasion of our territory. Yes, they want to come to Attica. We're convinced they're coming soon. Here's what we must do:

We will reinforce our manpower on Attica's frontiers. We're planning to double the number of forces on those outposts.

We'll bring in our veterans, those who completed military service. They'll have to go through a brief training program here on the Post. Space for them will be made when our men are sent to the frontiers and other areas of our City-State.

We'll significantly increase our weapons production in all areas.

We're sending our scouts far beyond the limits of Attica to learn of enemy troop movements.

We're continually assessing our needs as new information comes in.

As to each of you here, we'll be making assignments on an individual basis. Your assignment depends, in part, on how you've

*been rated in our current training program.
As for couples, all of you will receive the same
assignment. We've learned well that lovers
fight better as a group. All couples will remain
together.*

Assignments will be given out soon.

That's all gentlemen. We'll be in touch."

For the rest of the day, the clouds of war remained on everyone's thought. Deep concern about preparations dominated conversations all over the Post, well into the evening. "Fighting a war makes for a most different and difficult life," said one concerned recruit. Others wanted to know if they would be seeing their families before leaving Athens. It was the uncertainty of life that bothered the *hoplites* the most.

As Demetrius and Adonis returned to their quarters, Adonis said, "It seems our lives will be changing. Instead of preparing for war, we might find ourselves right in the middle of one."

"True," said Demetrius. "But we'll stay together. That's what counts. If the new emergency were six months ago, we wouldn't have been able to be together. I wasn't nearly ready physically to go to the battlefield."

It had been a difficult struggle for the two men. When they began their training together, it seemed Demetrius was never going to improve. That might still have been the reality if it hadn't been for the constant, persistent encouragement and patience by Adonis. It took months of hard, dedicated effort for Demetrius to get to the level of physical endurance needed to go to a battle zone. This was a case of erotic love fortifying *agon*.

Demetrius's motivation soared under Adonis's tutelage. Now he was ready. His arms, abdominal and leg muscles all showed he finally achieved a high level of physical fitness.

Now the men felt, despite the difficulties going on around them, they had each other. That would see them through no matter what the future had in store.

Conversations regarding the new reality continued unabated into the next day. In the morning on the athletic field, the recruits went through their usual maneuvers, long periods of calisthenics, each one followed by a period of running. The procedures were the same as any day. But one could feel in the air, something was different, something auspicious. No one could see this, but it was strongly felt. Above all, they wished to know when they would leave for the battlefield.

They didn't have to wait long. As everyone was leaving the athletic yard, they again heard the bell calling everyone to the Assembly Hall. "That's the second time in two days we've been called to a special meeting," said Adonis, as they changed their course.

"That's unusual," said Demetrius. "That's never happened before. Something's in the wind. Something important must have happened."

As the two young men came into the Assembly area, they could sense the concern of those around them. There were worries on their faces. "Will we be going into battle right away?" was the voice of one concerned recruit. The entire assembly room was filled with fear of the unknown. Soon, the Post Commander came to the podium.

Good morning.

I'll get right to the point. We're here today at an auspicious time in our City-State's history. We believe an invasion of our homeland by the enemy is imminent. Allow me to explain what that means for us and our basis for saying this.

Our scouts have travelled throughout the Peloponnese peninsula. We've also sent men to scout areas closer to home. What we've learned is undeniable. Sparta's army is on its way. They're coming here. The most traveled route for these men coming to Attica has always been over the narrow Isthmus of Corinth. It remains so today. That is the only land passage from Sparta to reach Attica, and today it's crowded with Spartan soldiers. We also know Sparta has plenty of reasons for coming here. Our relations have disintegrated into a tinderbox.

This is how we'll respond.

We'll be sending troops to the limits of Attica on all sides. Many of you will get notice of your departure in the next few days. Others will remain here to provide defense for our Post. But fighting on land will not be our main response. Sparta, as you know, has a powerful army. It would be folly for us to put most of our energy into a land response.

On the other hand, we have the greatest naval force the world has ever seen. The moment Sparta strikes an offensive that is deliberate and unprovoked, our ships, that is, our triremes will attack Peloponnesian ships. There's much we can do to destabilize the Spartans and their allies.

A few days ago, General Pericles, addressed the General Assembly. His words may hold interest for you. He advised our citizens on current affairs. He reminded them war will soon be with us. It may be unlike any war we've ever seen in Attica. We will not be able to protect those living outside our City's gates, should they remain in the countryside. They are not to go into battle. They must come into the City. They need to bring their possessions with them.

Since the time General Pericles gave the order for citizens to leave the Attica countryside, we have reports that is happening. Families are fleeing their homes in the countryside. They are taking their household furniture with them, including, in some cases, the very woodwork from their houses. As to their sheep and cattle, arrangements have been made to send the animals to the nearby friendly island of Euboea and a few adjacent islands. This isn't easy for our people. They've always lived in the country. Being uprooted this way may be the most difficult ordeal of their lives.

As to our preparations for war, General Pericles said we should be pleased to know how prepared we are. We have an army of thirteen thousand hoplites ready to fight in the Attica countryside. Also, there are sixteen thousand in the garrisons and battle stations here in Athens. We have twelve hundred horses mounted with archers along with sixteen hundred unmounted archers.

Pericles concluded by saying our naval forces are the most critical part of our defenses. We have three hundred triremes ready for service. One hundred have already left for Peloponnesian waters.

More details are coming. Tomorrow we're expecting General Pericles to address you. For the time being, as we remain in a state of crisis, these assembly meetings will occur every day at this hour. We intend to keep everyone informed. This meeting is now adjourned.

Like the others, Adonis and Demetrius gave rapt attention to the Commander. Also like the others, their fear was tangible. When the Commander finished, Demetrius asked, "What shall we do about this?"

Adonis said, "Whatever we're told to do. That's all we can do."

Recruits gathered themselves informally in small groups, all of them asking the others what the news might mean for them.

"Will I stay here?"

"Will I go to the frontiers of Attica?"

"Which is better?"

"Which is worse?"

"Will I see my family again?"

Such conversations continued all day and into the night. As for Demetrius, he thought of his family *How I wish I could see my family: my mother, my father, my sister, also our slave Chamus. And Nilo. My dear, little brother. Where could he be? What's he going to do? He's too young to be alone in warlike conditions. I hope and pray he returns home.*

Many didn't sleep that night. Few of the men had previously seen battle. They had, nevertheless, been well taught in the art of hand-to-hand combat and learned how to use all military technology. Sparta's reputation, however, was formidable. That's what they feared.

When morning light first reached them, the men were up and busy. Many would be leaving that day. Everyone knew not all of them would return alive.

At the normal hour, the men reported to their training field as usual. They didn't get far into their warm-up before the bell rang telling them to go to the Assembly Hall.

"Things will be different from now on," opined one recruit. "The life and death of our City-State Athens weigh in the balance."

At the Assembly Hall, both the Post Commander and General Pericles were sitting directly behind the podium. A more somber tone than usual was felt as soldiers continued filing into the Hall.

Demetrius said, "Ah. This is the first time I've seen General Pericles. What an impressive looking man he is. He'll be telling us what we will be doing."

"Yes," said Adonis. "Let's wait to hear his words."

The Post Commander was the first to rise to speak.

Good morning.

This meeting will be brief. There's no time for long discussions.

Today marks the beginning of all we've prepared for. Everything you've learned will be critical in the days ahead for your survival and yes, the survival of our City-State. Many are leaving today. We pray our gods and goddesses will be with you as you march into battle protecting our City-State. No higher honor can you have than to serve Athens. For those not leaving today, we hope to have your assignments soon. I now turn the podium over to General Pericles.

Thank you.

I'm humbled to be speaking to such a distinguished group of men: the defenders of Athens. All of Athens and Attica will be with you in spirit as you leave here today to meet the enemy. May the gods be with you in this noble endeavor.

Please note the following:

One. This war will not be decided on land. We know full well our limitations. We can only win this war on the high seas. One hundred triremes have left for the Peloponnese. We will invade their lands. Our war must have a naval component and the sea has to be the critical place for confrontations. That's our secret for victory.

Two. As far as Attica is concerned, we can no longer ensure the safety of our families living in the Attica countryside. They are coming to Athens. They're taking everything with them. They'll be permitted to enter the outer walls protecting our City of Athens and our Port town of Piraeus. We understand there will be hardships living in this nine by two-mile area. It will be difficult. This is the best we can offer until it's safe for them to return to their homes. There's not much time before the enemy arrives. We're praying to the gods, especially Apollo, Zeus and Athena to see us through this ordeal.

Thank you for your kind attention. I now turn you back to your Post Commander.

Thank you.

I want to add that those not having their assignments will receive them today. Those of you in partnerships living as couples are asked to remain for your assignment. Others are free to leave.

The Commander stepped down from the podium.

Demetrius turned to look at Adonis. "I guess we'll know soon where we're going."

"Yes. But again, what's important is we'll be together."

As the couples were huddling by each other waiting for news, the Post Commander approached them. He sat down beside them.

He began by saying, "I know you'll be glad to have your assignments. As stated from the podium, we've made our decision regarding partnered soldiers. Instead of stationing you with the others throughout the farmlands of Attica, we'd like to position all of you inside the walls surrounding Athens and our Port town of Piraeus. Your primary duty is to protect citizens living inside our walls. We absolutely cannot allow our enemy to penetrate these walls. If we do, it's certain defeat. We believe you, the partnered soldiers, to be the best suited for this job.

"You'll need to go to the wall's main gate, at the edge of Athens. You'll report to the local Commander Thanos. He's responsible for all operations concerning the wall's defense. He'll give you further instructions including your exact positions along the wall. There you'll also meet partnered couples from other Military Posts. You should arrive well before the sun sets this evening. And may the gods be with you. Are there any questions?"

"Yes Sir," said one recruit. "I have one. What type of facilities can we expect?"

"Good question. The answer is, almost nothing. You are to bring everything you'll need. In addition to your military equipment, you'll need to provide whatever bedding you wish to have, eating utensils, and whatever else you feel you most need. Your meals will be delivered daily from the nearest Military Post."

"That sounds fine," said another recruit. "But what about the people from the countryside? Where will they find food?"

"You've got to remember something. The situation we're in happened suddenly. The decision by General Pericles and our General Assembly is recent. We didn't have time to work out all the logistics before the countryside people pour into the area between our walls. This will take time to work out."

Another asked, "Are you going to give weapons to the farmers coming into the City?"

"We haven't decided on that. We'll have to see what our stockpile is, and many other things have to be sorted out. We're hoping many of them have weapons they can bring with them."

"That's all the questions I can take right now. You're free to go to your new assignment as soon as you've collected your belongings."

Nearly in unison, the soldiers responded, "Thank you, Sir."

When the meeting was over, Adonis and Demetrius collected their meager possessions together with their weapons and other military equipment and headed out to their assignment. As their Military Post was already within Athen's walls, they didn't have far to go.

On arrival, they were met by the local Commander Thanos. He explained to them what their area of responsibility will be. Their first job would be to help civilians from the countryside find a place to settle. "Do what you can to take care of their needs," he said. "But once the enemy arrives, your job will be mostly military. You must maintain our wall security and protect everyone inside."

Adonis and Demetrius decided to use this time to get an overview of their area. They would survey the area where they would have responsibility for its safety.

As they set out on foot, Adonis said, "This could be a difficult assignment, more so than anything we've ever done. Look around. There's no infrastructure here—nothing at all. The people from Attic's countryside must make their shelters. But they have nothing to make them from. They must find their own ways of getting food and water. There's no sanitation. And who knows how many are coming?" They also discovered *hoplite* couples from other posts had yet to arrive.

Demetrius asked Adonis, "Will we have the manpower to do our job? What do you think?"

"I can't say. There's too much we don't know. I wonder how things came to be the way they are. Too much suspicion perhaps. Too much mistrust between our city-states."

It wasn't long before the men had their first sightings of arrivals from the Attica countryside. A couple and two children were walking beside their mule pulling a small cart.

Adonis spoke first. "Do you see those people coming? Could they be some of our countryside citizens ahead?"

As they drew closer, the expressions on their faces showed how tired they were. As they were approached, Adonis spoke first. "Hello, my friends. How was your trip?"

One who appeared to be the father said, "Hello. We've been walking for three days. Our feet are sore. We're hungry and tired. We had to leave many possessions behind. We could only take what could fit in our cart."

Adonis said, "Let's help you find a place to lay down and rest. Here, please take this water for you and your family."

"Thank you. Thank you. How long do you think it will be before we can return to our homes?"

"We have no idea. War is unpredictable, as you know."

"Yes. Yes. You're right," said the man as he sat himself down beside a tree. "We could be here forever."

"Oh, this is dreadful," said the woman who appeared to be the wife.

"We hope you can return soon," said Demetrius.

As the man was making himself comfortable, they saw other arrivals. Some were elderly. Others were families, parents with children of all ages.

Adonis and Demetrius then returned to see Thanos, their local Commander. He was busy. He was also helping direct countryside arrivals to their places. Finally, Adonis was able to catch his ear. "Do you have any idea how these people can find food?" he asked. "Many of the arriving ones are hungry."

"Good question. We're working hard to keep open our Port of Piraeus. That way our ships can bring food from the islands. That's all we can do now. We're hoping shipments will arrive soon, but there's no way to tell when they'll arrive."

Meanwhile, the droves of country citizens continued pouring in without abating.

"We're going to have a major crisis," said Demetrius.

"We certainly will," said Adonis. "We can only try to guess how long this nightmare will last."

"And when will the Spartans and their allies arrive and try to break into our walls?" asked Demetrius.

"Yes. Things can get much worse."

Finally, Demetrius and Adonis decided they needed to arrange a place for themselves. It would be a while before the shelter for the *hoplite* recruits would be completed. They assembled a makeshift tent for them both. It would have barely enough room for them and their possessions.

Shipments of food did arrive, though not as plentiful as they wished. Shelters were also going up. Some of the construction was permanent; others were no more than tents. Day after day passed. There was no end in sight to the misery. News was slow getting to the people. They had little to no idea how warfare between the Athenians and the Spartans was going. Nor did they learn about how the Athenian naval fleet was doing in the Peloponnesian waters.

During this time the Spartans, with their allies, ravaged the Attic countryside where most of the families had left while taking refuge between the long walls. Those who remained outside the walls were either killed or taken prisoner. The devastation in the Attic countryside greatly demoralized the Athenians. The Spartans and their allies then laid siege to Athens itself. In the process, the Spartans cut off the food supply to those within the walls which included the City of Athens.

The long siege of their City-State left Demetrius and Adonis wondering about their fate. They tried to stay positive in their thinking. But they couldn't quell their pessimism. Demetrius particularly found it difficult not to feel alarmed.

"Are we witnessing the end of our beautiful City-State?" asked Demetrius.

"I don't know," said Adonis. "But you must know, Athens has shown resiliency in the past. Many decades ago it looked like the Persians were going to destroy us. Then Athens came back strong as ever and had them running home."

"We don't remember that, but it was taught to us."

"Yes. And as to our future, we must think positively. There's no other way."

The men were exhausted. They soon fell into a deep sleep.

CHAPTER 18

The Aftermath

I declare that later on, even in an age unlike our own,
someone will remember who we are.

— **Sappho**
630–580 BC

Historical perspective

The Peloponnesian War and the plague were the main causes that ended the Golden Age of Athens.

The arrival of families from the countryside in overcrowded, unsanitary conditions brought on the plague.

The Greek historian Thucydides referred to the plague as so extreme and lethal as to have no comparison. Physicians themselves knowing nothing of what it was. They were incapable of ameliorating their patients' condition. Physicians often died before the others as they had the closest contact with patients.

When Spartan soldiers entered Athens, they were stunned when they saw so many burning funeral pyres. When they learned they were burning victims' bodies from the plague, they backed off. They left the City, not willing to risk contacting the disease. Athens lost many of its finest soldiers to the plague, including General Pericles. In all, nearly half of the population succumbed to the disease.

Weakened by the illness, together with military defeats, left Athens too weak to successfully combat outside invaders. Despite its weakened condition, however, Athens won some battles elsewhere. But the overall situation did not bode well for the City-State. Facing a lengthy siege creating possible annihilation with the threat of starvation, along with the plague, proved too much for the beleaguered City.

Athens surrendered in 404 BC. The City-State would soon be governed by Spartan-controlled rulers who came to be known as the Thirty Tyrants.

The surrender took away much that had meaning for them. The protective walls instantly lost their function. Athens' army was disbanded. Its ships were destroyed or taken from them. They no longer had allies or overseas possessions. Compounding the situation, Sparta's allies, Corinth and Thebes, insisted the City of Athens be destroyed to rubble and its citizens be enslaved. It is noteworthy that Sparta overruled its allies. Recalling Athens past good deeds for them in previous wars, the City-State was spared. Athens became Sparta's unwilling ally.

Despite the difficulties, many functions of Athens continued. They included educational institutions, religious observances, businesses, the theater, *gymnasias,* and *palaestras.*

Back to our story

The war effort required ever more veterans to enroll a second time in the military. This included Demetrius's father. As it was, he fell early on to the enemy's aggression.

Following Sparta's take-over of Athens' Military Post, Demetrius moved into his father's home with Adonis. Around the same time, Demetrius's sister left home to get married. Their mother died earlier from the plague.

Nilo stayed away from the Theater for some time after Clio asked him to be his *eromenos*. But he did return. After a standoff, he accepted Horus's proposal that Clio could be his tutor if the arrangement excluded physical intimacy. This was accepted by all and seemed to work well.

Nilo continued living with Horus and spent much time at the Theater. He slowly took on various assignments. In time, Nilo became fully employed by the Dionysus Theater with significant responsibility. He learned to relish this work. Two years later, Horus invited Clio to move into his house. The time was then right for him to become Nilo's *erastes*. The difference was everyone approved the arrangement.

It still took a few more years before Nilo felt ready to see his family. When he returned, a joyous reunion took place between him and his brother. The brothers had much to share that was both heartwarming and sad. After learning his father was killed in action and his mother died from the plague, Nilo profoundly wished he visited his family years ago.

"You have no idea how much your father wanted to see you and help you," said Demetrius. "The trouble was, he didn't know how to go about that. So, with the help of

Adonis, myself and Chamus, he decided to go to Delphi to seek the advice of Apollo by way of the *Pythia*. It was a difficult trip over land and sea. But he felt he must go."

"What did Apollo tell him?"

"By way of the *Pythia*, Apollo told him to do nothing. His exact words were 'Let him be and you will see.' At first, your father and the rest of us believed the message was insufficient. But we came to see that nothing should be done, and in time your father would understand."

"Wow," said Nilo. "I never imagined father would go to such extremes like that."

"He loved you that much, and frankly, so did I."

This wasn't easy for Nilo to take. He so much wished he had returned to his home sooner. "But the truth is," Nilo said, "I had to leave home. Father was going to force me to continue my education. I had to have my freedom."

Demetrius and Adonis asked Nilo about his life after he left home.

"I started to live on the passageways, often at the mercy of strangers. I went to the *palaestra* because I couldn't think of another place to go. They let me stay there one night. The best part of that was the supervisor found someone to help me. His name is Horus. I moved in with him. I thought he was going to take advantage of me, sexually that is. That never happened. He took me to the Theater, where he worked and introduced me to many people. I learned much from being there and even met my *erastes*. I stayed with Horus until you asked me to return home."

"What a wonderful experience. Adonis and I were concerned about you for a long time. We were hoping you didn't need to stay on the passageways. We're so happy you returned to us."

For his part, Nilo was fascinated by his brother's account of his life in the military.

Demetrius explained that he would have been discharged early on if it hadn't been for Adonis's unrelenting help in getting him into good physical condition. Demetrius came to enjoy the military until the breakout of hostilities. "In wartime, military life is at best a living hell," said Demetrius, "but being with Adonis gave it a silver lining."

Conversations continued during their visits about once a week between Nilo, Demetrius, and Adonis. Nilo learned much about the horrors of living between the long walls with refugees pouring in from the Attic countryside.

Demetrius said, "If the city-states had united themselves into one nation, we could have had one strong country. Such a country could have defended itself from outside aggressors."

"Yes," said Adonis. "But there was far too much suspicion among city-states. Who can say that might've been possible?"

"So where do you feel Athens can go from here?" asked Nilo. "What do you think is in store for our City-State?"

"That's difficult to say," said Demetrius. "We're now at the mercy of other city-states. We have no idea what their plans might be."

"True enough," said Adonis. "But Sparta and its allies also lost much in the recent war. The time may soon be ripe for forces outside the Greek world to take advantage of weakened conditions that prevail throughout Greece."

As it was, Adonis would be more correct then he imagined. The Macedon Kingdom was slowly getting stronger. But it would take decades before its leader, Phillip II, began taking over Greek city-states. It would be well into the fourth Century BC before his rule would extend to Athens. Later, his son, Alexander the Great, created a Greek empire that he controlled. It would be maintained by Macedon until the Roman Empire arrived and dominated the landscape.

While the men enjoyed hypothesizing about the future, their main concerns remained fixed in the present.

In time, Nilo realized he was getting too old to be an *eromenos*. He and Clio decided the time had come to move on with other arrangements. On learning this, Demetrius invited Nilo to live with him in their father's house.

Nilo accepted. He moved in with his brother and Adonis. This turned out to be a perfect arrangement for him. Nilo was able to stay on his job at the Theater as well as maintain strong friendships with Horus and Clio.

One of the positive things coming out of Athens' apocalyptic upheaval was the concern and care fellow citizens gave each other, especially to those with the direst needs. Volunteer teams of citizens went house-to-house locating the neediest. "In that way," Demetrius told Nilo, "we met a boy in our *deme*. He lost his family from the war and the plague. He had nowhere to go. He was hungry when we found him. He had no idea what to do. We still visit him, give him food, and sustain him anyway we can."

Such talk made Nilo even prouder of his brother. "I'm so grateful that with all the problems you've had, this was important for you. It was in the same spirit that Horus helped me come out from a bad situation."

One day when Demetrius and Adondis were about to leave the house, they asked Nilo, "We're going to visit the boy we told you about, the one who has no family. Would you like to come with us?"

"Certainly," said Nilo.

And off they went.

It wasn't far to where the boy lived. Like most Greek homes at that time, the house was non-descript from the outside. Nilo got his first inkling of how things might be from the foul odors coming from indoors.

When the door opened, Demetrius said, "Hello Myron. How have you been?"

"Okay, I guess."

"Myron, this is my brother, Nilo."

Myron and Nilo shared greetings. Everyone went inside.

When they sat down, Myron said, "Thank you for coming to see me. You're the only visitors I have."

"It's a pleasure for us," Adonis said.

Myron was short. Nilo guessed his age to be twelve or possibly thirteen. It was obvious the boy hadn't bathed recently. His fingernails were black from encrusted dirt. His tunic was torn and dirty. And he smelled bad.

Nilo looked around. The house was in disorder. Things were not where they should be. The odor was stronger inside. Nilo asked the boy, "Could you tell me of your situation?"

"Yes. I live here alone. My father died in battle. When my mother took ill, and before she died, our slaves left. They feared contact with the disease. They never returned. They took all my parents' drachmas. I have no money to buy food.

I had little to eat for a long time until your brother and his friend found me. They've been kind to me."

Demetrius and Adonis then asked Myron about his present needs. They left him enough food to last another week.

The next day Nilo left home at the usual time to go to the Theater. On arrival, Nilo went to see Horus. He asked him if he could have the day off. He told him about his visit with Myron the day before. "The boy is in much need," said Nilo. He also explained how he wanted to help the boy.

Horus said, "Bless you Nilo. You're doing the right thing. Take all the time you need to help the boy."

Nilo left the Theater. He did not go directly to Myron's house. Instead, he went first to the *agora* to do some shopping.

When Nilo arrived at Myron's home, it was a surprise for the boy. He invited Nilo in, and they talked for a while.

Near the end of their conversation, Nilo said, "I don't want to be critical of you, but I'd like to help you clean your house. Do you mind if I help?"

"Uhh. I'm not sure," said Myron.

"I know you probably never had to clean your house before because you had slaves. Now you don't have them. It's not healthy for you to live in a dirty house."

"Yes, I know, but . . ."

"Tell you what. Let's go to your cooking area. That's the most important because that's where your food is kept."

Myron reluctantly followed Nilo.

Nilo was shocked when he entered the cooking area. Insects were everywhere. At one point he saw a rat race across the floor.

It took Nilo a while cleaning the floor and then the shelves where food was stored. He also made sure all the food was covered tight.

Myron stayed at Nilo's side the entire time, but he didn't help with the cleaning.

When he was finished with the cooking area, Nilo said, "That's all the housework we're going to do today. We'll do more during my next visit."

"Are you going to leave now?" asked Myron.

"No," said Nilo. "There's one more cleaning job to do. But it's not with the house. What we need to clean is you."

"Oh no, I don't need that—please no."

"If you want my help to continue, you must take a bath."

Myron reluctantly agreed while Nilo filled the tub.

When Myron was in the tub, Nilo checked occasionally to see that he was scrubbing the dirt off himself, including under his fingernails.

When Myron finished bathing, Nilo helped him dry off. Now, seeing him clean, Nilo noticed how handsome the lad was. *He looks nearly like a different person*, Nilo thought.

When he was dry, Myron reached for his dirty tunic.

"Oh no!" said Nilo. "You don't want to wear that." Nilo then handed the boy a new tunic he bought that morning at the *agora*. "Please put on this one," he said.

Myron thanked him. He confessed all this attention, especially the bath, made him feel better.

"Well, you're also looking better, like the handsome boy you are," said Nilo.

Myron blushed.

They continued their conversation before Nilo had to return home. While talking, Nilo learned more about Myron's background and how he lived before his parents died. The boy stopped going to school after hostilities broke out. He neither had money to pay for school nor to have a tutor. He was age thirteen, soon to be fourteen.

Nilo mostly enjoyed his time with Myron. But all this was taking its toll on him: his full-time job, responsibilities at home, his daily running, and exercise routines. Whatever time was left he would spend with Myron. He was thinking hard how to alleviate the situation for himself. He finally decided to ask his brother and Adonis if they could help a little more with the boy.

Back home with Demetrius and Adonis, Nilo explained how his day went with Myron. "The boy doesn't have friends. He's not going to school. He needs all the help he can get. Is it possible you can see him more often?"

"We'd love to see him more often," said Adonis. "But at this time, with everything else we must do, we're unable. But we'll continue to donate food. That is until he can stand on his feet."

"Okay," said Nilo. "If you supply his food, maybe I can take care of most of his other needs."

Nilo tried spending more and more time with Myron. But his commitments with the Theater made this difficult. Life began to be easier, however, as Myron was assuming more responsibility both in cleaning his house and with personal hygiene. Such progress warmed Nilo's heart to the point of seeing his friend in a new light.

One day after returning home from the Theater, Nilo was about to shed his tunic to do his exercise routines, including his daily run. At that moment a thought came to him. *Why don't I run with Myron? That way we can spend more time together.* He decided he would run to Myron's house as part of his routine.

When he arrived at the boy's house, Myron was a little surprised seeing Nilo standing there without his tunic. "What are you doing?" he asked.

"This is part of my daily run. Why don't you come with me? We can run together."

"Oh thanks, but I'm sorry. I can't do that. I've never been a runner."

"Don't worry," said Nilo. "Every runner has his first time. Today will be yours."

"But I can't keep up with you."

"I'll go slow. We'll run together as far as you can go. When you stop; I'll stop. We don't have to run far."

Myron, sensing he wasn't going to win the argument, stepped out of his house. He closed the door behind him. "I don't want to disappoint you," he said.

"The only way you can disappoint me is to not try. Come on, let's go."

Myron agreed and began to run.

"Stop," said Nilo. "You have to remove your tunic. It will get in the way and slow you down."

"Ah, yes. All athletes exercise without their tunics." He shed his tunic and placed it by his door.

They took off running slowly in the breeze.

"This feels nice," said Myron.

"You'll learn to love this someday."

The boys continued until Myron ran a slower pace; then he stopped.

"Okay, let's walk," said Nilo.

They kept alternating running and walking a few more times. Then, Nilo said, "You're doing well so far. Now let's return."

They returned in the same fashion, running and walking. When they arrived back where they started, Myron was tired. He had to lay down.

Nilo knelt beside him. "You ran well for your first time. I'm proud of you."

Myron smiled.

Nilo lowered his head and kissed Myron on the lips. It was his first intimate gesture to the boy. "I hope that's okay. Did you like it?"

"I don't know. No one's ever kissed me before, except my parents."

"Then maybe we should try it again." Nilo lays down beside the boy and gives him a gentle, but long held kiss as he also pressed his body close to Myron's flesh.

Myron didn't resist. When they finished, the boy said, "I think I like it."

"Perhaps we should go inside."

Immediately after entering the house, Nilo beckons the boy to lay down with him. Then Nilo shows him more about what close friends like to do.

Myron did not complain.

From then on, Nilo wanted to see Myron as often as he could. He tried committing several hours a week teaching the boy in academic areas. Whenever Nilo could get more free time, they visited the *agora* and later the *palaestra*. He also took the boy to the Theater and showed him around. They attended performances together.

On the day Myron turned fourteen, Nilo was able to persuade Demetrius and Adonis to go with him to the boy's house. There, the four of them shared a meal that Nilo prepared. The meal was followed with a lively conversation. When it was time to leave, Nilo told his brother, "You go on without me. I'm going to stay with Myron a little longer."

Myron and Nilo chatted for a while. Then Nilo said, "I have something important to say. It's like this. I've noticed a big change with you. You are someone who learns fast. I enjoy spending time with you, teaching you and having fun with you. I also believe you could use someone to guide you in more ways than I've been doing, at least so far. Please think carefully about what I'm going to say. The type of person you would benefit from most in your life right now is an *erastes*. I want to tell you, I'd like to be that person. And now that you're fourteen, how would you like to be my *eromenos?*"

Myron was surprised by the question. But he didn't take long to answer. As it was, the boy knew nothing about how the society-scripted game is played. He eagerly said, "yes," which was not the way boys in Athens respond.

Nilo, knowing Myron's lack of understanding, didn't hold that against him.

Nilo soon moved in with Myron. The two of them, *erastes* and *eromenos* went on to enjoy a formidable relationship.

The time had come when Nilo had everything he desired: a home, a good job, an *eromenos,* and most important, he had found his freedom.

The End

313

Bibliography

Explanatory note: A bibliography isn't normally included in a fictional work. An abbreviated one is included here because this book largely reflects conditions as they were in fifth century BC, Athens. Another reason is to provide resources to those desiring further reading on topics brought out in this book. The following do not comprise the entire scope of resources used by the author, which besides other books, include the Internet. But these are the primary sources. The following are all non-fiction.

Barringer, Judith —*The Hunt in Ancient Greece*; John Hopkins University Press, Baltimore, 2001. Hunting metaphors abound in ancient Greece and shed light on sexuality and gender roles. (297 pages)

Burckhardt, Jacob—*The Greeks and Greek Civilization;* St. Martin Press, New York, 1998. This book was first written in German and first published in Germany, in the late 19th century. Burckhardt devotes an entire chapter (53 pages) to the concept of *agon*, which he describes as a "motive power known to no other people." (504 pages)

Dover, Kenneth J.—*Greek Homosexuality*; Bloomsbury Publishers; London, New York, Sydney, Delhi, 1978. This landmark book changed the way historians write about sexuality in ancient Greece. Dover is a recognized expert on ancient Greece. He writes objectively with strong background knowledge. His book is a breakthrough in how sensitive topics relating to sexuality in classical Greece can be discussed. In a foreword to Dover's work, Mark Masterson and James Robson wrote, "[A]ncient Greeks found it normal for adult men to find handsome youths sexually attractive and the primary form that same-sex relations took in classical Athens was pederasty." (319 pages)

Garland, Robert—*Ancient Greece: Everyday Life in the Birthplace of Western Civilization*; Sterling Publishing, New York, 2008. A textbook-type read on daily life in classical Greece brimming over with interesting facts. (366 pages)

Golden, Mark—*Children and Childhood in Classical Greece;* 2nd Edition; John Hopkins University Press, Baltimore, 2015. This is about the place of children in their public and private lives from 500 to 300 BC. (373 pages)

KIRKUS REVIEWS

THE ISTHMUS, Stories of Mexico's Past: 1495-1995
By Bruce Stores
iUniverse, Inc. (392 pp.)
ISBN: 978-1440174889;
Publication date: November 16, 2009

Stores explores the history of Mexico's Isthmus of Tehuantepec in this short story collection.

The author presents fictionalized accounts of five centuries worth of invasions, rebellions, and elections in the Isthmus of Tehuantepec—a region of Mexico long renowned for its unique culture and fiercely independent spirit. The stories range from Zapotec peasants receiving Aztec merchants in Tehuantepec in 1495, to the city of Juchitán establishing local, leftist autonomy in the 1980s. In these tales, the isthmus is a place of passions and legends, with a long history of exploitation by outsiders; as Mexico-based author Nancy Davies writes in her foreword, it "historically has been an area of conflict, like all geographic areas that serve as crossroads, trade routes, and strategic guardians for empires made or in the making." Stores' tales take readers through these many conflicts, from the final free days of the Zapotec *Binni gula'sa'* people to the Spanish conquest, through the Rebellion of 1660 and the French intervention two centuries later, up to the Mexican Revolution and the clashes between national and local parties in the second half of the 20th century.

The eleven stories, along with supplementary materials, offer a glimpse at this little-visited area of Mexico, where the gulf is closest to the Pacific Ocean. Stores is a capable writer, adeptly handling the shifting languages and cultures that enter and exit the narratives. His characters sometimes feel a bit flat, as their emotional complexity is generally secondary to their participation in significant events; the didactic aim of the book reveals itself in long passages of historical exposition. This is less a book of historical fiction than one that uses fiction as a tool to teach history. Once readers realize this, however, the collection becomes quite enjoyable, as the landscapes, cultures, and clashes are engaging and likely unknown to most English-language readers. The comprehensive historical coverage persuasively contextualizes the troubles and political desires of the region's modern population. Like every contemporary place, it continues to experience a long, difficult birth.

A rich, fictionalized account of a little-known region's past and present.

**CHRISTIAN SCIENCE: Its Encounter With Lesbian/
Gay America**
By Bruce Stores
iUniverse, Inc. (274 pp.)
ISBN: 978-0595666584;
Publication date: September 9, 2004

A lifelong gay Christian Scientist explores his religion's
history and its largely uncharted, turbulent relationship
with sexual minorities.

Mexico-based American journalist Stores (*The Isthmus*,
2009) looks at the controversial Church of Christ, Scientist,
from the 1950s to the present day. Specifically, he tells of
how the church, once devoted to outdated, exclusionary
practices regarding gays, has come around to adopting a
policy of leniency. Stores includes numerous profiles of
intrepid, trailblazing gay activists who advocated changes
within the church, such as defrocked Pentecostal Rev. Troy
Perry Jr., who established the Metropolitan Community
Church in the 1960s, and Chris Madsen, an outspoken
lesbian cub reporter who was terminated from her position
at the *Christian Science Monitor* in the 1980s due to her
sexual orientation. Madsen's story ignited a momentous
scandal and lawsuit, which would rock the church's steely
foundation. Stores also presents profiles of several other
people who wished to exclude sexual minorities from church
membership, such as the staunchly anti-gay letter-writer
Reginald Kerry and singer and LGBT rights opponent
Anita Bryant. By offering such divergent viewpoints, Stores'
intelligent, thought-provoking narrative strives to "provide

new frameworks in defining the place of sexual minorities in ecclesiastical institutions." The author's closing notes reflect the latest positive inroads, including pro-gay-equality activism by the author's own son on the Christian Scientist Principia College campus. Ultimately, Stores' narrative coalesces into a fair-minded look at the evolution of Christian Science's stance on gay rights, the responses of its leadership and followers, and the hope for change.

A meticulously researched educational tool, particularly for readers with a casual interest in Christian Science and LGBT issues.

About the Author

Bruce Stores did not begin serious writing until after retiring. His first book came out at age sixty-six.

He believed he was unfairly ex-communicated from his Church due to its lack of understanding of sexual orientation issues. This led to his writing, *Christian Science: Its Encounter With Lesbian/Gay America* (iUniverse 2004, 248 pages). It wasn't until five years later that his second book was published.

A long interest in Mexico's unique history and a special interest in the Isthmus of Tehuantepec led to the publication of *The Isthmus: Stories From Mexico's Past, 1495-1995* (iUniverse 2009, 360 pages).

Nilo and Demetrius is his third book.

Bruce Stores was a Peace Corps Volunteer in Guatemala working in community development programs near Quetzaltenango in the early 1960's. Later he was a community development officer involved with refugee resettlement in Vietnam at the height of that war with the U.S. Agency for International Development (USAID). His third venture overseas was to serve as Recreation Coordinator for American employees and their families with Bell Helicopter/Textron in pre-revolution Iran. He also served the YMCA as Youth

Director in Vineland, NJ and Branch Director in Midland, TX. He later worked with self-help housing projects near Seattle, WA and was a contributing reporter for many years with *Seattle Gay News*. After relocating to Mexico in 1995, he was an English teacher for six years. He has lived in the Mexican City of Oaxaca since 2007.

He is a graduate of Springfield College, Springfield, MA with B.S and M.Ed. degrees in humanities.

He was married in 1967 and divorced in 1980. He has one son and two grandchildren.

Printed in the United States
By Bookmasters

Printed in the United States
By Bookmasters